**Flirtin**

From the midst of all the fear and confusion, she knew one thing clearly: At the heart of this duplicity was a young woman out on her own for the first time. She was experiencing life in the fast lane and—worst of all—a dangerous desire for this man. Her life had always been so predictable. She'd always known what was expected of her; how to feel, how to behave. But now her life was filled with uncertainty, volatility, and an intense sexual craving she'd never before felt.

As he kissed her hand again, she began to cry. The fear, the tension, the desire—all finding release in the hand of the enemy. . . .

# ONE FALSE MOVE

## Stacey Sauter

A SIGNET BOOK

SIGNET
Published by New American Library, a division of
Penguin Putnam Inc., 375 Hudson Street,
New York, New York 10014, U.S.A.
Penguin Books Ltd, 27 Wrights Lane,
London W8 5TZ, England
Penguin Books Australia Ltd,
Ringwood, Victoria, Australia
Penguin Books Canada Ltd, 10 Alcorn Avenue,
Toronto, Ontario, Canada M4V 3B2
Penguin Books (N.Z.) Ltd, 182–190 Wairau Road,
Auckland 10, New Zealand

Penguin Books Ltd, Registered Offices:
Harmondsworth, Middlesex, England

First published by Signet, an imprint of New American Library,
a division of Penguin Putnam Inc.

First Printing, July 2000
10  9  8  7  6  5  4  3  2  1

Cover art partly based on a design by Dana Ellyn Miller.

 REGISTERED TRADEMARK—MARCA REGISTRADA

Printed in the United States of America

PUBLISHER'S NOTE
This is a work of fiction. Names, characters, places, and incidents are either the
product of the author's imagination or are used fictitiously, and any resemblance to
actual persons, living or dead, business establishments, events, or locales is entirely
coincidental.

*Dedicated in loving memory
to
Charles A. Federline*


*A tough cop, a devoted father,
a trusted friend.
You are missed.*

# ACKNOWLEDGMENTS

I am deeply indebted to many people who provided love and support during the course of writing this novel, particularly my family.

I am deeply grateful to the following, who provided support and expertise: Mark Sauter; Detective Elizabeth Foley, Lt. Tony Giorgio, and Officer Kevin Tryrell of the New York City Police Department; Rex Tomb and Ed Cogswell of the FBI; Matt King and Kevin Murphy of U.S. Customs; Carole Mehrling, Lt. Mike Garvey, and Jennifer Huffman of the Montgomery County, Md. Police Dept.; Brian Hagburg of Montgomery County's HAZMAT team; volunteers at the Thoreau, N.M. Fire Dept.; Tino Merli at the Waldorf; Janet Muller, Pat Brennan, Nancy Brown, and Eric Young (formerly) of Paul, Weiss; Dr. Glenn Yago; Mike Matusewicz; Howard Segermark; Kathy Brown; Howard Goldman; Mary Lou Wood; Eddie Warner; Ron Sayler; Ray Friedlob; Dan Reiss; David Street; and Father Milton E. Jordan. Also to Dana Miller, for inspiring the cover's design.

As always, to my editor, Hilary Ross, and my agent, Pam Bernstein, and her associate Donna Downing—many thanks.

A special thanks to Lisa Walker and Kathy Jo Horan for their insight, guidance, and friendship. And finally to Bob, Lynda, Mary, and Peggy for their enduring love.

# PROLOGUE

Day by day the drugs had whittled away at her conscience, leaving only a brittle twig of self-control. Which on this day snapped.

She was tall and skinny, clad in a pair of tight black jeans and braless under a baby blue tank top. Her short, gel-spiked hair was dyed a Tabasco red; her skin was pale as wax paper. Chronic malnourishment had hollowed her eyes, while years of affection for drugs had darkened them. The New York City coroner guessed her age to be thirty. She was twenty-four when she died.

She had entered a branch of the Chase Manhattan Bank with a stolen check, waiting anxiously to cash it. It was the lunch hour, and a long line waiting for tellers snaked before her. She had reached the middle of the line when she caught sight of two armed guards carting sacks of cash on a dolly through the lobby, watching as they stepped onto an escalator toward the lower level. She had just come up the opposite way, and knew down below were doors leading to a concourse. And the concourse led to the subway.

Fixated on the money, she stepped over the velvet rope between two stanchions and moved swiftly toward the escalator.

*Idiot,* she thought, seeing that the rear guard had his back to her. His partner was likewise facing forward. Advancing catlike up behind the first guard until she could practically count the hairs on his neck, she grabbed the pistol hanging from his right hip. Before he could even turn to look, she fired a shot at the back of his head.

In less than five seconds she lay dead on top of him. As her shot rang out, his partner reacted automatically, landing two shots in her chest. Her body turned and toppled on top of his partner. Nervously glancing around for accomplices and seeing none, he pushed her body aside to determine if his partner was still alive. His glazed blue eyes were locked open in a bizarre, almost embarrassed, look. Within seconds a small army of New York City cops burst into the bank.

"Drop the gun," bellowed the first cop, his own gun drawn. The guard immediately obliged, knowing that protocol meant relinquishing his weapon until police had control of the scene. He held up his hands in surrender. They would soon know he was one of the good guys.

Officer Jack Jennings Jr. edged forward, barking orders into his walkie-talkie. "I need an ambulance," he said.

"No, no, you don't," said the guard. "They're both dead. She shot him. I shot her."

Jennings moved closer. The woman was slumped in a heap at the bottom of the escalator, her head and shoulders drooping to the right. As he leaned directly over her body, he caught a strange flash of metal. It was a steel earring pierced into the nape of her neck, with a shark's head protruding from one side, a tail jutting out from the half-inch of flesh behind it.

# CHAPTER
## 1

Mrs. Malcolm V. Rutland III freed the last bobby pin holding her heirloom bridal veil in place, then hesitated before removing it from her thick, dark hair. She let out a bittersweet sigh, thinking how sad it felt to take it off—as though her vibrant youthfulness would suddenly transform into matronly plainness.

*Never!* Candace thought emphatically, while swiftly tossing it on top of the nearby king-sized bed. No, the twenty-six-year-old bride didn't want the perfect day to end. But she'd landed the perfect man, someone she believed would make her feel vivacious for a lifetime.

Candace smiled affectionately while listening to Malcolm's off-key whistling in between drags of his Dunhill Double Corona—one of the twenty-dollar cigars he'd liberally distributed among their three hundred and fifty wedding guests, all still waiting in a downstairs ballroom of the luxurious Waldorf Astoria Hotel for their grand exit. She knew he was sitting on the john, perusing the sports section of the *New York Times,* and that he was happy. Drunk, happy, whistling, and, as usual, taking his time.

Always punctual, Candace tempered her impatience over Malcolm's loitering. She didn't want to keep everyone waiting, and besides, she was ready for a quiet and sexy night alone with her new husband.

"Mal," she said sweetly, "We're not on the honeymoon yet. Are you going to be ready to leave in ten minutes?"

Through the white louver doors of the marble bathroom she could hear him turn the newspaper pages.

"I can't believe Derek Jeter broke his foot playing a pick-up game of basketball," he responded nonchalantly. "There goes the season."

"Malcolm!"

"Good God. Ten minutes. I heard you!" he said, turning yet another page. "We've only been *married* ten minutes," he muttered loud enough to be heard, "and already she's nagging me!"

Candace smiled as she heard the toilet flush, then entered the master bathroom's adjoining dressing room. As she went to open one of the mirrored closet doors, she spotted Malcolm behind her, the bathroom door open just enough to reveal his nakedness. In his free and easy manner he blew a smoke ring in her direction.

"Sure you don't want to start the honeymoon right now?" he jested, a broad smile consuming his handsome face. She loved his immodesty.

"Oh my God," she cracked up, turning to face him. "What are you doing?"

"Getting in the shower," he slurred. "You wanna join me?" His usually smooth, resonant voice was raspy from three days of nonstop socializing.

"A shower! Are you nuts? Why do you want to take a shower now?"

"'Cause I feel like it, and I wanna smell sweet for my baby." He winked as he opened the door all the way. "You surc, now?"

Candace relaxed. "Believe me, it's tempting. Just be sure you're out of there and ready to leave in ten minutes."

"Heartbreaker," he groaned.

"Ten minutes!"

"Ten minutes, ten minutes," he chanted. "You know, I'm doing this for you." He winked again and shut the door. Immediately the shower began, along with his off-key whistling.

Candace opened the closet door to examine her going-away outfit. It was a simple navy blue linen suit that she planned to adorn with a fresh white orchid. With her twelve-foot train trailing behind her, she left the bedroom suite and crossed the expansive entry hall, cutting through the over-sized formal dining room and on into the kitchen. Opening the refrigerator, she found her orchid set atop a half-filled case of Heinekens, the remnants of his bachelor party.

Claiming he wanted to pay final respects to his bachelor-hood by honoring the greatest womanizers of all time—the presidents of the United States—Malcolm had stayed in the $5,000-a-night suite for three days. For more than fifty years this suite had been home to every U.S. president when he visited New York City. In fact, Malcolm's favorite rogue—President Clinton—had slept here just last week. And, as re-vealed in confidence by Malcolm's best man, during the bachelor party a Monica Lewinsky look-alike dressed as Uncle Sam performed a stupefying striptease in front of Malcolm as he sat in the suite's genuine Kennedy rocker smoking a fat cigar. *He's crazy,* she thought. *Rich, but crazy.*

Candace buried thoughts of what might have happened that night as she scurried back to the bedroom where Mal-colm, still in the shower, was now singing.

Candace giggled while picking up a hairbrush, feeling un-threatened by the thoughts of his antics. She knew he loved her madly, and had to wonder at her luck in snagging this

delicious man. Flinging her head over upside down, then
vigorously brushing her long hair, she smiled inwardly.
*Manhattan's most eligible bachelor is eligible no more,* she
thought happily.

She was only aware of the man's presence for a split second. The same moment after tossing her head into an upright
position Candace saw him standing directly behind her in
the mirror. She never had a chance to scream. In a blinding
flash his knife cut deeply across her slender neck, severing
her vocal cords. Within seconds she lay in a bloody, crumpled heap—her perfect day coming to a deadly end.

# CHAPTER
# 2

Jack Jennings Sr. laughed aloud at one of Jimmy O'Neill's ribald tales, but inwardly felt relief that his son had never been arrested in the young man's company. Jack Sr. had spent the last three decades with the New York City Police Department, and now his eldest son and namesake was with him on the force. Tonight several of Jack Jr.'s friends from his Catholic prep school days had joined him for a casual twenty-eighth birthday party. Having polished off a few bushels of crabs, they were now downing pitchers of beer while regaling one another with personal stories of lust, petty larceny, and assault—the latter both on and off their alma mater's football field.

O'Neill was nearly finished telling an indecent story when the growing rumble of a nearby motorcycle made him stop and look around. The rider of the bike decelerated and turned into the Jenningses' driveway, parking close by. Jack Jennings Sr. smiled broadly as two riders, the first a young, jean-clad woman, climbed off the back of the bike. She removed her helmet, then shook out her long wavy hair. Wiping her Ray-Ban sunglasses on her ribbed white tank top, she placed both helmet and glasses on the seat before joining the group.

"Hey, baby," said Jack Sr. warmly.

"Hey, Dad." She grinned back, pecking him on the temple.

Her fourteen-year-old brother, the youngest in Jack Sr.'s brood of four, was right behind her. "Hi, Dad," said Robbie.

"Oh, no," said Jack Sr. "I know what that grin says, and say it ain't so."

"It was so cool!"

"Robbie! I thought I told you. You're too young to ride that damned motorcycle."

"Relax, Dad," said Carla. "He did great. Besides, it was just around an empty parking lot."

"You guys remember my brother Robbie? And my sister, Carla?" Jack Jr. interrupted.

For the first time that evening Jimmy O'Neill was nearly speechless. It had been a while since he'd been to the Jenningses' house. "Carla, yeah, sure," he said. There was astonishment in his eyes and a sudden self-consciousness in his voice.

"Hey, Carla," a few of the other guests echoed.

"Hey, guys," she greeted them after throwing back the first swallow of a cold brew. "How you doing, Jimmy? Long time, no see."

"I'll say. What are you up to these days?"

"Not much. How 'bout you?"

"Same old same old."

Jack Sr. let out a muted laugh over O'Neill's newfound constraint and Carla's characteristic modesty. She had recently been sworn into the ranks of the NYPD and was already one of the top cadets at the Training Academy.

"Jack, did you save me some crabs?" Carla asked, turning to her brother.

"Did somebody say McDonald's?"

"Aw, come on! You promised."

"They're inside," he said, standing up to his full six feet.

"I'll go get 'em. Had to hide 'em from the vultures, you know."

"Sit down, birthday boy. I'll find them." She turned to Robbie. "You hungry?"

"Naw. I'm going down to the McNallys' to shoot some hoops."

"Have fun." She lightly squeezed his shoulder, then turned and headed inside, revealing a well-toned thigh through a tear in the back of her jeans.

O'Neill let out a soft wolf whistle as she disappeared. "Good God, almighty!" he muttered. "I think I'm in love."

"Forget it, O'Neill," said Jack Jr.

"What the hell happened to her?"

"What do you mean?"

"I mean, the last time I saw her she was, well, you know, cute. But now she's—"

"Vavavavoooooooom!" another male guest jumped in. The crowd laughed.

"Is she seeing anyone?"

"Don't even think about it," Jack Jr. said protectively, his eyebrows furrowing.

"What? Are you her bodyguard or something? I'm really scared," O'Neill mocked him.

"Actually, she doesn't have much time for anybody," Jack Sr. broke in, his voice edged with pride. "She's a cadet at the Academy right now."

"Get outta here! She joined the NYPD?" responded Jimmy incredulously. "Oh, man. I dig a chick with handcuffs."

"O'Neill's definition of commitment," quipped Jack Jr.

"Yeah, boy. Lock me up," he said, prompting more laughter. "Seriously, though, she's joined the force? How come?"

"Catholic school. Can't shake the urge to wear a uniform," Jack Sr. said, then laughed himself. "Though I'd kinda like to think it's 'cause she's following in her old man's footsteps."

The back door swung open, and all eyes were on Carla as she quickly crossed the patchy lawn toward the picnic tables. She was holding the portable phone, which she promptly handed to her father.

"For you, Dad. Sounds urgent."

"What the hell?" he muttered after thanking her. "Jennings here."

The group remained respectfully quiet as he listened, then rose out of his seat, his well-defined features expanding with alarm.

"Someone picking me up?" Jack asked. "Stand by, then. I'll be there," he said, turning off the phone.

"What's up, Dad?" asked Jack.

His father shook his head in disbelief. "Some socialite bride was just found murdered in the Presidential Suite at the Waldorf Astoria."

"Jesus!" blurted Jimmy. "See what marriage does to you?"

A collective groan went up. Jack Sr. tempered a grin while tousling Carla's hair, then handed her the phone. "I've got to go."

"You need help down there?" asked Jack Jr.

"I'll let you know. Happy birthday, son." He kissed Jack Jr. on the crown of his head and then left.

After twenty-two years as a New York City cop Liz Phillips thought she'd seen it all. Yet the sight of the brutally murdered bride caused her unexpectedly to wince, then nearly gag. The victim's gown, once a satin river of white, now rippled around her in gruesome waves of crimson. On the floor beside her lay a damp hotel bath towel, and in the blood-stained carpet next to it, the bare footprints of her new husband where he'd stopped in shocked horror upon discovering his nearly beheaded bride.

She could hear the young man sobbing in the adjacent room. Phillips knew it would be best to get him out of the suite. But over the years she'd dried many crocodile tears off the faces of husbands turned murderers, and wasn't about to let him go without getting a statement from him herself. The fact that a prominent Manhattan socialite, on her wedding day, no less, had been brutally murdered in a room designed to meet Secret Service security standards, meant that nothing could be left to chance in solving this crime. As chief of New York City's Homicide Division, Liz Phillips knew the hue and cry to find this woman's killer would be unrelenting. Already a horde of reporters had staked out every conceivable exit of the hotel. Immediately upon arriving at the Waldorf, Liz Phillips had declared the entire building a crime scene. No one but police personnel was allowed to enter, and no one was allowed to leave without first being questioned. Over a hundred cops and technicians were at work gathering evidence and questioning every staff member, wedding guest, and hotel guest alike. Already she'd commanded seizure of every photo and videotape taken at the wedding, and then the video from the hotel's internal security system.

Phillips ran a hand through her short, wavy brown hair, then scratched the back of her head while watching the medical examiner, Ken Matsunaga, do his job. She recalled an assignment covering this suite during a visit by President Ford when she was a rookie detective. She knew that access to the Towers, where the suite was located, was extremely limited. Having thought through every conceivable entry point, she'd dispatched investigators to search them.

Her thoughts were interrupted by her friend and senior colleague, Jack Jennings, who'd been supervising the questioning of wedding guests. Jennings gave her a no-nonsense shake of his head.

"You wouldn't believe," he stated with soft disgust, "the number of paranoids in that crowd of snobs. Say they won't talk without their attorney present." He snickered. "Can you imagine paying someone three hundred bucks an hour just to confirm you were doing the Electric Slide?"

Phillips managed a slight smile, knowing the man had little patience for whiny socialites.

"What are you hearing down there?" Phillips pushed up the sleeves on her casual black cotton shirt. She too had been called while enjoying a backyard barbecue with friends at her Brooklyn Heights home, and had arrived wearing jeans and Birkenstocks. As chief of the division she was rarely out in the field now. But the extraordinary nature of this murder demanded her presence. Among the wedding guests were several close friends and colleagues of the mayor, and enough bluebloods to sink the Mayflower.

"Same thing over and over," Jennings responded. "She was so sweet . . . so in love . . . came from such a good family . . . how could anyone do such a thing . . . can't imagine the husband had anything to do with it. Basically don't know or didn't see a damned thing."

Phillips sighed, turned her back on the corpse, and led Jack into the hallway. "Of course they didn't see a damned thing. You know as well as I do, Jack, that this woman didn't have a petty argument with someone downstairs that suddenly escalated into murder. It took some planning to get into this place. Plus, nothing appears to be stolen; her perfect two-carat diamond in its platinum setting is still on her hand, and Matsunaga pulled a pearl and diamond pendant out of that gash on her neck. From what I've heard, nothing else has been touched."

He remained silent for a moment while watching Matsunaga at work, then let out a frustrated sigh. "Lizzie, if there's one thing I've learned in all our years on the force, something this hideous is usually a professional hit. Which means there's revenge scrawled in that pool of blood. And God only knows who's intended to read it."

# CHAPTER
## 3

Mitchell Cunningham quietly followed his wife and two teenage daughters into their spacious Park Avenue apartment. He flipped through some junk mail on the hall table, and finding nothing of interest, retreated to his mahogany-paneled study, where he gratefully closed the door against his family.

He spent most of his Sundays the same way. Waking his wife, Sydney, around six-thirty for a brief sexual interlude—their only one for the week, if she let him get lucky—he'd next head to the kitchen and eat while scanning each page of the Sunday *Times*. Around eight-thirty, and regardless of the weather, he'd jog four miles in Central Park, come home, shower and shave, and then join his family for Mass at St. Ignatius. This was always followed by brunch at a trendy Manhattan restaurant.

Back home, Mitchell would withdraw to his study to pore over financial reports and analyze the latest market trends while tuning in to whatever business news he could find on television. Briefly rejoining his family for a traditional home-cooked dinner, he'd slip back into his study and sip scotch on the rocks while channel surfing, finally heading to bed around eleven. When they were younger, his daughters used to cozy up with him to watch Sunday night TV. But their adolescence had robbed them of needing that slice of affection. Now all they wanted was his money—just like their mother.

In spite of getting to bed at 3:00 A.M., this Sunday's routine was hardly any different. He'd had indifferent sex, devoured the newspaper, jogged, dutifully attended church, and then taken his family to brunch in a must-be-seen place. He talked mostly with the girls during the meal, feigning interest in their trivial pursuits while wondering if either of them would graduate from prep school with any ambition beyond finding the best bargain on stupid and expensive accessories. It was an exercise in patience for him, as he much preferred the seclusion of his study to the boring prattle of his wife and children. To some extent, Mitchell Cunningham's success as an independent investor hinged on the latter part of his Sunday routine, and he was always fidgety about getting on with it. He was a self-made man, and no one knew better than Mitchell Cunningham how to squeeze money out of each minute. And no three people knew better how to squander time and money than the members of his immediate family.

But today it wasn't earning money that had him so uptight. Images of Candace and Malcolm Rutland burned in his mind. And not just from this morning's paper. He and Sydney had been wedding guests of the young couple, watching them exchange vows, then later spin merrily around the dance floor.

It seemed like an eternity before they learned why the couple never returned after going to change their clothes, and only then after a detective announced resolutely from the bandstand that no one was to leave the room. A small horde of uniformed cops simultaneously converged on the ballroom, causing shock and then a brief eruption of pandemonium. Teams of detectives followed shortly thereafter, and it was 2:00 A.M. before the last guests were questioned and released, Mitchell and Sydney among them.

The questions were fairly straightforward. They were asked how they knew the couple; what did they give as a wedding gift and could they confirm it had been received; did they notice anything odd—any fights, any strangers that didn't belong; did they know of anyone dangerous with whom either Candace or Malcolm might have been involved; how would they individually describe the bride and groom; had they personally loaned money or anything else of value to them; when was the last time they'd seen them before the wedding, and did anything unusual occur at that time; etc., etc.

Mitchell stated he did not know the bride or groom personally, that it was actually Sydney who knew Candace through a couple of charitable boards on which they served together.

"Very efficient and very organized," Sydney told them. "Something of a lighthearted chatterbox, but very generous. She also loved that boy dearly. She'd had her sights set on him for some time until *he* finally focused in on her."

When the Cunninghams were politely asked if they minded a follow-up phone call should investigators need to ask any further questions, the couple nodded agreeably, and much to Mitchell's quiet relief they were released.

No, he did not know the bride personally. But he did know why she was dead.

# CHAPTER
# 4

Jack Jennings pushed his black plastic reading glasses back from the tip of his nose. Cheap and flimsy as they were, he'd managed to keep the same pair for the past twelve years—a small success for the notorious tightwad. He glanced over his paper at Jack Jr., who was sitting across from him at the Blue Bay Diner and was likewise absorbed in a New York rag.

THERE GOES THE BRIDE! splashed the front page tabloid headline with the news of Candace Courtland Rutland's funeral. The deceased had been buried in a Hudson River Valley plot alongside her philanthropist father, the late Phillip Courtland.

Jack Jr. rustled the newspaper. "Jesus, Dad," he said, "this is unbelievable. What's up with this case so far?"

"I gotta tell you, son, the *New York Post* seems to know as much about this one as we do, and that's not much. There are absolutely no leads right now."

Jack Jr. studied his father's face for signs of deceit, as it was unusual for him not to confide what he knew about current investigations. Occasionally there would be a case where, despite Jack Jr.'s status as son and fellow cop, his father kept him in the dark. But the young man could read the truth in his father's eyes.

"C'mon, no fat insurance policy somewhere?"

His father grinned wryly. "Don't you think there'd be easier ways to go about knocking off the girl if insurance was involved? Besides, we were surprised to find only a meager policy naming her mother as sole beneficiary. About a quarter million, which is chump change for that crowd.

"And," he went on, "the husband's statements consistently stand up. He seems genuinely distraught and for now, at least, he's not a suspect." He took a long sip of his coffee, then motioned for Bobby, a cheerful and longtime waitress of their favorite Queens diner, to give him a refill.

"Christ, would you look at that?" he said to Jack and Bobby, directing their attention outside. The three laughed while witnessing an attractive, young blonde jump out of her late-model Mazda convertible after parking in a Handicapped Only spot.

"Some handicap!" Jack Jr. quipped at the slender beauty as she jogged across the street in a revealing pair of shorts and a thin tank top.

"Must be a real pain for her to keep up with those long legs," his father remarked.

Bobby chortled, then sighed. "Guess now isn't the time to ask your help on a ticket I got last week, huh?"

"Here's your help!" Jack Sr. laughed, then dipped into his pants pocket and produced a set of well-worn rosary beads.

"Hail Mary! Pass the collection plate, you jerk!" She playfully whacked him on the arm, prompting both Jenningses to raise their arms in mock protection of their faces.

"Don't worry, pretty boy." She affectionately rubbed Jack Jr. on the head. "I wouldn't touch that gorgeous face of yours." He blushed in embarrassment as she walked away. Jack Sr. beamed, thinking how much his son looked like him when he'd first joined the New York City Police Department. *Handsome,* he thought proudly, *damned handsome.* Jack Jr. had inherited his father's hearty Irish looks, with thick, wavy, black hair; dark lashes under heavy brows that framed violet-blue eyes, and a creamy complexion that turned ruddy from the first whip of a wind—or a compliment. Fortunately, Jack Jr. had been spared the hardships his father had endured as a young man.

An Irish immigrant, Jack Sr. became orphaned after his working-class parents died of polio just two weeks apart from each other. He was sixteen years old then, and the oldest of three surviving children. He steadfastly kept his promise to his dying father to finish high school, and did so while struggling with two jobs to keep his family together. It was a hardscrabble existence. But still, he managed to keep a roof over their heads and food on the table, supporting his brother and sister until they were both married with families of their own.

After high school graduation he worked full time as a stevedore, with dreams of one day running his own shipping business. But his firsthand observation of the mob's strong-arm tactics down on the wharf led him in a different direction. Instead he joined the New York City Police Department, and in the thirty-six years since, his mixture of toughness, street smarts, and compassion had turned him into one of the city's finest and most respected cops. It was also what propelled him to become commander of Manhattan South.

Sitting across from each other in uniform, he and Jack were doing the same thing they did every Wednesday—eating dinner at the Blue Bay Diner. For Jack Sr., it wasn't just a chance to catch up with his oldest son or to get a hot

meal. The place was filled with warm memories of his late
wife, Donna, who at age fifty-eight and after thirty-five
happily married years had died of ovarian cancer. Every
Wednesday night for nearly twenty years, he and Donna
would retreat to this restaurant alone to sort out problems
and celebrate small joys across a blue-and-gray speckled
Formica tabletop. Donna good-naturedly joked about the
food, but wouldn't have traded a single one of those greasy
meals if it meant giving up a date with her husband. In
fact, just a few weeks before dying she'd insisted on their
regular evening out at the Blue Bay. Jack Sr. never told his
son that this was the last booth they shared before her
death.

Jack Jr. knew. He too missed his mother. And while he
had since moved out, he was back at their Bayside home in
Queens so frequently that practically everyone agreed his
rent was a waste of money.

Jack Jr. scooped up the last ketchup-drenched French fry
from his plate and popped it into his mouth. "Dad," he said
while still chewing, "are you at all concerned about Carla?"

Jack Sr. smiled at the thought of his twenty-two-year-
old daughter, dark-haired and olive-skinned like her Italian
mother. His only daughter, she'd learned early how to hold
her own against her brothers—and not because she could
easily outrun any of them. As a teenager, she'd earned a
black belt in Hapkido and could knock the daylights out of
just about anyone. She was athletically gifted and smart,
having received scholarships at several major colleges. But
instead of going away, she'd decided to commute to
Queens College while caring for Robbie, who was only ten
when Donna died.

"What do you mean?"

"Suppose she lands a foot patrol in the Bronx?" Jack Jr.

went on, then paused as Bobby dropped the check on the table. His father picked up the bill.

"This one's on me," he said, a toothpick clenched in his teeth. He exited the booth, stood, and gently patted his girth. Jack Jr. slid out behind him and dropped a healthy tip on the table before following his father to the register. He still hadn't said anything about Carla.

"You got your book with you, son?" he asked as they walked out into the warm June evening.

"Yeah."

"Good. Give that handicapped Rockette a ticket. And about Carla?" He paused, as if collecting his thoughts. "After she kicked the shit out of that kid down the street . . . what was his name?"

"Dennis Diffley?" Jack said incredulously.

"Yeah, that's the one. Remember the beating she gave him after he stole her bike?"

"Dad, you're joking. That was over ten years ago."

"Doesn't matter, son. I guarantee you if she knew how to stand up for herself back then, well, let's just say I would pity anyone who gets in her way today."

Moaning between short, uneven gasps, she slowly and painfully pulled herself up. The farthest she could rise before feeling a need to puke was a humiliating doggie-style. *He broke one of my ribs,* she thought fiercely. She glanced up briefly at her opponent's smug expression. If she'd had any strength left in her body, she would have flown through the air and landed a side kick square in his jaw.

The thunderous wake of a jet taking off from nearby LaGuardia filled the silence in the cavernous warehouse, while the crowd remained still. Carla knew they were all watching, and waiting.

"Are you okay?" the referee finally asked. An acute pain

in her right side made breathing more difficult and talking nearly impossible. But she refused to give up and pushed even harder, rising halfway up before painfully resting her hands atop her knees. Worse than the bruising kick was the sting of humiliation. In all her years of martial arts competition, she'd lost only a handful of matches. But this defeat hurt the most, as it was the only time she'd publicly competed—and then lost—against a man.

"Do you need help?" said the ref somewhat impatiently while leaning in toward her.

"No, thanks," she whispered hoarsely, finally pushing one foot in front of the other. She could hear the small crowd begin to stir, and as she shuffled off the mat her opponent gleefully raised his arms in victory. His contingent of supporters broke into cheers, making Carla wonder if it was more for defeating a woman, or for bringing her down in particular. Regardless, she thought, they'd gotten their money's worth today. He'd won the privilege of squaring off with her after seven rounds of hard-fought competition among the toughest martial arts competitors in Queens. Regardless of age, gender, or discipline, at least twenty-five black belts from the various martial arts schools challenged one another in an unsanctioned, no-holds-barred tournament. And after five hours of rigorous matches, Carla Jennings, a third-degree black belt in Hapkido, and Hans Kim, a second-degree black belt in Taekwondo, were left standing.

At last Carla shuffled her way off the mat, and was met halfway by her longtime coach, Master Judd Tompkins. A former Green Beret commander and Vietnam veteran, Tompkins possessed nerves of steel and laserlike concentration. He was one of the few Hapkido instructors on the entire East Coast with a sixth-degree black belt. At age fifty-nine the man was in better shape than most men half his age.

"Please, don't—" Carla said. She was going to say "lecture me now," but the pain seemed to grip even her voice.

"He cracked your eighth rib. It'll take about seven weeks to completely heal."

Carla didn't doubt him. He'd gained valuable knowledge of the human body as a onetime Army medic; the most ironic time in his life, he'd once told her, as he was simultaneously trained to kill and heal.

"I can barely breathe," she uttered.

"To the hospital," he responded. "He might have punctured your lung, too."

Carla didn't resist the suggestion, as she was desperate for a full gulp of air.

Halfway to the emergency room he finally spoke again. "You were watching his feet."

"What?" she groaned.

"You were watching his feet."

Carla grimaced. That was the extent of his lecture, something she'd often heard in full. "If you've got your eye focused on the attacker's weapon, then you're not concentrating on an opening—on a way to escape or hurt your opponent."

"Faster, please," she whispered.

It turned out he was right: eighth rib, probably seven weeks to heal, fortunately no lung damage.

Tompkins dropped Carla off at home. Once inside the modest but charming Tudor-style house, she settled onto the oversized brown corduroy sofa in the family room, wrapped herself in a hand-crocheted afghan made by her mother, then drifted off to sleep from a mild painkiller. She was grateful for the sedative, since it meant she might sleep through her father's arrival home and be spared, at

least temporarily, another lecture—this time for fighting in
an illegal competition. When she finally awoke the next
morning, it wasn't her father nudging her shoulder, but
rather her twin brother, Tommy.

"Oouuchh!!" She grimaced, before discovering his
handsome, smiling face.

"What's the matter with you?" He laughed. "You got a
hangover?"

Carla momentarily massaged her eyes, then affectionately grabbed hold of Tommy's hand and nuzzled it against
her face. "God, Tommy, I wish. I got cracked in the ribs
last night in a local version of Ultimate Fighting. Eighth
one down. Right side. It's broken, and, man, does it hurt."

"That sucks. How does he look?"

"Not a scratch. And worse, he's only a second degree in
Taekwondo. I don't know what hurts worse: my aching
side or my wounded pride. Where's Dad?"

"Don't know."

"Man, is he going to be pissed off at me."

"What are you going to tell him?"

"The truth. I got hit in a competition. Problem is, it was
unsanctioned. Basically illegal."

Tommy laughed. "Look at the positive. At least it was
only a rib, and not you, that got busted."

Carla moaned.

"By the way, you little miscreant, how's the Police
Academy?"

"Until now, good. Thank God today is Saturday." She
moaned again, this time over trying to turn her body. "I've
screwed up, Tommy. This injury will definitely interfere
with my training."

"Relax, sis. It won't be the first time a cadet got hurt."
He squeezed her hand, and she saw the empathy in his
face. Better than anyone, he understood her competitive

nature, and knew her dilemma was not graduating from the Academy so much as finishing at or near the top without the appearance of favoritism.

Carla squeezed his hand back. He made himself comfortable beside her. "Where's your bike?" he inquired of her Kawasaki motorcycle, which was typically parked in the driveway.

"In the shop. Nothing major, but I won't be riding for a while anyway. How's your new love?" she asked, switching to a more interesting topic.

"Kinda scary."

"Marriage?"

"You know it. They all want to get married."

"To *you*?" she said with a laugh. "Tell me you don't want to get married and raise a family someday."

"Yeah, maybe someday. But right now, the only thing I want to do is curl up beside the only one I know who truly loves me," he said, resting his head on her hip.

"Now *you're* starting to scare *me*!" she exclaimed. "Help me get up, please." She winced as she rose off the sofa. Tommy laughed at her disheveled appearance. Her mane of dark locks was bursting from the confines of a twisted headband on top of her head, looking like a wild, hairy geyser, while her soft brown eyes were barely visible beneath overgrown bangs. With deep-set dimples and finely shaped noses; dark, wavy hair and brown, wide-set eyes, they both resembled their mother.

The T-shirt she'd slept in was confiscated property from their brother Jack's extensive collection. It was faded navy blue with white print, and part of last year's NYPD softball uniform. It featured a macabre picture of the Grim Reaper with the slogan "Our day begins where your day ends." Tommy always found it hard to believe that someone with Carla's warmth could find comfort in something so morbid.

"You want me to make you some breakfast?"

Carla blew Tommy a kiss and smiled, the corners of her mouth folding into her endearing dimples. Their behavior today was starkly different from their youth. Back then, they'd fought constantly, but as older teenagers became nearly inseparable. Especially after they started to develop romantic interests in each other's friends, and needed each other's help to pursue their tender fancies.

In spite of his roguishness, Tommy was cerebral and gentle-natured like their mother. He shared her love of all things classical—literature, music, and opera. And as their father disliked the latter, it was often Tommy who had accompanied his mother to Lincoln Center performances, and to watch her perform. As a young single woman, Donna Jennings had joined the chorus at the Metropolitan Opera. Although she abandoned dreams of stardom when she married Jack Jennings, she never left the opera, performing as a part-time member of the chorus almost until her death.

"You can fix me breakfast if you want, but why do I feel the demand for a favor coming in return?" Carla responded.

"God, I love your legs," said Tommy. Her T-shirt stopped just beneath her buttocks.

"Tommy, now you're *really* starting to scare me," she said, then laughed. "What do you want? My motorcycle?"

"Naw, honestly I don't need a thing. I've missed you."

"Me, too."

"Seriously, can I fix you breakfast?"

"Sure," she smiled, adding coyly, "Anything I want?"

"Anything you want. By the way, when will your bike be out of the shop?"

"See, I knew it was something. I just knew it!" She said laughingly, while wrapping herself in a well-worn chenille robe.

"I'm teasing," he laughed, tossing a pillow in her direction.

"Careful, careful," she cried playfully, while earnestly protecting her right side.

"Careful—with you? I don't think soooo!" He smiled. "They just don't make 'em any tougher than you, babe."

# CHAPTER
## 5

At 9:50 A.M. Sydney Cunningham was about to leave for her weekly tennis match when she suddenly remembered dinner plans with a college friend visiting New York. Typically she'd knock on Mitchell's study door and then tell him in person. But he'd been so edgy all week that she didn't feel like dealing with him directly. Instead, she wandered down the long hall and into the kitchen, where she retrieved a piece of paper and jotted a note.

The size of their apartment, styled to resemble an elegant French country house, considerably exceeded the typical cramped existence of most New Yorkers. Occupying the entire top two floors of a pre-war Park Avenue building, their five-thousand-square-foot apartment was a six-bedroom unit, featuring not only large, formal living and dining rooms, but a comfortable family room, servant's quarters, an office for Sydney, and an extra room that served as her home gym. Their two girls each had her own room, there were guest bedrooms with private bathrooms, and best of all, according to Sydney, there were four working fireplaces. Of course, Mitchell had his own study, which privately Sydney considered the nicest feature as it kept him out of her hair for extended periods of time.

Passing by the pantry, which doubled as a service entrance, she noticed something odd. The door leading to the back stairs was slightly ajar.

"Manuela," she shouted out. There was no answer. Though it was early for the maid, Sydney assumed she'd arrived early and had already started her routine chores. She always came through the front, but frequently opened the back door when placing the garbage on the rear landing for collection by the building's staff. Sydney entered the pantry and then opened the door all the way, peering down the darkened stairwell. There was no sign of Manuela.

"Hmmm, that's strange," she said, then shut the door tightly and proceeded toward the front hallway, where she planned to leave the note. She stopped, however, listening to the sound of something stirring upstairs, thinking perhaps she'd heard a door click shut.

"Manuela," she shouted again. Only silence followed.

"Must be Mitchell," she muttered aloud. She dropped the note on the table then retreated to the powder room for a quick pit stop. Uneasiness nipped at her, however, as she thought about the back door. Once when she had shut and locked it, it turned out Manuela had been out there, only out of sight on the landing below. Sydney had left home shortly thereafter, and the poor woman had had to walk down fourteen flights of stairs, exit the building, and reenter through the lobby.

Flushing the john, Sydney decided to check once more. Grabbing her tennis racquet en route, she moved briskly down the hall and back to the pantry, where she quickly unlocked the door.

"Manue—" she started to shout when out of the shadowy darkness a man's black-gloved hand clamped firmly down on her mouth. Impulsively she thrashed his arm with her racquet, and for a split second saw pain register in his dark eyes as he let go, cussing aloud in what sounded like Russian. He was tall and heavyset, wearing the uniform of the building's work crew. But Sydney, who as a board member of their co-op building knew all the staff by name, did not recognize him.

Quickly retreating, she desperately tried pushing the door shut against him.

"Mitchell!" she screamed feverishly. *"Mitchell!"* There was no response. Thrusting the door wide open, her attacker delivered a powerful punch to her jaw. Grabbing her by the hair, he spun her around, then wrapped his beefy arm across her chest and under her armpit, constricting her upper body movement. Catching the flash of a silvery knife as it passed in front of her face, Sydney thought of her two daughters away at camp, and began pleading.

*"No, please, no, don't,"* she cried.

Within seconds she was dead.


"What the hell does she want now?" Mitchell wondered aloud after hearing Sydney scream his name. He had no intention of answering her, as she was probably incensed over something as inane as his dirty breakfast dishes. It wasn't enough to leave them for Manuela. Or even to be grateful that she was married to someone who could afford a house-keeper. *No, she has to absolutely control me,* he thought angrily.

*What am I going to do? What the hell am I going to do?* He left his desk and moved over to the window, peering down at the pedestrians strolling along the sun-filled street. Two mothers were pushing strollers with fat, joyful babies. A beautiful brunette was slipping into a taxi. A maintenance man was just exiting the rear of the building. Mitchell felt sure that by comparison to him, all of them had manageable and happy lives.

He glanced at a hand-cut crystal table clock, realizing that by now Sydney must have surely left for tennis. Still, he would give it a few minutes longer before venturing out for another cup of coffee.

"What the hell am I going to do?" Mitchell plunked down in a richly upholstered chair, then put his face in his hands. He was doomed. Rand Emmerson and Roman Petrovsky had him just where they wanted him, and unless he fled, there was no way out.

Leaning back, he closed his eyes and wondered where in the hell he would go. He'd recently read an article about the beautiful and remote regions of Patagonia. But it was fast becoming a spot for the ultrarich and famous, and increasingly a place where he might get found. Anxiously he rose from the chair, and began pacing back and forth.

Finally Mitchell opened the door just a crack and listened for Sydney. It was very quiet, and he presumed she'd left. He was walking through the living room and toward the kitchen when he spotted the note on the hall table.

*Mitchell, in case I miss you, I will not be home until late this evening. Olivia Scotland is in town, and we're having dinner together. I'm off to tennis and then some shopping. Sydney.*

"Translation: I do not want to spend any time with you, but I do want to spend your money." He balled up the note and tossed it onto the table. He headed to the kitchen, fully expecting to find cold coffee, as Sydney inevitably turned off the brewer.

"Wonders never cease," he muttered upon seeing the red light aglow on the appliance. Pouring himself a cup and adding cream and sweetener, he had started back toward his study when he spotted the rear door propped open.

"That's odd," he said; then suddenly his senses went cold

with shock. His coffee mug went crashing to the floor. He could see a hand, and there was no mistaking the French manicure or the multicarat anniversary ring.

*Is she dead?* He began trembling. Forcing himself forward, he lightly pushed the door against her hand. She didn't budge.

*Oh, my God! She is dead!* Terror consumed him as he leaned forward and opened the door all the way. Beneath Sydney's prostrate body was a pool of blood. Her head lay sideways and at a lopsided angle, showing the severe wound on her neck. He could see the bone of her spine.

His knees buckled, and he unwittingly fell on the floor beside her, feeling momentarily immobilized. But instead of feeling pity for his wife, he could think only of himself.

*They're going to get me. They're going to get me. I've got to get out of here!*

Not knowing whether her killer was on the other side of the door or lurking somewhere in the apartment, he took her racquet as a means of defending himself, then moved backward across the tiled floor, finally leaning against a pantry cabinet.

*"It's pay or play,"* Rand Emmerson had told him several weeks ago. *"They're threatening to kill us and family members if that's what it takes. We've got to be firm, Mitchell. We're not going to pay. If we start, there will be no end to their demands."*

"Oh, God, get me out of here," Mitchell cried. "No one will understand. No one."

Candace Rutland was dead, and now Sydney. And any ensuing investigation was bound to reveal the truth. He didn't care about the money. All he wanted was out.

*I'll run,* he thought. *They will never find me. I'll go, I'll go . . .* His imagination was spinning wildly when sounds in the hallway made his heart nearly stop. The front door opened and shut. Footsteps shuffled across the foyer. Stand-ing up, Mitchell immediately replaced the racquet with a carving knife from a pantry drawer.

Peering around the corner and down the long hallway leading to the foyer, he felt immeasurable relief at the sight of Manuela, who was unfolding Sydney's crumpled note. His relief was quickly replaced by panic. Placing the knife on the countertop, Mitchell took several large breaths and began proceeding down the hallway. Suddenly realizing his hands and trousers were now covered with blood, he quickly retreated and instead peeked out from the pantry.

"Manuela," he yelled out with forced cheerfulness. "What are you doing here? Didn't Sydney call you?"

"Oh, hello, Mr. Cunningham," she responded brightly in her thick Cuban accent. "No sir, she didn't call me."

"Well, you know how forgetful she can be. Listen, since the girls are away, Sydney and I have decided to take a brief vacation, starting today." He added nervously, "And we just didn't think it was necessary for you to clean house until we returned. We thought you'd like the time off."

"Oh?" she said.

"With pay, of course." She smiled at him, though still rather curiously. "That is okay with you, isn't it?"

"Yes, of course." She was still staring at him. She'd never once seen him in the pantry, and then to have him address her with only his head poking out seemed very peculiar. "Are you okay?" she asked.

"Me? Of course, why do you ask?" he responded. "Oh," he immediately rejoined, "I'm sorry, Manuela, you caught me off guard. I'm in my underwear." By her smile she seemed convinced. "Okay, well, you enjoy this week off. And listen, just in case Mrs. Cunningham and I decide to stay away longer, we'll call you."

"Yes, of course," she responded haltingly. "Have a nice trip."

"That I will," he said, waving good-bye as she left. For several minutes afterward he stayed frozen, staring down the hall as a kaleidoscope of thoughts and fears consumed him. Not knowing the killer's whereabouts, he was afraid to move one step beyond the pantry. He knew that should he survive, his life as he'd known it was over.

Slowly he turned toward his wife's slain body. "I'm getting out of here," he said, as if casually discussing his dilemma with her. He could take a flight out of JFK International Airport. He proceeded to open his wallet and count his cash. He had four hundred and thirty-five dollars. Not including cab fare to the airport, it was hardly enough to buy a one-way, last-minute ticket, preferably to Geneva, where he could tap one of his largest accounts. Using a credit card would leave electronic footprints, and he knew it would be unwise to stop first at his New York bank.

As he glanced once more at Sydney's hand, a deranged thought crossed his mind. He'd foolishly spent thirty thousand dollars for that ring on her finger, and he wanted it back.

Surrendering his wits, Mitchell bent down and worked the ring off her limp finger, then jammed it in his pocket with astonishing satisfaction. As for cold, hard cash, she must have money in her purse. He peered down the broad hallway that cut through the apartment, and seeing nothing suspicious, he ventured forth in search of her handbag, unaware that he was leaving faint bloody footprints behind.

"Bingo!" he exclaimed after finding her wallet. Another six hundred dollars. Still, it was hardly enough to cover a trip to Switzerland. That's when he remembered his daughter Sarah had a hidden stash. Though she spent his money with abandon, she hoarded every cent of her gift money, keeping a fair portion of it stowed in her bedroom. Mitchell dashed upstairs, where he feverishly tore apart her room looking for the money. She'd done a remarkable job of hiding it, as there was nothing to be found in any of the better hiding spots. Then he opened the top drawer of her French antique bureau.

"What a dope!" he said aloud over the obvious site. But his criticism quickly gave way to awe, as he discovered over two thousand dollars in a plastic bag beneath several of the thirteen-year-old's training bras.

"Good God, I should have been charging her rent."

He knew the accumulated three thousand dollars was enough to get him started, and as he was already upstairs, Mitchell entered his bedroom suite to pack a suitcase. It turned out to be a grave mistake. After he flipped on his closet light, Mitchell Cunningham's life went permanently dark.

# CHAPTER
# 6

Liz Phillips retreated to the nearby restroom, and for the first time in over twenty-four hours she got a close look at herself. In spite of practically no sleep for two straight nights, and a ripening tension headache, she managed an inward nod of approval. In a week she would turn forty-five. Notwithstanding sleep deprivation, a stress-packed career, one divorce, and a recovered fractured vertebra compliments of a high-speed chase gone awry—she thought she looked pretty damned good. She gingerly plucked two stray gray hairs from her head, rinsed the lingering taste of coffee laced with thick, powdered artificial creamer from her mouth, then headed back to the war room, where over a dozen detectives were at work.

Settling down at a worn metal desk, she scanned her surroundings before digging through her notes yet again. Posted on the south wall was an oversized mural featuring the minutia of Candace Courtland Rutland's life on Post-it notes and index cards; while the north wall harbored the details regarding Sydney and Mitchell Cunningham. Hunches about all of them were posted on a wall in between.

It had been two weeks since a maintenance man found Sydney's body, a bloody trail leading him to the horrifying discovery in the service stairwell of their apartment building. Police later found Mitchell's body in the couple's master bedroom closet. For Liz it had been two weeks of pure hell as the pressure remained unrelenting on the NYPD to find the killer. She opened her binder and read the medical examiner's notes again.

> *Each victim's throat was slashed open with a clean, horizontal cut, seemingly with a surgical scalpel that cut from left to right—carotid to carotid. Bruising of the oblique muscles beneath each victim's right arm suggests that the killer is a large man capable of wrapping his left arm over the victims' upper torsos, holding them tightly under their right armpit with his left hand while using the instrument in his right. Given that Mitchell Cunningham was six feet tall, we can assume the attacker is at least that height.*
>
> *Only Sydney Cunningham bore injuries consistent with a struggle, as there was a contusion on her right lower jaw, suggesting that she'd been struck.*

The coroner said the Cunninghams had been dead less than two hours before being discovered. Their maid confirmed that she'd spoken with Mitchell around ten-fifteen, meaning that sometime between midmorning and noon, the killer climbed fourteen flights of stairs and picked the locks on the Cunninghams' back door. Whether Sydney caught him in the act was unclear, though it was obvious that she'd been murdered first. More puzzling was whether or not Mitchell had been involved in her death. His footprints were found in a pool of her blood and more of her blood was found on his clothing. If he'd innocently discovered her, why didn't he call for help? Was it because the killer was in the pantry with him when he spoke to Manuela, perhaps dictating his actions? If not, then after finding Sydney, why did Mitchell rummage through his daughter's possessions, take her cash and then apparently his wife's anniversary ring? Two sets of male footprints were found in the apartment, yet his were the only ones found in his daughter's bedroom, bearing traces of Sydney's blood. It seemed unlikely the killer would have allowed him to move alone at any time. And as far as his children and the maid could tell, nothing else in the apartment was missing, eliminating burglary as a motive.

Furthermore, the family's travel agent, someone who'd been doing business with them for twelve years, had no record of the vacation plans Mitchell had suggested to Manuela. In fact, Sydney spoke with the agent two days before her death about getting train tickets home from camp for their children. She had commented on how delightful it was not having to be anywhere for the next couple of weeks. She wasn't even planning on going to their country house.

Another perplexing twist was that both Cunninghams had attended the Courtland and Rutland wedding. Malcolm Rutland was brought in for extensive questioning again; every conceivable aspect in both couple's lives had been scrutinized, and still no explanation, with only one possible lead.

"Commander Phillips," one of her subordinates hollered from across the room while muffling the phone against his chest. "It's Hizzoner."

"Tell him I gave at the office," Phillips snapped back. Still, she shut her notebook and picked up an extension. With feigned politeness she addressed the city's caustic and intrusive two-term mayor. "Good morning, sir."

"Liz, good morning," said Alan Perkins.

"What can I do for you?" She pinched her forehead and momentarily closed her eyes. A few detectives nearby went silent, and not out of respect for the mayor. He was unpopular among the police rank and file, having subjected them to serious budget cutbacks for two years straight. Liz

Phillips hated the man because of it. The loss in department
dollars meant that some homicides went unsolved, which
Phillips felt was an incalculable crime in and of itself.

"Listen," he began in a light, informal tone. "I talked to
Stevens this morning about the phone records," he said, referring to the commander of the NYPD, Joseph Stevens, and
then to the phone records of each victim. Long distance
charges were easy to investigate, but the local phone company charged $500 per day for each phone number under re-
view. In this case, Hizzoner had provided enough cash for
the department to examine the past three months, even six if
necessary. And while it was crucial in this case to examine
those records, it was infuriating to Phillips that his largesse
was prompted by a desire to satisfy his wealthy constituents.

"Uh-hm," she muttered, wondering when he would get to
the real purpose of his call.

"Liz. I can understand why you might wonder about Rand
Emmerson. But what do you really have? Not much." He
paused. "Wouldn't you agree?"

"What are you suggesting?" she said.

"What I'm suggesting is that you think about this. I've
known Rand since he was twelve years old. He was a solid
kid, a very good student, and now he's a respectable young
man. I cannot imagine that he'd have a single thing to do
with these murders. Though I can imagine that he might
have socialized with these folks, or even done business with
them, hence the phone calls."

Phillips had anticipated this. Rand Emmerson's father,
Ham Emmerson, was the mayor's best friend and largest
benefactor. He was a highly influential investment banker,
and his son was a very successful commodities broker. The
local phone records revealed calls between Rand's office
and the homes of the deceased on several occasions, though
preliminary financial records showed no trace of business

with him. According to an invitation list provided by Malcolm Rutland, Rand Emmerson had been invited to the wedding, but he'd sent regrets. Phillips wanted to inquire about his calls with the victims, and hoped to learn his whereabouts on the wedding day. It did not mean he had anything to do with their murders. But his presence in their lives was a common denominator, and if nothing else he could hopefully provide the police with a lead—something in short supply right now.

"Sir, I don't mean to be rude. But could you be a little more clear what it is you want me to think about? He's not a suspect. We just want to know why he talked to them. It's that simple."

Perkins sighed heavily into the phone, which was his customary way of conveying impatience. People struggling to impress him might be intimidated. Liz sighed back.

"What I'm suggesting, and believe me, I'm not trying to tell you how to do your job. I'm only suggesting that bringing him in for questioning might create a media maelstrom around him and his family. I've known his parents for twenty years, Liz. Even if there was nothing to it, something like this might destroy them. Think about it."

Liz shook her head in disbelief. Three people were dead, a killer was at large, and the mayor's top priority was protecting a crony.

"What did Stevens have to say about this?"

"He told me to take it up with you. Again, I'm not trying to tell you how to do your job. But please weigh what evidence you have a little more closely before bringing him in. The press is bound to get a hold of this and . . . who knows what, turn it into some preppie murder case."

"Sir, do I need to remind you that preppie is in jail for committing murder?" she said snidely of Robert Chambers, the young man convicted in the late eighties of killing a woman after having sex with her in Central Park.

He sighed again. "Do what you need to do," he said, then hung up.

"All right, sir," she said. "And have a good day"—she hung up—"you prick."

Two nearby detectives laughed.

"Jesus Christ, I'll be so glad when this is over," Phillips said.

# CHAPTER
# 7

Through hazy smoke from a Cuban cigar clenched between his teeth, he never lost eye contact with the young woman. Tucking her business card inside the jacket pocket of his hand-tailored suit, he managed a grin. She'd approached him under the pretense of business. He would call her under the pretense of the same.

"Thanks," he said smoothly. "I appreciate the compliment."

"Well, like I said," she responded eagerly, "I heard you were one of the best."

One of Randall Hamilton Emmerson III's cohorts at the trendy Manhattan nightclub laughed out loud at the double entendre. Rand, however, restrained himself. Within seconds he'd sized her up. Financially she was nowhere near the league of his investors and would never become his client. But physically she met his criteria—female, firm ass, and cute. He would definitely keep her card.

She looked at him, waiting for an invitation to sit down at his table, one of the most coveted spots in the underground nightclub. He said nothing. "Well, I guess I'll see you," she said with an obsequious grin. He nodded as she turned and walked away.

"Another anemic," he pronounced, "desperate to suck my blue blood." Laughter erupted among his male friends.

"Through your dick," said his longtime friend, Dr. Cameron Bulloch.

"Ohhh, I feel a blood drive coming on," Rand quipped back, sustaining the laughter. "In fact, maybe I'll give blood tonight," he said, pulling out the young woman's card.

Their audacity was cut short by the appearance of Sergei Fedorov, a former Harvard Business School classmate and friend of Rand's. Extroverted and glib, and quite a ladies' man himself, he would have normally enjoyed the conversation. But tonight he appeared agitated as he slid into the semicircular booth beside Rand. Compliments of the club owner, there was always a tray of liquor sitting at Emmerson's table, helping the influential patron avoid any unnecessary wait for service. Fedorov reached over for a tumbler and poured himself a glass of vodka, then took several belts.

"Hard day at the office?" said Rand mockingly.

Fedorov sneered. "We made a big exchange today," he replied.

Rand slowly exhaled cigar smoke. "Really? Everybody happy?"

Fedorov downed the rest of the vodka. "An even exchange," he said while plunking down his glass.

"Business was good, then?" said Rand dryly.

"Very good." Fedorov nodded.

Rand Emmerson slept quite well that night. The next morning before leaving for his customary jog around Central Park, he scanned the *New York Times*.

FORMER KGB AGENT VIKTOR MALAKOV FOUND DEAD OF APPARENT SUICIDE. Rand smiled as he read the short mention about the notorious spook. He had been found dead in his Moscow apartment from a self-inflicted bullet wound to the head, it reported. He smiled.

"Finally, an even exchange."

# CHAPTER
# 8

The hard, progressive beat of the Foo Fighters played so loudly into Gerrold Evans's headset that he barely noticed the police siren wailing behind him.

He could sense a car bearing down on him as he sped wildly along Manhattan's Seventh Avenue on his beat-up bike, swerving recklessly among cars and pedestrians in the dense rush hour traffic, but he didn't dare slow down by turning around to look. Making his last delivery, then getting to Giants Stadium on time for tonight's U2 concert was his chief concern. He'd had tickets to the sold-out show for months now, and wasn't going to miss a minute of it. And though a pager nestled deep in his pocket buzzed incessantly, and his walkie-talkie crackled with the voice of his supervisor, he ignored them both, knowing his boss would demand "just one last" pickup and delivery.

Singing loudly in unison with the band's lead vocalist, he sat upright, and releasing his hands from the bike, began banging madly to the rhythm on a set of air drums.

"Shit!" he said as the light ahead of him at Thirty-eighth Street suddenly turned red, and heavy cross traffic abruptly cut him off. Quickly grabbing the handlebars, he brought his bike to a shaky halt, fighting for balance as he did, finally wiping his sweaty brow with the back of his grimy hand.

The temperature was well into the nineties. He glanced at his neon-green plastic watch—it was 4:31 P.M. With any luck he'd be down on Wall Street by five, then out partying with his friends by six.

"What the fuck?" he shouted as his headset was forcibly ripped from his ears. Gerrold angrily spun around, and in a desperate move to distract the thief he spewed a large, mucousy spit ball. Immediately he regretted the move. His unwitting target was a New York City cop, who grimaced while wiping the saliva from his face.

"Whoa! Not a bad hit," the young man foolishly joked, hoping to ease the cop's anger.

The cop rubbed the sticky mess on Gerrold's sweat-soaked Tommy Hilfiger shirt. "You gotta driver's license?"

"What for? I'm not driving."

The cop was not amused. "I said, you gotta driver's license?"

"I suppose," Gerrold replied more respectfully, less from the cop's pressure and more from the realization that he might be late getting to his concert. He began fumbling with his backpack, searching in vain for his wallet. "What exactly have I done, Officer Jennings?" Gerrold asked, reading the man's name badge.

"Have you ever been to driver's education?" Jack Jennings Jr. snarled. He was tall and well built, reminding Gerrold of a Greenwich Village club bouncer with whom he'd recently quarreled after being refused admittance to a popular night spot. The bouncer got the better of him.

"Why?" Gerrold questioned, ignorant of any wrongdoing.

"Why?" Jennings repeated. "Because you might have learned that it's illegal to pass through a red light. I got you down for at least three of those. You found that driver's license yet?"

Gerrold dug furiously for his wallet, first pulling out the T-shirt and jeans he planned to wear that evening, followed by his lunch trash.

"I can't seem to find—" he stopped, gasping at the sight in his hand. What he'd believed to be lunch remains turned out to be his stash—a Baggie with an eight ball of coke. Hoping the cop hadn't noticed the blunder, he quickly jammed it back down in the sack.

"Wow, you know what, Officer Jennings? I must have left my wallet at home; which I do remember from driver's ed is not good." Gerrold laughed nervously. He'd never been caught with dope before, and couldn't believe that on this of all nights he might get busted.

"I mean, what do I do, man? Can't you just take my name and address and give me a ticket or whatever?" he asked with feigned composure. The patrol car's flashing lights, the rush of heavy traffic around him, and the curious looks of passersby seemed to suddenly crowd in on him, making Gerrold feel claustrophobic and panicky. In spite of the heat and his profuse sweating, a chill rushed through his body.

"I'll tell you exactly what to do. Hand it over," said Officer Jennings.

"Hand over what? I just told you I don't have my wallet."

"Give me the backpack."

"Don't you need a search warrant or something?" Gerrold asked shakily.

"Give me the backpack," Jennings commanded.

Gerrold knew there was no escaping now. He was going to be busted. He handed it over, unable to watch as Jennings went straight for the dope. He cautiously opened the plastic bag and smelled the contents.

"I'd say this is my lucky day. I got me a smart aleck and a dope peddler at once."

"Isn't this where you read me my rights, or something like that?"

"Yeah, and tell you you might want to shut the hell up before you get into any more trouble."

Gerrold's long, dirty blond hair was completely soaked now and sticking to the back of his neck. Realizing he was about to be handcuffed, he quickly pulled a rubber band off his wrist and gathered his hair into a ponytail.

As he did, a look of incredulity covered Jennings's face. There in the nape of his neck was a steel earring with a shark's head protruding from one side, its tail jutting out from the half-inch of flesh behind it.

In the glare of the midafternoon sun aboard the Staten Island ferry, Detective Frank Kelley caught the glint of something odd on the right cuff of his navy blue blazer. Bending his arm for closer inspection, he realized he'd failed to remove the tin foil used by the dry cleaners to protect a short row of brass buttons. *Incredible,* he thought, as he realized he'd escaped a ribbing from his colleagues over this. It was unlike him to miss such a detail, but even more unlike them to miss poking good-natured fun at him. *Well, usually good-natured,* he concluded.

A twelve-year veteran of the NYPD, Detective Kelley had spent the last five years battling a rare adult onset of Tourette's syndrome. His case was mild, but still obvious, and though he wasn't blurting any unintentional expletives, at times his face twitched uncontrollably, prompting him to squint and rapidly blink his eyes. His co-workers had nicknamed him Twitch, which he'd accepted with outward good humor but truly resented. It made him seem like some buffoon. He was, in reality, one of the brightest detectives on the force. And sadly, as the disease progressed, his days doing undercover detective work ceased. It made him too recognizable, his superiors told him. He could have claimed disability, but opted to stay put instead. Which suited the department just fine as they didn't want to sacrifice his keen mind, keeping him at work behind the scenes on some of the more perplexing cases.

He began peeling off the layers of tin foil while thinking about his mission ahead. He was out to learn the identity of "Red," or "Simply Red" as some of his colleagues referred to her because of her flaming red hair. Following Officer Jennings's astute observation about the identical body piercings of Gerrold Evans and Red, Kelley's assignment was to interrogate the boy and learn about any connection between the two. He shook his head, thinking how different today's youth culture was compared to his own. Back then, tatoos on your upper arm were considered risque. Today, however, it seemed there were no boundaries as kids tattooed and pierced every conceivable body part to gain some sort of delusive status.

Kelley arrived at Staten Island, then took the bus to the Port Richmond neighborhood that Gerrold Evans called home. He walked past some empty storefronts in the decaying business district, and turned right onto Gerrold Evans's street. He lived in a small, detached house with light blue vinyl siding that gave the impression of a mobile home. It had darker, faded blue shutters, and no garage, though there was a driveway in which a tire-less 1970s Pontiac LeMans sat perched on concrete blocks. Weeds had choked off most of the grass, and a small cluster of peaked azaleas framed the front stoop.

Detective Kelley tried the doorbell, which was broken, then knocked twice. He could hear a television, and figured someone must be home. He knocked again, and this time a yellowed sheer curtain parted in the window, behind which stood a woman wearing curlers. Moments later the door cracked open, and she spoke over the chain lock.

"What can I do for you?" she asked in a clipped, raspy voice.

Kelley tried hard not to twitch while presenting his badge. "Detective Frank Kelley, NYPD. I'd like to speak with Gerrold Evans. Is he here?"

"What for?"

"I have a couple of questions I'd like to ask him."

"What about? He done something stupid again?"

Kelley laughed. "You must be his mother."

"Good guess," she responded, adding, "He ain't here, and I'm gettin' ready for work."

"Any idea where he is?"

"He's supposed to be out looking for a job. I sunk a few hundred into his bail, which he promised to pay back. Fat chance I'll ever see it." Kelley could see beyond her hard edge that she was neither bad looking nor old—probably in her midforties. She was wearing a frayed pink housecoat that snapped up the front, and had half-finished her makeup while waiting for the hot curlers in her dyed blonde hair to cool.

"You know," she said, "my kid's never been in trouble. I mean never. I just don't get it. It wasn't like he was some Einstein in school or nothing. But it was pretty much like he did what he was asked and was always where he was supposed to be. And now, well, it's like he's making up for lost time."

Kelley twitched, which he hated. During moments like this he could usually get someone to open up even further. He could see in the woman's soft blue eyes a look of bewilderment over his unnatural jerk, as if she wasn't sure whether to feel sorry or scared. People who didn't know him often looked the other way, pretending not to notice.

"Well, he's not in any more trouble over the drug charges, if that makes you feel any better. The reason I'm here is to follow up on a missing persons report. Someone he might have known." Kelley pulled out a photocopied sketch of Red and flashed it in front of Evans. He noticed a perceptible change in her countenance, from frustrated to just plain worried.

"Do you recognize her?" he asked.

Shirley Evans looked up at him, squarely meeting his eyes. This time he didn't blink. Neither did she. "I didn't think she was classified as missing," she nearly whispered. "Gerrold told me she was dead."

Kelley's energy intensified. "Actually, *he's* right. Do you know her?"

Closing her eyes, she released a huge sigh, as if preparing for an emotional bungee jump. "I never met her."

"But Gerrold knew her."

"Yeah, I guess. Kinda. Listen, I can only talk for a few minutes. You wanna come in? I'm usually supposed to be at work by three o'clock. But I gotta quick errand to run and told them I'd be in at four today." She opened the door and held it while Kelley entered the house. He was not surprised to find outdated furniture against cheaply paneled walls. But it was clean. A soap opera blared on a large, old television, which Evans promptly turned down.

"*As the World Turns,*" she said. "The story of my life. Have a seat."

Kelley sat on a worn-out sofa with blue, brown, and gold polyester fabric. A skirt surrounding the bottom of it was ragged, and sagging cushions were bolstered by foam reinforcements. Shirley Evans sat across a heavy oak coffee table from him in a worn-out recliner. She looked at him nervously and rocked gently for a moment before reaching over for a pack of Salems on the table.

"Care for one?" she asked, while lighting up.

"No, thanks. Never smoked, actually."

"Good thing," she said after blowing smoke sideways and away from Kelley. She started to take another drag, then paused. "Pardon my manners. Do you mind if I smoke?"

He did mind. "Go right ahead." He smiled, nonchalantly scratching the back of his balding head.

"Thanks." She continued rocking while taking a few more drags, momentarily watching the TV. The living and dining rooms were joined in an L-shape, the whole area covered in gold shag carpeting. Kelley guessed by the interior that the husband must have split around 1975.

"What's wrong with you?" she asked bluntly.

"Excuse me?"

"Your head. You keep jerking it. Is it some nerve disorder?"

Kelley rubbed an ever-tense muscle on his shoulder blade. "Tourette's," he responded.

"That sucks. Don't get me wrong. It don't really bother me. Believe me, in my twenty years as a licensed practical nurse, I've seen it all." She took another long drag, but never fully exhaled, instead allowing smoky words to escape her mouth. "I'm sorry for you. I know it's not easy."

"Thanks. And you're right. It's not easy. But life goes on. I'm happy to still be doing my job. Speaking of which, what can you tell me about this woman?" he asked, placing the sketch of Red on the table between them so that it faced Shirley Evans.

She shook her head and rolled her eyes. "He said he bought some drugs from her, and the next thing he knew he was watching the news reports of her bizarre death."

"Did he also hear the reports that she's unidentified? Why didn't he call if he knew who she was?"

"Probably 'cause he's in enough trouble. That boy is

scared to death, and frankly so am I. I shouldn't even be talking to you about this. He made me promise not to tell no one he knew her, and now look what I've done. But I don't need any more trouble, and he don't neither."

"What can you tell me about her?"

"She was a drug source. And she's dead. That's all I know. Gerrold usually don't talk much about his personal life. But he did confide that he recognized her, and then amazingly told me how he knew her. You gotta believe me when I say I was floored. That kid rarely tells me anything. But she was the first person he'd ever known that died. Plus, I think the arrest really shook him up, and like I says, he's scared. Anyway, he promised me it's the only time he'd ever bought dope, and that he bought it from her."

"Trust me, he'll never know you told me. Any idea when he's expected home, or where I might find him?"

"Yeah, but first, how'd you link them two together anyway?"

"You know the 'earring' he wears in the back of his neck?"

"Yeah," she said, then stubbed out her cigarette.

"The victim had an identical earring posted in the exact same location on her body."

"Oh, shit."


The sun's warmth forced Kelley to remove his jacket and roll up his sleeves. Despite the heat he didn't mind setting out on foot in search of the young man. Shirley Evans had told him about a pool hall that Gerrold frequented in Port Richmond's nearby business district.

Easily spotting the local establishment, Kelley crossed the street. But not before adjusting his sunglasses, something needing frequent alignment due to his facial spasms.

Rubbing the back of his tense neck and adjusting his glasses once more, he entered the bar.

It was dark and reeked like a stale keg. The wood floor was rough and dull, while shellacked, burly wood tables and benches ran along the north wall. An equally burnished bar filled the opposite wall, its sole occupant a thin, older man drawing hard on a filterless cigarette while nursing a bottle of Budweiser.

"Ah, kiss my ass," he muttered at a large overhead TV as an umpire declared a third strike against one of the Yankees. Kelley, an avid Yankees fan, leaned on the bar for a moment, contemplating buying a beer. But the bartender was in an adjacent storeroom talking with a vendor, and in the rear of the joint he saw Evans. He was resting on his pool cue while watching a challenger sink two balls from a single shot. Evans didn't flinch. He waited patiently as his opponent sank one more, then missed the next. Evans moved in and easily sank six shots in a row to finish the game. Kelley wondered if this was how he made money now, and wouldn't blame him if he did.

Kelley moved closer to the action. "You're pretty damned good," he said.

A slight, appreciative grin crossed Evans's boyish face. "Thanks, man. You play?"

"How much would it cost me?"

"Coupla quarters."

Kelley chuckled, and twitched. "You're letting me off easy," he said, fishing in his pants for some change. "Actually, I wondered if there wasn't some kind of wager involved."

Evans eyed him with a mixture of sympathy and curiosity, as if Kelley's malady made him too easy a mark. "Well, I suppose if you want . . ." Evans started, then paused as Kelley twitched again.

"Naw. Why don't you two play?" Evans suggested, nodding at his former competitor.

"I don't think so," said Kelley, reflexively pulling out his badge. "Detective Frank Kelley, NYPD Homicide."

"What now?" Evans snarled, rolling his eyes upward. "I haven't killed anybody—yet."

"Nothing to worry about then—yet," responded Kelley. "I was just wondering what you could tell me about this woman," he went on, pulling out the sketch of Red.

"I don't know her," Evans said, barely glancing at the picture. He turned to walk away.

"You know, that's interesting," Kelley continued. "Because here's something you might recognize."

Evans let out an exasperated sigh, then stopped. "What?" he snapped, his back toward Kelley.

"Take a close look." Kelley reached into the breast pocket of his jacket and, retrieving a Polaroid snapshot, walked in front of Evans and held it up to his face.

"So? What is it?"

"It's a picture that the coroner took of this woman's neck. Did I mention that she's dead? Anyway, one of my colleagues noticed that her earring matches the one you wore on the day of your arrest—posted in the same location."

He walked behind Evans. "In fact, it looks a lot like the one you're wearing right now. Shark head on the front, tail fin out the back. What a coincidence. Wouldn't you say?"

"Yeah, what a coincidence. See ya later," Evans declared, walking away again.

"Any coincidence that we found your name and number on her when she died?" Kelley lied.

"Yeah, that would be a coincidence, because I never knew her."

"Any coincidence that you bought dope from her?"

The young man visibly blushed. "What is it you want from me?"

"The truth. That's all. She's dead, and no one seems to care. You must have cared a little when you turned your necks into shish kebabs together. I'd guess she was more than a source, maybe even a pretty good friend."

Evans began to speak, but lowered his head instead. When he finally looked up, Kelley could see tears brimming in his soft hazel eyes. "Man, this is so unfair. Why is all this shit happening to me?"

"What do you mean, to you? She's the one that's dead."

"You know what? That really sucks. As if I had something to do with her getting blown away in a bank heist."

"So you do know who she is?"

Evans released another sigh conveying jumbled emotions, fear among them.

Kelley pressed on. "Somewhere I'd imagine is someone who'd *care* to know she's dead. I thought for a moment that person might be you. Anything you want to tell me about her?"

Evans's macho demeanor withered. He slid into a booth with the solemnity of someone stepping into a confessional. "Am I in some kinda trouble?" he asked with a tentative voice. Kelley couldn't tell if it was an act or not.

"Discounting possession of cocaine and riding your bike like a psychopath through Manhattan, I'd say no," Kelley responded between two jerks of his head.

"What's your problem, man?" Gerrold stiffened uncomfortably. "You're making me nervous."

"I'm supposed to. I'm a cop."

"No. I mean your head. What's your problem?"

"None of your business. But what is my business is this girl's identity. And all I want from you right now is help finding her next of kin."

Gerrold cast his eyes downward and spoke softly. "I don't know much, man."

"Yeah, but you seem to know more than anyone else right now. Listen, Gerrold, you've got to trust me. I'm just trying to do my job, which right now is identifying a woman who, in a foiled bank heist, killed an armed guard. Unless you had something to do with *that* act of insanity, then you've got nothing to worry about."

Evans looked over at the bar and gave a nod to the bartender, who promptly poured a draft, then delivered it to the young man.

"Can I get you anything?" the bartender asked Kelley.

"Whatever he's drinking," Kelley replied, watching Evans take a large swallow of his beer. Moments later the bartender returned, and as the two shared a cold draft, Gerrold calmed down enough to open up.

"I met her about six weeks ago," he started. "It was a fluke thing. She was trying to get into the same bar as me, and we both got bumped out of the line by the bouncer. I felt kinda sorry for her, 'cause her English wasn't so great, and the bouncer was a real dick to her because of it. So I got in his face. He was threatening to kick my ass when she cut in, and for some reason he just let us go. So we went off together, looking for some other place to get in."

Kelley remained silent, not wanting to interrupt.

"Anyway, turns out she was pretty down on her luck. She'd recently moved to the States from Russia, after following some boyfriend to Louisiana. When she got there, he told her to leave and that he didn't want anything to do with her. Said she was devastated, 'cause she'd spent nearly all of her money gettin' over here, and didn't have enough to get back. He wouldn't help her at all, and so before she left Louisiana, she broke into his apartment and found some dope, which she stole. Then she hitchhiked up to New York, supposedly because her boyfriend knew someone up here, and she was hoping that he might help her get a job, or a place to live, or something. Turns out he pretty much told her to fuck off.

"Meanwhile, she's broke, which is why she went to the club. She was looking for someone to buy her dope. Which I did," he said, shaking his head in regret. He took another swig of beer and pursed his lips before continuing.

"She really had nowhere to go and noplace to stay. A courier friend of mine had just taken off on a bike trip across the country, and left me with the keys to his place in case I wanted to crash in the city. I told her she could stay there till he got back, 'cause I knew he wouldn't mind."

"What's the address?" Kelley asked, retrieving a notebook from his jacket.

"Down in the Village," he said, stating the precise location. "I don't know who she was, really. I mean, she said her name was Suzanne, which didn't sound too Russian to me. Anyway, she had some great coke, some of which she gave me in return for the favor. We got high a coupla times at my friend's place, and one of those times, on a kinda lark we just went out and did this," he said, touching his pierced neck. "And this," he stated, boldly lifting his shirt and revealing a pierced belly button. Kelley cringed. "She talked me into it. Pretty fuckin' crazy, huh?"

"Simply put—yes. Did Suzanne mention anyone that you can remember? Any family members in the U.S.? The name of her boyfriend or his friend?"

"Naw. You know, it all sucks too, because she was pretty sweet. And scared. I remember that." Evans looked the other way for a moment. A dozen years of police work told Kelley that Evans had probably slept with the girl too, though he'd probably never admit it.

"Listen, for what it's worth, I'm sorry she's dead. She was

obviously a mixed-up character, and fortunately you didn't get involved any more than you did. But what I need to know first, is her stuff still at your friend's apartment?"

"Yeah, far as I know."

"Do you still have the keys?"

"Yeah."

Kelley thought for a moment about getting a search warrant, then decided he wouldn't need one if Evans joined him. "You wanna take a trip into the Village with me and let me in so I can take a quick look around?"

Evans finished off half his beer in one swallow. "I suppose. This mean you might help *me* out down the road?"

"I'll see what I can do for you. By the way, think hard. Do you remember the name of the guy she tried to reach up here?"

"Hmmm," he struggled for the moment. "Not really. All I remember is it was kinda different. I think it was something like Rand." He thought for an instant longer. "Yeah. It was definitely Rand."

# CHAPTER
# 9

Kelley rapped on the door of the Greenwich Village loft. As expected, no one answered.

"Go ahead," he motioned to Evans, then watched as the courier-cum-criminal fumbled with a set of keys, opening three dead bolts on the thick metal door.

"Shit," decried Evans. It was sweltering, stuffy, and reeked of stale Chinese food inside the one-room loft. Strong beams of sunlight poured through two westward-facing windows, revealing an amazing amount of clutter. Old newspapers and magazines formed various heaps about the place, competing for space with scattered clothes and shoes. On a breakfast bar to Kelley's left were open and moldy cartons of Chinese take-out, along with a plate containing half-eaten portions of sesame noodles, moo-shu pork, and an egg roll.

Evans claimed the last time he'd seen the girl alive was nearly a week before the bank incident. He'd pretty much left her alone amid his friend's rubbish, stating that that was the way he'd left it, and typically preferred to live. A futon centered along one wall was buried beneath sheets and a couple of skimpy dresses—the first visible evidence of a female presence. On the floor was an oversized dark green duffel bag, in which clothes were carelessly stuffed.

Kelley immediately walked to it and began inspecting the garments. They were cheap and bore mostly Russian labels. Placing everything in a neat pile on the bed, he dug farther, finding a number of personal effects, including a box of condoms. He noticed Evans blushed as he placed them on the bed. From the confines of the bag, Kelley retrieved a pair of jeans, and began fishing around the pockets. Beaming, he discovered a passport.

"Natasha Sorokin. Born August 12, 1974. Look anything like your friend Suzanne?" Kelley inquired, passing the document over to Evans.

The young man instantly recognized the girl's face framed in natural brown hair. "That's her," he said softly.

Kelley pulled out the rendering of the young woman, then compared the two. "Yeah, I'd say it's a pretty good match."

Evans sat dejectedly down on the bed as Kelley finished searching the contents of the bag and then scoured the room. He found nothing particularly interesting anywhere else, and after collecting the young woman's possessions, he thought to do one last thing. He picked up the phone and hit the redial button. It rang twice.

"Good afternoon, Rand Emmerson's office," came a pleasant female voice.

"Oh, I'm terribly sorry. I must have just dialed the wrong number," Kelley said politely, while jotting down the name. "Would you mind telling me what number I just called?" he went on.

"Why, certainly," the woman replied. Kelley then wrote down the number.

"Hmmm, right number; wrong person. What company is this, please?"

"Hartson, Devlin and Burns," she responded professionally. "May I transfer you to someone else's line, sir?"

"Well, actually, just put me through to the switchboard, please."

"Hartson, Devlin and Burns," an operator soon said.

"May I get your street address, please?" Kelley inquired. It was a Wall Street location.

"Oh, and one other thing. I need to send something to Rand Emmerson. What is his full name, please?"

"Just a minute while I look that up," she said. Seconds later she was back on the line. "That's Randall H. Emmerson the third."

Detective Kelley rubbed his right shoulder while waiting for the coroner to pick up. It was late on Friday, and he still hadn't eaten lunch. But he needed to close as much of this matter with "Red" as possible before the weekend.

"Henderson here."

"Dave, how ya doin'? This is Kelley."

"What's up?" Dave Henderson answered hurriedly. Like most high-level public servants, he had too much to do and too little time to do it, and was a master at cutting to the quick.

"Listen, I think I've got a positive ID for you on Red. She still in the morgue?"

"Oh, yeah."

"I've got a passport with her pretty little picture in it. Bet says you can't guess her age. Five bucks for each year." Kelley loved goading Henderson, a forensics fanatic who became angry at himself for even slightly miscalculating guesses.

"I already said she was about twenty-nine, perhaps thirty. How far off?"

"Five bucks for each year. You game?"

"Fuck you. How old?"

"Twenty-four."

"Only if the passport is valid."

"Good point. Anyway, don't send her to Potter's Field just yet."

"You got it. Any next of kin?"

"Don't know yet."

"Keep me posted," Henderson responded, then in his characteristic "gotta go" manner, hung up the phone.

"Too bad," said Kelley, flipping through the passport's mostly blank pages for the umpteenth time. "Thirty bucks woulda covered pizza and beer tonight." Apparently Natasha Sorokin had just gotten a new passport, or hadn't traveled much. He glanced at the wall clock, which read 5:14 P.M.—too late to get through to Immigration and Naturalization and find out what they might know about her.

He thought through all he knew already. Supposedly she was twenty-four years old. Had lived just outside of Odessa and, according to the April 21 entry posted in her book, had first entered the U.S. through Miami. According to Gerrold, she'd been in New York for at least three weeks when he met her. A week after he'd partied with her at the loft he learned someone matching her description had been killed at the bank. He tried calling her twice afterward, but no one answered. Because of his pending trial he was fearful of getting involved, deciding some time before his friend returned to the loft he would get rid of her belongings.

In addition, Henderson had told him she was a drug addict, strung out on heroin when she died. Gerrold claimed to know nothing of that, maintaining they only did coke together, and that she was the source of the stash found on him by Officer Jennings. So, Kelley concluded, she was a drug addict, thief, murderer, and—thinking sardonically about her pierced neck—a masochist. Other than that, he still didn't know very much.

He rubbed both hands over his head and through his thinning hair. Late Friday afternoons were always bustling in headquarters. Even though detective work went on twenty-four hours a day, those fortunate enough to wrap up a thing or two could call it quits and enjoy the weekend. He hoped to be among them when he spotted Liz Phillips passing through the Homicide Division while chatting with Cliff Blackman, the chief of the Narcotics Division. Kelley got up from his beat-up metal desk and quickly crossed the office.

"I've got something you may both want to take a look at," he said, flashing the passport in front of them.

"Jesus, where'd you get this?" Phillips asked, immediately recognizing the woman.

"Long story. Short answer: loft in Greenwich Village. Might have been dealing drugs, sir," he added for Blackman's benefit, then proceeded to tell them how he came to interview Evans and how he'd then acquired the passport.

"What else? Any contacts other than Evans?" asked Blackman.

"Well, sort of. The kid told me she came here from Louisiana looking for help from someone named Rand. I hit the redial on the phone at the loft, and got the office of Rand Emmerson, or Randall H. Emmerson the third—"

"Stop. Stop right there." Liz Phillips's skin prickled. She looked around to see if anyone else was listening. Somewhat flustered and uncertain if he'd done something wrong, Kelley remained silent.

"Come into my office, both of you," she commanded. The three silently paced down the hall into her average-sized office with its big view of the East River.

"Kelley, who else knows about this?"

"Only Henderson at the morgue." Sensing it had more to do with Emmerson and less with Red, he offered clarification. "The only thing he knows is that we may have a positive ID on the girl. I asked him not to send her body to Potter's Field just yet, that's all."

"Good," said Phillips decisively.

She cast a concerned glance at Blackman. "Have you spoken with Emmerson?"

"No, not yet."

"Does Gerrold Evans personally know Emmerson?" Blackman interjected.

"No. He couldn't even remember his full name."

"Did you mention anything about the results of your phone call to him?" Phillips asked.

"No, but he was in the room and could clearly hear what I said."

Phillips bit her lower lip for a moment, then spoke. "Listen, Kelley, let me have the passport. And do not say *a thing* about this to anyone. I'll deal with Henderson directly. But you understand, not a word about this to anyone in or outside this department. Clear?"

"Clear."

"What's the address of the loft?" she inquired, removing a pencil from behind her ear and grabbing a steno notebook off her desk. Kelley fired off the address.

"I want Evans's file," she directed. "Please give me everything you've got."

"You want the girl's clothes? I brought 'em in with me."

"I want absolutely everything."

Kelley's head unnaturally jerked as he mocked a friendly salute to his boss, then left the room.

"Way to go, Twitch," she said with muted jubilation after he'd closed the door. "This is just the piece of luck I've been waiting for."

\*       \*       \*

Jack Jennings Sr. surveyed the commemorative plaques and photographs on the beige walls of Liz Phillips's office. A framed *New York Times* magazine cover featuring the woman during her days as a narcotics agent grabbed his attention. Young, tan, and athletic, back then she wore her hair in feathery layers, which Jack remembered well. The photo featured her standing on a New York dock with a heavy gray cloud mass over her head, hands on her hips, wearing a sleeveless white shirt, jeans, and a leather shoulder holster. At first glance she might have looked like one of Charlie's Angels, but beneath the fluffy mane was one of the gutsiest women to emerge on the force. At the age of twenty-nine, she'd infiltrated a ring of drug smugglers with direct links to the Mafia crime lord Alfonse DeCarlo. She'd personally busted Big Al—an arrest that sent him to prison for life and had her forever looking over her shoulder. She was undeterred by threats, however, and once her cover was blown she joined Homicide and established herself as a tenacious detective.

Jack looked over at Carla sitting quietly in her rookie's uniform. In spite of her outward calm, he knew she was nervous. Neither one knew why they'd been summoned to Phillips's office, and Carla would not even openly guess. Secretly she was afraid that her superiors might have learned how she truly injured her rib cage, and that she was in for a reproach.

*I will never fight in one of those damned illegal competitions again!* Carla admonished herself. *But why would the chief of homicide have anything to do with a reprimand?*

"I'll put in a call to the D.A. and I'll get back with you on it later," Liz declared dryly to the party on the other end of her phone line. "Thanks." She hung up with a sneer.

"Defense lawyers," she said, and shuddered. Both Jenningses laughed.

"What's up, Lizzie?" Jack asked.

"I need your help." She removed a pencil from behind her ear and began tapping the eraser end on the desk. "I've got an interesting and highly classified development to share with you," she said. She looked at Carla. "None of what I tell you can leave this room. Understand?" Carla nodded deferentially.

"Frank Kelley investigated Jack Jr.'s lead on that chick that blew away the armed guard in Chase Bank a few weeks ago. 'Red,' remember her? Earring in the back of her neck?"

"Yeah, sure," said Jack. "So what's up?"

"Kelley found out the kid Jack Jr. busted, Gerrold Evans, bought his dope from her, did body piercing with her, and had also put her up in a friend's loft who was away."

Carla tensed up again. *Oh, God. What if Jack is in some kind of trouble?*

"So Kelley checked out the loft and discovered this young woman's passport. Her name is Natasha Sorokin— she's Russian. Just came to the States in April. While he was there, Kelley picked up the phone, hit the redial, and presto, gets patched right into one Mr. Randall H. Emmerson the third's office."

"Mary, Mother of God," Jack uttered. He was aware that the investigation into the Rutland and Cunningham murders had been stymied by the mayor over his relationship with Ham Emmerson.

"You can say that again," Phillips responded tersely. "That slimy . . ." Her voice trailed off. "The mayor tells the whole world he's doing everything he can to solve these murders. Then he essentially obstructs the investigation for personal advantage." She shook her head in disgust.

"Why the hell would she be calling him?"

"Apparently she was fixated on some Russian who'd moved to Louisiana. New Orleans, Baton Rouge. Who knows where and for what? And who knows why in the hell she would be calling Rand Emmerson."

"What do you need from me, Lizzie? You know I'll do anything I can to help you."

"Good. Because I want your daughter."

"Carla?" His brow wrinkled with perplexity. "What the hell do you want from Carla?" He asked the question while glancing over at Carla's startled face.

"I want both of you to hear me out before you say anything. And bear in mind, Jack, that I'm asking you for something for which I don't necessarily need your approval.

"Here's what the task force knows about Emmerson. He works hard, plays hard, and runs in some pretty fast circles. Princeton undergrad, Harvard Business School. He's a commodities broker with an apparent Midas touch. Even so, and though he comes from money, it's hard to fathom how at such a young age he could have accumulated his purported net worth of at least thirty million dollars. But that's the word on the street."

"How old is the guy?"

"Thirty-one. Anyway, what in the hell would a hard-luck, drug-addicted Russian in New York via Louisiana have to do with him? And as you already know, we found footprints in the Cunninghams' apartment made by a Russian shoe. It's all coincidental. But you know in this business, what's coincidence today is evidence tomorrow."

"You think he's dealing dope?"

"Big time."

"So what does Carla have to do with this?"

"Undercover, Jack." She looked over at Carla. "I want you to go deep undercover. Get near him. I want to find out who he hangs out with. I need to know his business sources, how he spends his money, and what, if anything, he had to do with the murders of Candace Rutland and Mitchell and Sydney Cunningham."

"Lizzie, have you lost your mind?" Jack promptly interjected. "Carla isn't even a real cop yet!"

"Which is precisely why I want her, Jack. No one knows her. If Emmerson is dealing dope, you've gotta believe that it's not minor league. The dealers are getting more and more sophisticated with their police intelligence—once in a while they know more about our cops than we do. I could send out a veteran, but I think our greatest chance of success with Emmerson lies with sending out a complete unknown. And someone I know I can trust.

"Jack, listen to me. I've known Carla since she was a kid. Not only is she a fresh, attractive face, she's unknown. She's tough and smart as hell, and she already knows a lot about this business from her old man. Furthermore, Rand owns a Harley, and *she* possesses a business degree."

Jack Jennings wished for a moment that this was some ridiculous joke. Emotionally he'd believed himself ready for his only daughter to join the force, and was prepared for her slow and eventual entry into the ranks. But this unforeseen development caused every primal instinct to protect and guide her to tug at him like a riptide.

"Lizzie, family business or not, Carla's not ready. She doesn't know the first real thing about police work."

"That's crap, Jack, and you know it. Look, let me tell you how I envision this. The mayor is out of the loop on this. Meaning no one except for me, you, the chief, Blackman, Frank Kelley, and my 'specialists' from the Federal task force who will train and make her over will know."

"Jesus, Lizzie. What about our family?" he blurted.

"Jack, this," she said, rising and placing her hands firmly on her desktop, "is her family too."

Her expression was thoughtful but stern. Jennings nodded in appreciation, as he identified all too well with the fraternal bond of which she spoke.

"Just tell your sons she changed her mind about joining the force, and decided to take an extended motorcycle trip to clear her head. She cannot, under any circumstances, have any contact with them. And as much as I'm grateful for his help so far, that includes Jack Jr."

Jack remained silent as Phillips pressed on. "She'll spend the next three weeks with U.S. Customs agents at the Federal Law Enforcement Training Center in Georgia doing intense undercover training. Then another three being transformed into a believable socialite. After that, I have access to a chic Central Park West address that she'll call home for as long as it takes."

"C'mon, Lizzie. With all due respect, why a woman? And why Carla? I mean, she's smart, attractive, and tough. But she's not tough enough yet. Think about it. Why not send in one of the boys? Even someone nearer his age?"

The look on her face and the tone of her voice strongly suggested he was pushing his luck. Jack Jennings knew better than to play the gender card with Liz Phillips. But he wasn't thinking like a colleague. Instead, he wanted to protect his only daughter.

"Two reasons," Liz said firmly. "From the sketchy information I've gathered about Rand Emmerson, he's quite a womanizer. The male friends are more of a constant, but the women come and go. I think Carla would possess a greater chance of getting near him."

"She gonna be wired?"

"No. Not at first. I want her to roam about freely, then report her findings back directly to me. Look Jack, you and I both know she can do it."

*This is insane! She's not ready,* Jennings continued to think. *She may find herself in over her head and ruin her career before it starts. Worse, she could end up dead.*

Phillips looked him squarely in the eye, intuitively sensing his turmoil. "Jack, I'm not going to play down the danger of this. Emmerson may turn out to be as harmless as a tadpole, or as ruthless as a shark. But I desperately need inside information that I can't get through traditional means.

"I know this is unorthodox, Jack. But I'm not looking for your permission. Only your blessing."

"May I speak now?" Carla interrupted sharply. She was incredulous that this conversation was now taking place as if she weren't even in the room.

"What?" her father snapped.

"Does it at all matter here what *I* think, or what *I* want?"

He looked downward for a moment, then met her determined look. "I'm sorry, Carla," he said, clearly distressed.

"What would you like to say?" said Liz. She sat back down in her green leather chair and calmly folded her hands in front of her.

While briefly collecting her thoughts, Carla scanned Liz's display of trophy photos, focusing on the cover shot of her after the Al DeCarlo bust. *She wasn't much older than I am now,* Carla realized. She took a deep breath.

"Commander Phillips, with all due respect, my father's concerns are legitimate. I mean, let's be honest. I can hold my own against three badgering brothers and a tough-cop father. But Queens isn't exactly cosmopolitan. And besides, I've spent most of the past five years helping my father raise Robbie. In reality, I've led a pretty sheltered life."

Jack let out an audible sigh while Liz raised a discerning eyebrow. "Do you think I'm unaware of those things?"

"No, of course not. But let me finish." Carla faced her father.

"Dad, don't forget. We discussed the perils of this job when I first decided to join the force. I told you then, and I'll say it again. I want to make you proud. In fact," she hesitated, "one day I'd like to command the entire NYPD."

Phillips chuckled softly, but otherwise she and Jack remained silent. Carla went on, looking her father square in the eye. "In choosing this career, I decided to face whatever risks come my way. But they're *my* risks now. Not yours. And if Commander Phillips thinks I'm capable of doing this job, then I'm fully prepared to do it."

"Bullshit," he blurted.

"Bullshit, nothing!" Carla shot back. "Why are you being so hard on me? If it was Jack sitting here, you'd be patting him on the back and saying 'Way to go, son.' Like it or not, Dad, I'm taking this assignment."

Jack ran a hand over his careworn face, then stood up, his six-foot stature in dark blue uniform casting an imposing presence. "Well, then, young lady," he said, affixing his hat to his head. "Best of luck."

He walked toward the door, then turned and looked directly at Liz. "And if I were you, Lizzie, I'd watch my back, or she might have your job before you know it."

He abruptly left.

*You'll see, dammit!* Carla thought angrily, fighting back tears as the door slammed shut behind him. After a pause, she turned toward Liz. "I guess I'm all yours."

Liz nodded, but was momentarily quiet while gently tapping her fist against her chin. Finally she put her hand down.

"Let's get to work," she said softly while standing up and joining Carla on the other side of her desk. "By the way," Liz went on, "how's your rib cage?"

# CHAPTER
# 10

*Fake it till you make it. . . . Fake it till you make it. . . .* The
mantra kept running through Carla's head as she fumbled
with her mascara.

*You must first convince yourself of your new identity.
Here's the portfolio on Charlotte Desmond's life—memorize
it. Read thoroughly the sections on rare book collecting, sailing, and the publishing industry. Start thinking that money is
no object—you can afford whatever you want. Only remember, you don't spend or purchase like the nouveau riche. You
are old money, noblesse oblige, a trust funder. Which means
you don't flaunt it. There is nothing garish or ostentatious
about Charlotte Desmond.*

*Keep this in mind: Charlotte is a classically tailored,
well-educated, and well-bred young woman. Think ele-
gance; think Tiffany taste. Just imagine with Charlotte's education, refinement, and unlimited resources where she'd
most like to live and vacation; what kind of clothes and jewelry she'd wear; what she would do for entertainment. Let
those answers be Charlotte Desmond's answers. Remember: The trick to sounding confident is to thoroughly know
the basics. Then fake it till you make it.*

It was uneasy adjusting to her own transfiguration. Vanished was her wavy dark hair and all natural beauty. Under

her new guise, straightened honey-colored locks styled in a
page cut framed her Elizabeth Arden–enhanced face. Nothing looked or felt the same, she thought, while rooting
around for just the right lip gloss. Even wearing makeup
was an awkward adjustment. At first her eyes watered
under the weight and unfamiliarity of it all. Curled eyelashes were now considerably thickened and lengthened
with black mascara. Lids covering her golden brown eyes
were dusted in muted tones of taupe and brown and ac-
cented by a dark-plum eyeliner. Once naturally thick eyebrows had been tweezed into thin half-moons; which,
ironically, she had to pencil in for a more shapely effect.
Her olive skin was now covered with a light foundation,
while already high cheekbones were newly defined by a
soft, rosy blush.

Her new makeup and hair-care ritual took more than an
hour to complete, approximately fifty minutes more than
her standard grooming routine. The result, however, by
anyone's standard, was stunningly beautiful.

But this was not Carla Jennings getting ready for the day.
It was Charlotte Desmond staring back at her from the mirror of her new Manhattan apartment. Charlotte Desmond,
who'd just spent six weeks being transformed from a fresh-
faced rookie into a striking sophisticate.

Outwardly, everything about her now said privilege and
class. From her highly buffed nails down to her well-
pedicured toes, Charlotte Desmond appeared the embodi-
ment of a stylish, worldly debutante who'd recently settled
in Manhattan. After two years abroad working for a London-
based literary publisher, she'd decided to move stateside
and look for a new job. Originally a Seattle native, she was
a sailing enthusiast and a rare book collector besides.

Already Carla had discovered a number of dirty secrets
regarding her undercover metamorphosis. Primarily, where

dope peddling, murder, and high society were involved, money to manage such an investigation seemed the least concern. Secondly, the subculture of covert police operations provided an amazing depth of furtive support. True, there was a St. Dunstan's Press in London run by a group of academics, but it was also a well-disguised front for Scotland Yard. A handful of Yankee spooks had even found "employment" with the publisher, and on occasion an undercover cop from a large American city found his or her résumé padded with a St. Dunstan's credential. Charlotte Desmond was one of the privileged few.

Additionally, Charlotte's apartment carried a rent far greater than Carla's entire monthly paycheck. It was a spacious two-bedroom unit in a high-rise building, with an unobstructed view of Central Park and a backdrop of neoclassical apartment buildings on Fifth Avenue.

The apartment itself was another remarkable police resource. The purchaser was a gentleman who preferred leasing it out to occupying it himself. The owner, as it turned out, was the NYPD, and the gentleman a fictitious front. When Carla had first entered the apartment, she found it hard to believe something managed by a government bureaucracy could be so appealing.

Decorated in creamy, neutral colors with a variety of rich, textured fabrics and gold accents, the rooms with their twelve-foot ceilings and heavy crown molding, gray bleached floors and hand-painted sisal rugs, felt at first like a decorator showroom. But after a week the gallery feeling gave way to an odd sense of being at home. Especially when she spotted herself in framed photos scattered throughout the apartment. Smiling brightly in the pictures was Carla as Charlotte, superimposed into family snapshots with people who looked like Ralph Lauren cut-outs. Carla smiled at the sight of them. Her adopted father, white-haired and tan in his cotton swimming trunks, looked the picture of health and success as he managed a tiller aboard a sailboat on which the family clan was happily gathered. Carla couldn't even remember the last time her father had a tan.

There was a photo of Charlotte Desmond receiving her bachelor's degree from the University of Michigan, and another with a group of college classmates, arms stretched out across one another's shoulders; smiles broad and bright with birthright and promise.

The kitchen, with its granite countertops and glass-fronted cherry wood cabinetry, boasted the finest Royal Doulton china, Tiffany silverware, linen napkins, and crystal stemware. In the bedroom, the cotton sheets on her antique four-poster bed were the softest available, while the expensive and fluffy comforter offered an irresistible and downy retreat against any of a day's shortcomings.

The bedroom's walk-in closet was filled with designer clothes, and the bathroom was stocked with what Carla referred to as "pricey human condiments." Bottle after bottle of fragrant lotion, bath oils, and expensive soaps filled the shelves and drawers. Softly scented candles in graduated lengths and thicknesses occupied a ledge near the Jacuzzi tub, while thick white towels awaited the well-relaxed bather.

Immersing herself in the world of Charlotte Desmond, Carla learned from experts how to shop, dress, and behave like a privileged and hip young woman. She knew now the distinction between things stylish and faddish, and which were a combination of the two. She could speak knowledgeably on any number of new subjects, rattling off the names of top vintners one minute, while discussing coveted vacation spots the next. Her vocabulary grew exponentially with sailing terms and the jargon of the publishing world.

She could discuss, though only superficially, the merits of contemporary artwork, telling you whose work was currently hot, and whose was not; and she could readily identify the most famous works by Old Masters.

The *New York Observer* and the *Wall Street Journal* became part of her daily reading, as well as a host of other magazines popular with her supposed peers. She could tell you which caterer to choose for which special event, the more desirable Hampton townships, which charity balls in New York were must attends, the short list of truly successful socialites, and the much longer list of socially successful wannabes. She knew which restaurants in Manhattan were in vogue, and which to avoid. Carla became familiar with Madison Avenue's finest shops, and knew the better florists, gift shops, and rare book dealers besides.

Charlotte Desmond, the daughter of Walter Desmond, an entrepreneur, had been raised with a sister and brother in Seattle's exclusive Highlands community. She'd attended the private Lakeside School before leaving for Michigan, where she'd graduated with a B.A. in economics and a minor in English. Aspiration: to one day own her own publishing company. Hobbies: sailing, running, the History Channel, collecting rare books, and reading biographies of famous people. Personal estimated worth: four million dollars. Source: family trust.

About the only item remaining of Carla Jennings's was her mother's rosary beads, which she refused to forsake in the transition. They were suspended from her bedpost, serving as a source of connection to the two most important things in her life—her faith in God and her family.

On the last day of the first week occupying her new West Sixty-second Street address, Carla Jennings was entirely familiar with Charlotte Desmond's trap. Carla checked her image in the mirror one last time, then glanced out her living room window at dark and thickening clouds. *Perfect*, she thought.

Glancing at her borrowed Rolex, Carla realized she had only fifteen minutes left to reach the Metropolitan Towers on West Fifty-seventh Street. It was only 7:45 A.M., but already she felt smothered by the August heat. On Seventh Avenue, she hurried her pace, making a quick left turn on to West Fifty-seventh. Wishing she'd made time for breakfast, Carla looked longingly at a street vendor hawking coffee and sweet rolls, but passed him by. The gleaming, black-glassed Metropolitan Towers were now in sight, forcing her to stop and peek at her watch once again. She was several minutes ahead of schedule, but pressed on.

For five straight mornings she'd gone through the same drill, only not quite so dressed up as today. The first day she'd staked out the exclusive address was at six o'clock on Monday morning from a coffee shop across the street. She never saw him, and four dispiriting hours and several cups of coffee later, she briefly gave up for the day. The next morning, at seven, she spotted him leaving the building in jogging attire. He returned thirty-five minutes later and then disappeared, only to reemerge around eight, and only then after the doorman hailed him a taxi.

The next day Carla arrived early, again observing Rand Emmerson's exercise ritual followed by a predictable return to the Metropolitan Towers, where he disappeared for approximately twenty-five minutes to shower and change. Again at 8:00 A.M. he reappeared, relying on the doorman to flag him a cab.

Today, however, she intended to insert herself into his routine. Positioning herself east of the building's entrance, she feebly tried summoning the first available taxi. Fortunately, several occupied cabs drove by. It was now 7:59, and like clockwork the doorman appeared. Ignoring Carla, he rudely stepped ahead of her to secure a taxi for his tenant. As if receiving a telepathic dispatch, the driver of a vacant cab abruptly cut over two lanes of traffic before halting beside him. Rand promptly exited the building under the cover of a canopy and began climbing into the car.

"Hey!" Carla shouted. Emmerson stopped. She quickly dashed up to the car.

"I've been standing here waiting for a taxi," she said, directing her criticism at the doorman.

"I'm sorry, I didn't see you," he lied, while protecting the car's access for Rand.

"This is really frustrating," she said firmly. "I need to be downtown soon, and have had no luck getting a cab." She looked imploringly at Emmerson, worried that her hands might begin trembling in time with her quivering nerves.

"The subway's just a block away. That might be faster," the doorman suggested smugly.

"Where are you headed?" Rand intervened.

"Broadway and Twenty-second," she fibbed. Carla was as honest as the day was long and felt her heart jump over the lie.

"Listen, climb in." Rand gestured. "It's a little out of the way for me, but we can certainly share a ride."

"Are you sure? I don't want to put *you* out."

"C'mon," he insisted, his mouth curling into a slight grin.

"Thanks, I really appreciate it." She smiled gratefully as he moved out of the way, allowing her to slide in first. His gallantry faded, however, after giving the driver directions. Whether he was detached or playing at it, he managed to ignore her. Out of sheer nervousness, Carla opened up her purse and began fumbling around, searching in vain for

God only knew what, while Emmerson rustled open his copy of the *Wall Street Journal,* the *New York Times* propped on his lap.

"Mind if I have to look at the *Times*?" she inquired.

"Not at all. Here," he said, politely handing it over to her. She scanned the front page.

"Paper says sunshine today, all day," she said aloud. It was now drizzling. "Do you suppose they'll run a retraction tomorrow?" He turned slightly to face her, let out a low, throaty chuckle, then resumed his reading.

Carla remained silent. With each succeeding light they passed, she grew increasingly nervous. She knew small talk was essential, but she was afraid of a rebuff and so remained absorbed in today's news. Finally he spoke.

"You heading to work?" he inquired, while turning newspaper pages, not looking at her.

"No," she replied, being deliberately vague herself. As he was looking straight ahead, he appeared unaware that she was taking in the details of his appearance.

His ears were slightly oversized and low-set, making the rest of his head seem somewhat enlarged. He had tight waves in his short, dark blond hair, a dash of gel making it look like wet, rippled sand. His complexion was smooth and lightly freckled, his nose proportionate to his face, and though the groove beneath his nose and upper lip was somewhat elongated, his lips and mouth seemed a perfect shape for his strong chin and firm jaw. His eyes drooped slightly, but they were keen and golden brown, giving the appearance of seriousness. And while feature by feature he was not ugly, overall he did not strike her as particularly handsome. But he had a discernible charisma that Carla found appealing.

He was also a large, muscular man—six-foot three, she guessed—and his clothing was impeccable. With its seemingly invisible stitching and perfect fit, his light gray double-breasted suit appeared to be hand-tailored. He possessed an obvious fashion flair, wearing a light purplish-blue shirt with a striking tie and pocket handkerchief ensemble. The fresh scent of his cologne competed nicely with the stuffy, humid interior of the cab.

"Do you live in the building?" he suddenly asked.

"The building? You mean Metropolitan Towers?" she responded. He nodded.

"Oh, no. I just met someone for breakfast nearby. Obviously, though, you must live there. How do you like it?"

"I like it," he answered rather nonchalantly.

"That's it? You just *like* it. I have to admit it's not my style, but I understand it is a really fabulous building."

He chuckled. "Yes, it is a nice place to live. Where do you live?"

"West Sixty-second, next to Central Park. You know, old plaster walls and moldings, twelve-foot ceilings and arched doorways," she offered, knowing how much it contrasted with his starkly contemporary building.

"I grew up with that," he said. "This is more *my* style. Where do you work?" he asked, now folding the paper atop his lap and turning slightly toward her.

"I don't, really."

"Must be nice."

"Don't get me wrong. It's not by choice. I just recently moved here, and I'm off this morning to meet two prospective employers."

"Well, good luck. Where are you interviewing?"

"A couple of publishing houses."

"Oh, really, which ones?" he asked, his curiosity piqued.

She was prepared for this, but nonetheless felt her stomach clench as she rattled off the names of two legitimate publishing firms.

"Too bad," he responded genuinely. "I have a good friend who works in publishing. Thought she might be able to help you out. In fact, I bet she can," he went on. He reached inside his jacket and pulled out his wallet. He retrieved his business card, glanced at the back of it to make sure it was clean, then obtained a designer pen from another pocket and began scribbling the woman's name and phone number on it.

"Sylvia March," he stated. "She's an editor at Gilbert Brown," he added, then wrote down her number. "I'm Rand Emmerson, by the way. You should give her a call and tell her I told you to do so. In fact, I'll probably speak to her later today. Why don't you give me your name and number, and I'll have her call you directly. You never know, maybe they'll have something there."

"That's nice, and very brave of you," Carla remarked, then laughed. "I mean, how could you possibly vouch for me?"

His mouth turned up at one side, and he looked briefly out the window. "Because I'm a good judge of character, and something tells me you're all right," he blithely defended himself while turning back. He had already done his own inventory of her appearance, and was suitably impressed. "I'm happy to help."

*Remember, you aren't playing hard to get. You are hard to get. You're a* Rules *girl if there ever was one. Move slowly and cautiously.*

"Thanks, I appreciate it," she said, reaching for his card, then reading the front and back of it. "And what do you do at Hartson, Devlin and Burns?" she inquired, smiling. Emmerson smiled back as her cheerful grin was made all the more endearing by charming and deep-set dimples.

"Trust me, nothing special."

They were suddenly interrupted by the cab driver who'd

just pulled up to Carla's contrived destination. She scrambled for some cash to pay her share of the fare.

"No, no, I'll get it," he said somewhat proudly.

"Oh, no," she insisted back, then handed him a ten-dollar bill.

"I don't see your name and phone number on here."

"Sorry." She smiled as she climbed out onto the sidewalk. "And thanks for sharing the cab."

# CHAPTER
## 11

Sylvia March was one of those rare women whose combination of height, resonant voice, and elitist upbringing gave her the unique status of unofficial queen wherever she went. Not particularly beautiful, she was beautifully well kept, managing the details of her appearance like an advance man pondering every conceivable aspect of an upcoming event. Nothing about her image was left to chance. At five-foot-ten, blonde, well built, and impeccably groomed, she commanded immediate attention in any setting. Strangers fumbled deferentially when first addressing her, and those that knew her stretched themselves even further, as they quickly learned she was not someone with whom to trifle.

She was a true manipulator, warming up to people just enough to gain their confidence, only to use to her advantage whatever information they imparted. Careful to cover her tracks, she was usually never viewed poorly in connection with someone else's sudden misfortune. Which was how she'd managed to rise rather rapidly at Gilbert Brown—from an editorial assistant to senior editor in a matter of four years.

She was raised in the same neighborhood and privileged class as Rand Emmerson: wealthy parents, a Park Avenue address, a prep school education, then a degree in English from Vassar College. She never worked a day in her life until after graduation. She didn't intend to work for long either, as her true goal was to marry well and enjoy a life of luxury similar to that in which she'd grown up. But as long as she had to work, she was determined to make the best of it. Her job at Gilbert was interesting, but what she mostly enjoyed was that men found her position impressive without being threatened by it. Plus, it beat working for some financially undernourished charitable organization, a career path chosen by many of her equally privileged girlfriends.

On arriving at work this morning, she settled down with a cup of tea in fine bone china, then began sorting through her in-box. There were three new manuscript submissions, one of which she would certainly reject as she personally knew and disliked the author. Without reading it, she put a rejection memo on it. She had just finished reading the cover sheet of another when the phone rang.

"Sylvia March," she answered.

"Ms. March," was all he said.

She beamed.

"Rand. And how are you this miserably hot summer morning? Will I see you out at the Hamptons this weekend?" she said, her voice soft and pleasant.

"Don't know yet."

"I'm leaving early this afternoon; you can ride out with me. I'll even put the top down for your benefit."

"Oh, and who could resist such a joyride?" he said sarcastically, then laughed. "I'd offer you a ride on my Harley, but I'd have to get a side car for all your luggage."

"Oh, puh-lease," she responded in her naturally haughty drawl.

"Oh, puuuuhhhh-lease nothing. The last time I went somewhere with you, I got a hernia from hauling all your crap. But listen, that's not what I called to discuss. I have a favor to ask."

Sylvia straightened up in her chair. She'd do anything for this man.

"I met someone who's looking for a job in publishing."

She slumped in her seat. Translated, that meant he'd met some new woman he was trying to impress at her expense.

"What is she looking for?" she asked with feigned interest.

"To tell you the truth, I don't know. Just a job in a publishing house. I hope you don't mind, but I gave her your name and number."

"Oh, and thanks for asking me first."

"Well, at least I'm giving you a heads up."

"That's big of you. What's her name?"

There was a moment of silence, followed by a muted chuckle. "Well, that's the second part of my requested favor. I don't know her name. I was hoping she'd call and then you'd pass it along to me."

"So let me get this straight. You gave some total stranger my name and number, no doubt telling her I could get her a job? What a creep!"

"I didn't say you'd give her a job. Only that maybe you would talk to her. Fair enough. She recently moved to Manhattan, and I thought it was a nice way of saying welcome to town."

"What? So you can show her the town?" She let out a low throaty laugh. "You know, it's a bit unlike you not to get a name and number yourself. What's the matter? Losing your touch?"

Rand was unwilling to admit that he'd tried and failed. "Not at all, I'll have you know. We were both in a hurry, and . . ." He paused, feeling somewhat irritated. "Listen, if she calls, just tell her I told you about her and then be sure to find out how I can reach her."

"What if I think she's a creep, too?"

"Then we're a perfect match. Just be gracious about it."

Sylvia responded with lighthearted impertinence. *"I'd do anything, for you, dear, anything. . . ."*

"Good God. If it comes to this, then forget it!" he said, then laughed.

"Ride with me to the Hamptons?" she adroitly asked again.

"Promise you won't sing?"

"No."

"Then, no."

"Okay, I promise. Can you leave early?"

*"I'd do anything . . . anything for you . . ."* he whistled back.

"Good, I'll pick you up at three o'clock."

"See you then," he answered, and hung up the phone.

It took Sylvia a few seconds before hanging up herself. Any connection with this man, however tentative, was hard to let go. Even though they'd soon be sharing two straight hours together and would furthermore socialize over the weekend; no matter that they were investment partners with a variety of reasons to chat; hanging up with him always made her edgy. Like a junkie on a drug buzz, contact with him always produced a high. Likewise, his easy dismissal of her could sometimes yield immeasurable depression.

Sylvia looked at the calendar as she replaced the receiver, then grinned. Ironically, this was the second anniversary of when they'd first made love, something they'd done in the Hamptons following a madcap party. Drunk as she had been, though, Sylvia could recall every detail of that evening. She had long desired that kind of intimacy with him. For six weeks they'd had a sexual relationship; one she'd hoped would last. His subsequent rejection of her at summer's end at first came as a crushing blow, and then a test of time.

"If you're not patient with him, someone else will be," said her mother after hearing from her heartbroken daughter that Rand wasn't ready for a commitment. Mrs. March made it clear she considered him worth the wait in this obvious endurance test. Sylvia should appear patient and understanding without ever making him feel threatened. Eventually he'd realize those assets were what he needed in a partner.

"What a man really wants, darling, is a companion and an ally. Someone who is a confidante, and shows that in spite of his flaws he is loved."

For two years now Sylvia had endured, swallowing her pride as scores of women flung themselves at him, some capturing his attention enough to enjoy his customary six-week affair. Sylvia had stopped feeling jealous of those women; instead she almost pitied them, as the pattern was inevitable. For the first two weeks after expressing interest in a woman, he carefully seduced her with his mixture of elusiveness and charm while deliberately abstaining from sex. By the third week the woman was ready to screw him on Fifth Avenue in broad daylight. For three or four weeks an intense physical relationship ensued, with him providing just enough attention for her to believe it was something real. By the sixth week, and after he'd exhausted his physical interest, his work would suddenly start to interfere with their nights together and he'd become hopelessly inaccessible. The poor woman would call him; he wouldn't call back. She'd get frantic, sometimes showing up at his office, his apartment, or any of his favorite haunts looking for reasons and reassurance. She would get the reasons, never the reassurance. Knowing what good friends they were, some women tried working their way back into his good graces through Sylvia—a guaranteed kiss of death. Sylvia only had to mention that so-and-so had called her, not even why, when Rand would smell excessive neediness and then dismiss the woman altogether, leaving Sylvia to do his dirty work.

A more level-headed woman was let down with slightly more care. He would say, after making her wait it out several days, that he thought she was very sexy and a lot of fun, but that his work was growing more demanding and he simply wasn't ready for a committed relationship. When she professed to understand and offer ways to work it out, he made it simple. No, he would insist. But I promise we'll still be friends. He'd never call her again.

Because Sylvia had kept a lid on her own despair, and because they ran in the same social circles, a solid friendship had developed between them. Rand finally became comfortable sharing his stories of wayward love. Sylvia always laughed and safeguarded his secrets. Through it all, she was the only one of those women with whom he had remained true friends.

And so, why not help the mystery woman? Sylvia concluded. *Six weeks from now she'll be history.*

# CHAPTER
# 12

No one could understand how he'd slipped so deeply into trouble. Not even he'd fully understood it, as the truth was a variable in his life, something he'd manipulated for so long that in the end he couldn't even level with himself.

Rumors abounded. Was it a suicide?

*No, he would never kill himself.*

He must have been depressed.

*Impossible. He seemed so happy.*

How could he have lived like that?

*He died so pathetically.*

No one who knew Dr. Cameron Bulloch wanted to believe that he could have possibly taken his own life, or that he'd been so hopelessly addicted to drugs. He was so handsome, vibrant, intelligent, so lovable. He came from good stock. His wealthy parents had given him everything. And now their only son was dead at the age of thirty from a heroin overdose.

A neighbor first suspected something was wrong when the pungent smell of his decaying flesh permeated the hallway they shared. They were not friends, just friendly. Ever since he'd moved into the walk-up building in Manhattan's Upper East Side, she'd been trying to get to know him better, even once inviting him over for dinner. He'd politely refused on the grounds that he was involved with someone.

Which wasn't a lie. He was always involved with someone, but not in the manner in which he'd let on. He'd thought the neighbor was sort of cute. But he could see the eventual outcome of dinner, and she wasn't cute enough to pierce his highly guarded privacy on a regular basis. Women were naturally drawn to him, which turned out to be both a blessing and a curse. If he showed any level of interest, they clung tight. Any indifference resulted likewise, only with a strangely intensified effect. One dinner and she'd be knocking on his door with any number of contrived excuses to see him. And with the exception of a few friends who knew his recreational use of coke had slipped into a full-blown addiction, he wanted his private life to remain just that.

He'd frequently tried kicking the habit on his own, repeatedly resolving to temper his need by focusing on exercise and work. Newly centered, or so he thought, he'd start those mornings with a glass of orange juice, a handful of vitamins, fifty stomach crunches, and a half-hour run on his treadmill. On those days of resolution, he'd even walk to work, arriving invigorated and ambitious—a bright young doctor on his way to becoming the chief resident. Or so he thought.

But his resolve would always vanish in an itch for the drug, something he'd have to scratch with a few hits during lunch. That usually calmed him enough to get through the afternoon. But work demands often prevented a lunch break, and by day's end the doctor would be so agitated he'd end up consuming twice as much cocaine as normal to make up for the deprivation. Lately, following those binges, he could barely get out of bed—more than once even puking on his treadmill.

To battle the inevitable hangover, he began injecting small

quantities of heroin. It was during such self-prescribed therapy that Cameron Bulloch died. Still wigged out from the previous night, he'd mistakenly injected a lethal dose of China White into his system. Death, in his case, was quick and kind.


Commander Phillips tried imagining how two such seemingly nice people could have raised such a wayward child. Along with Detective Frank Kelley and a Russian translator, Natasha Sorokin's parents were sitting in her office nervously answering questions about their daughter, whose body they'd come to claim.

He was a mechanical engineer, she was a music teacher from Odessa. Ostensibly they lived a clean and simple life. And like most parents, they had harbored high hopes for their child. They couldn't understand where they'd gone wrong, as they'd given her everything within their means. In return she developed a drug addiction, kleptomania, and an obsession with a man they claimed not to know.

"What's his name?" Kelley asked through the translator. The couple looked sheepishly at one another, and then the husband spoke. Roman, he said. He knew nothing else.

"Did you ever meet him?"

*"Nyet."*

"Do you know where he's from?"

*"Nyet."*

"What happened with Roman?" Phillips asked gently.

The mother sighed heavily as she looked up at the ceiling, tears falling.

"She was in love with him." The mother spoke softly. "My heart was so broken for her. She wouldn't talk with us about it, but I heard her on the telephone telling someone that he'd left for the States."

She went on to say how for over a year Natasha became

obsessed with finding him, and saved all her money—which in Liz Phillips's mind meant she'd stolen as much as she could—then bought herself a one-way fare to Louisiana, a nonrefundable ticket to hell. According to the translator, her parents hadn't seen or heard from her since her abrupt April departure.

"Any forwarding address?" Kelley inquired.

The wife began crying again, prompting her husband to gently rub her plump knee. They did not have one.

"Do you know what he did for a living?" Kelley asked.

Mr. Sorokin's face suddenly grew brighter. *"Da,"* he said. Then in English: "Fertilizers."

"Sounds like shit to me," said Kelley, grateful for the translator's silence.

Liz Phillips was also quiet. But for a different reason. Her eyes had fallen to the daily homicide report—something she typically read first thing in the morning, but today had postponed to meet with Mr. and Mrs. Sorokin. It offered a brief synopsis on homicides and other suspicious deaths that had occurred the previous day. The word "Princeton" popped out at her.

> *Dr. Cameron Sebastian Bulloch, aged thirty, died at home of an apparent drug overdose. ME believes decedent OD'd at least four days ago. It is not clear whether or not anyone else was in the apartment at the time of his death. There was no suicide note.*
>
> *He was a resident in internal medicine at East Side General. A Manhattan native, he took his medical degree from Cornell University and his undergraduate degree from Princeton.*

She looked up and realized all four people were watching her.

She stood up and addressed the translator. "Please tell Mr.

and Mrs. Sorokin we don't have any more questions at this time.

"And, Frank, after you get them squared away, I need to see you alone."

He nodded approval, then disappeared with the three others.

Phillips immediately picked up the phone and dialed directory information in Princeton, New Jersey, asking for the university's Admissions office.

"Good morning," she said politely to the receptionist. "I need to confirm dates of matriculation." She was shortly dispatched to someone else, and introducing herself only as Ms. Phillips, she waited patiently while the clerk clicked away on a computer seeking information on Cameron Bulloch.

"Our records show he graduated in 1990."

Phillips repeated, "1990," jotting it down.

"Anything else I can help you with?"

"Actually, yes. Also check your records for Emmerson, Randall H. Emmerson. I believe he also graduated in 1990."

"Just one second," the woman said, typing away yet again. "Appears they were in the same class," she said, then chuckled softly. "I sure hope they aren't competing for the same job," she went on.

"Trust me," Phillips responded, "one of them is completely out of the running. Thank you very much for your help."

In accordance with police procedure, cops from the Nineteenth Precinct had sealed off Cameron Bulloch's apartment the previous night with a DO NOT ENTER WITHOUT A POLICE OFFICER OR PUBLIC ADMINISTRATOR placard, and bright yellow CRIME SCENE DO NOT CROSS tape across the doorjamb. Everything legally allowable in the investigation of Bulloch's death had already been collected, including the drug paraphernalia he'd last used. But without a warrant, the cops had no authority to search extensively through his belongings. Liz Phillips was taking care of that today.

Opening the door, she was instantly sent reeling backward. Though Bulloch's putrefied body had been removed twelve hours earlier, the stench hung heavy in the air.

"Jesus Christ!" Frank Kelley exclaimed from behind her.

"Oh, how I've missed this," she said, drawing her arm across her nose.

"Ladies first."

Phillips cast him a damning look.

"Okay, clear the way," he said, then lightly chuckled.

Pushing ahead together, they discovered a handsome, one-bedroom apartment. The living room had a dark, hardwood floor covered with a nine-by-twelve antique Oriental rug, a high ceiling with plaster crown moldings, and a well-used brick fireplace surrounded by an elaborately carved mantel. Flanking it on either side were floor-to-ceiling bookshelves, each brimming with textbooks, hardback classics, well-thumbed paperbacks, and various framed photos. Phillips, wearing latex gloves, inspected a sterling silver framed photo, presumably of the deceased on the occasion of his medical school graduation. He was sandwiched between two obviously proud and happy parents, a confident smile on his handsome, preppie face.

"What a fool," she said. From her early patrol days in some of New York's most crime-infested neighborhoods, Liz Phillips had learned dope was a cunning companion that would just as soon cozen a well-heeled socialite as a welfare mother.

"Anything in particular we're looking for?"

"Rand Emmerson," was all she said, and got right to work.

With the exception of a few articles of clothing dangling from a treadmill, his apartment in the converted walk-up brownstone was relatively tidy. A white-tiled breakfast bar dividing the kitchen and living area was clean; the sink and stove were spotless. Phillips opened the refrigerator and discovered a quart of orange juice, two bottles of expensive white wine, a spoiled apricot, moldy bread, and an unused stick of butter. The vegetable crispers were empty, and the freezer contained one empty ice tray and a frost-covered box of Lean Cuisine.

"Pretty pathetic," she said, then peeked out a window over the kitchen sink. Below was a well-tended garden of a neighboring townhouse; a peaceful oasis in the otherwise gritty city.

"You know what else is really pathetic?" she went on.

"Can't imagine."

"Bulloch paid $2,000 each month in rent. Forget his gruesome death. By next month some sucker will probably be paying $3,000 for the privilege of calling this home."

"No doubt. Help me out here," said Kelley, who'd picked up a far corner of the hand-woven rug. Phillips picked up the other corner, and together they rolled it back. At first all they found were several flattened dust bunnies, and then a small, empty, white paper bag. Phillips recognized it as something used by confectioners when selling candy by the pound. She dropped it into an evidence bag.

Removing the four cushions from a love seat, she discovered several more of the bags, collecting each one in turn.

"An addiction to candy corn?" Kelley wisecracked.

"A sweet tooth, my ass," said Phillips. "Look at this."

In two of the sacks were waxy envelopes with a white powdery substance.

Kelley looked at the contents of one. "Definitely not powdered sugar." It was a glassine envelope, the kind heroin dealers commonly used. "Looks like the Good Ship Lollipop has diversified."

"Well, I can tell you two things for certain. Carla Jennings is going to a funeral this week."

"And?"

"The Good Ship Lollipop is going down."

# CHAPTER
## 13

Carla arrived early and slid quietly into a rear pew of the Madison Avenue Presbyterian Church, then closed her eyes and prayed. Though it would be a Protestant funeral service for Cameron Bulloch, she clung to her mother's rosary beads as though sitting amid her family at St. Bellamine's in Queens. One concession Carla had extracted from Liz Phillips was that Charlotte Desmond be Catholic, allowing her to attend weekly Mass without raising anyone's suspicion.

Crossing herself, she opened her eyes. The church was built of polished marble and granite, with dark mahogany pews and a thick, scarlet carpet. An elaborate, oversized European tapestry was suspended behind the altar. *Waspy,* she thought.

As the church began filling, it became evident to her that Bulloch had been a well-liked man. People familiar with one another from various phases of his life began clustering together, breaking the pall with warm embraces and soft but cheerful chatter. The contingent from his undergraduate and medical school days was easy enough to spot: young, attractive professionals with an obvious affinity for socializing—funeral or not—as they flocked together in the back near Carla. Their conversations mixed the sad confusion

over their friend's untimely death with "glad-to-see-you-
what-have-you-been-up-to" small talk. More somber members of Bulloch's extended family congregated near the
front.

How could someone with seemingly so much going for
him end up dead from a drug overdose? Carla wondered.
And how was it that no one here, all apparently bright and
educated people, had suspected anything about the extent of
his addiction?

A hush fell over the congregation as the minister, a large
man with swept-back, graying hair, stood before them. Bulloch's casket was wheeled in, followed by his bereaved parents, each gripping the other tightly for emotional support.
In spite of never knowing the deceased, Carla felt an unexpected sadness.

Taking a deep breath, and looking upward at the ceiling,
she pulled herself together. As her eyes returned to the procession, she saw him. Just across the aisle and a few rows
up, she spotted Rand Emmerson and a tall, handsome
blonde as they hurriedly slipped into the end of a pew. The
woman whispered something close to his ear, then looked at
him as he turned left and responded. It was a comfortable
gesture, as if they knew each other well. Contrary to the sad
faces around her, the woman smiled at his remark, and then
whispered something back. Their conversation was broken
only by the minister's opening prayer.

Rand respectfully bowed his head, next focusing his full
attention on the minister, a man who quickly gained everyone's interest with his sonorous voice. He delivered a mean-
ingful and heart-warming service, causing the congregation
to break into both tears and laughter. Carla couldn't help but
notice that twice during the service, Rand wiped his eyes
dry.

Observing how truly affected he seemed by this loss, she

wondered how it was possible he could effect any kind of tragedy himself—particularly murder.

Cameron's mother was a petite, well-tailored Southerner with short brown hair worn in a dated, but nonetheless flattering, upswept bouffant style. Her face was sweet and round, with creamy, nearly flawless skin that defied her true age of sixty-three. Wearing a black crepe dress and black patent pumps, she stood in the foyer of her friend's Fifth Avenue home, and, in her ever hospitable manner, received the many guests gathering for the post-funeral reception, quietly thanking each of them for being present. Her husband, a prominent Manhattan neurosurgeon, was overwrought with grief and retreated to the apartment's study, leaving his wife to cope with the mourners.

"Thank you, darling, and thank you for coming," Carla overheard Mrs. Bulloch say to the woman just ahead of her. They moved on, leaving Carla in the spotlight.

"Hello, Mrs. Bulloch," she began sympathetically, then took a deep breath. "I only recently met your son. But he impressed me as a genuinely warm and sensitive person. I am so sorry for your loss."

"Thank you, darling. You were a dear to come today." She cordially squeezed Carla's hands.

Carla politely excused herself. She was entering the expansive penthouse apartment when she turned briefly and saw Rand Emmerson and his female companion waiting in the vestibule beside the elevator for their chance to speak to Mrs. Bulloch. Carla paused, grateful for a guest book, over which she lingered.

"Sylvia," Mrs. Bulloch said in her drawling manner.

*"I have a good friend who works in publishing . . . Sylvia March. She's an editor at Gilbert Brown. I'm Rand Emmer-*

*son, by the way. You should give her a call and tell her I told you to do so."*

The two women lightly and awkwardly hugged, Sylvia's height making it difficult to fully embrace the diminutive woman without pressing Mrs. Bulloch's head into her breasts.

Sylvia stepped back and dolefully confessed. "I wish I knew what to tell you, Mrs. Bulloch. I was so fond of him. He will be greatly missed." Slightly cocking her head while blinking back tears, she took Mrs. Bulloch's hands. "Please don't hesitate to call me if there's anything I can do."

"Thank you, dear." Mrs. Bulloch squeezed back.

"Also," Sylvia added, "Mother and Daddy wanted me to send their condolences. They were so sorry they couldn't be here today. But you know, if there's anything they can do, they'll be happy to help."

Her statement smacked Carla as disingenuous. If her parents were truly supportive, wouldn't they have made the offer in person?

"Yes, I'm sure," Mrs. Bulloch responded, with a note of skepticism, Carla thought. Sylvia graciously proceeded, leaving Rand to move into her place. The two looked at each other for only a moment before Mrs. Bulloch's reserve dissipated.

"Oh, Rand," she cried. Bringing her hands up to her face, she began weeping. He pulled the woman in and held her tightly, communicating his own sense of loss.

"It's going to be okay," he said, holding fast, then bit his lower lip as if to keep from crying. For an unusual length of time she clung to him, and then, finally distancing herself a bit, she looked up at him past her wet, clumped eyelashes, managing a smile.

"Oh, how he loved you," she said tearfully.

"I loved him, too," replied Rand, tears standing in his eyes. "You know, all I can say is this really sucks."

His unexpected crudeness made the woman chuckle. "Oh, Rand, only you!" she gently chided.

"Listen," he said more thoughtfully. "We'll get through this. But I want you to know if there's anything, and I mean *anything,* I can do for you, will you please call me?"

"Absolutely." She smiled warmly. "Just promise you won't be a stranger."

"I promise." She finally released him, then excused herself from the next guest and headed to the powder room. As soon as her back was to him, he rolled his eyes and released a low, whistling sigh. "I need a drink."

Quickly turning her back, Carla waited until they'd moved well into the apartment before diverting her supposed attention from the guest book. She watched as they disappeared out onto a spacious, canopied veranda. It was unclear to her just what kind of relationship he had with Sylvia. He had claimed they were good friends, but they seemed almost intimate.

Carla wandered into the dining room and prepared herself a small plate from a table overflowing with catered and homemade food. Smiling at a few unfamiliar faces, she moved into the living room and positioned herself in the crowd so she could see outside. Rand and Sylvia had now separated, as Sylvia had joined a group of smokers, and he was nowhere in sight. Realizing this was as good a chance as any, Carla handed her plate to a uniformed servant and eased her way outside. There was a bar set up in a far corner, which was where she spotted Rand standing in a short line. Cutting cautiously through the crowd beneath the yellow-and-white striped awning, Carla quietly sidled up beside him.

"Who's first?" the bartender queried lightly.

Rand turned to see the subject of this competition, his face breaking into a heartened smile.

"Well, by all means, the lady!"

"Hi. Rand, right?"

"Good memory. How are you?"

"Fine. Just fine, I mean, considering the circumstances."

A somber look crossed his face, and he lightly shook his head. "Unbelievable."

"Does anyone here want a drink?" the bartender interjected.

"Oh, sorry." Rand returned his attention to the man. "I'll have a gin and tonic. And what about you?" He smiled again at Carla.

"Just a Diet Coke, please."

Gathering their drinks, they moved away from the bar, standing on the fringe of the crowd.

"And what brought *you* here?" He said. "Actually, what I mean is, I thought I knew everyone Cameron knew."

"Oh. I didn't know him long. I met him while visiting a good friend who was recently hospitalized at East Side General. He was one of her attending physicians. It's so sad," Carla added. "I mean, he was such a nice guy, and he seemed like such a good doctor. In fact, my friend is still in the hospital, so I promised her I would come today."

"Hmmm. Too bad. I hope she'll be all right." He paused. "You know, I'm sorry, but I never caught your name."

Carla let out a light laugh. "Alexander Hamilton."

His face screwed into a puzzled expression. "*Alexandra* Hamilton?"

"No. Alexander Hamilton," she said affirmatively.

Rand appeared confused for only a moment longer, then chuckled. "Oh, you are a piece of work," he mused, suddenly realizing she was referring to the Secretary of the Treasury, whose face appeared on the ten-dollar bill she'd handed him in the cab.

"Any other aliases, Ms. Hamilton?"

Now it was Carla's turn to laugh. "I'm sorry," she said. "My name's Charlotte Desmond. And it's Emmerson, right? Rand Emmerson?"

"You're sharp. By the way, did you ever call my friend Sylvia?" He took a swallow of his gin and tonic, then began chewing nonchalantly on an ice cube. He was dressed more conservatively than when she'd first met him, though still with a flair, in a dark blue double-breasted suit with pleated trousers and a starched white shirt handsomely embellished by a black-and-cerulean blue geometrically patterned tie.

"No, I'm sorry, I just didn't get the chance. I hope you didn't tell her to expect my call."

"Actually, I did. But that's okay. How did your interviews go?"

"Very well. In fact, I got some freelance work out of one of them. Which is fine with me, since it gives me a chance to see if I like working for the company."

"Good for you. Which company?"

"Small operation. Nothing glamorous," she offered vaguely.

"You should meet Sylvia. In fact, she's here with me today, Charlotte. And I'm sure she'd be happy to speak with you."

"I hope you don't mind my asking, but how did *you* know Cameron Bulloch?" Carla changed the subject.

"Princeton. We were really tight. Played rugby, were in the same eating club. You know, he liked to party. But he was smart, and always had his act together. This really came as a shock to me. I had no idea he'd gone down so deep." Rand shook his head sadly. "I had no idea."

"I could hardly believe it myself," Carla responded. "He seemed like such a good doctor. Who would have ever guessed he was involved with drugs? I can't imagine how he functioned, can you?"

A funny look crossed his face. "Everyone's different."

"What do you mean?"

"Tolerance level. Everyone's different. You'd be amazed at the number of people standing here right now that probably inhaled a line or two before heading out, and you'd never suspect it."

Carla took a sip of her soft drink. "And what about you? Am I missing something?"

He laughed. "Me? Definitely not. I never touch the stuff."

"Really?"

"And what about you?"

*Mention that you tried it a long time ago, and it didn't agree with you. But don't get yourself trapped into proving that you're a user.*

She was about to answer when, uncannily, Carla sensed the woman's presence before she saw her.

"There you are!" Sylvia rudely interrupted. "I've been looking all over for you. Where's my glass of wine, you creep?"

Rand's composure remained sanguine. "Sylvia, I'd like you to meet someone. Remember the gal I mentioned who was looking for a job in publishing?"

Sylvia blinked back her surprise, then with all the enthusiasm of an insect caught on flypaper turned toward Carla.

"Hello," she said with cultivated politeness. "I'm Sylvia March. Nice to meet you."

*Unless a hand has first been extended to you, do not offer yours to shake. It may come across as gratuitous.*

"Thank you," said Carla with cool detachment, wrapping both hands around her glass. "I'm Charlotte Desmond."

Sylvia was about to speak when Rand interrupted. "Charlotte recently met Cameron at East Side General while visiting a sick friend."

"Really!" The word took a roller coaster ride off her

tongue, sounding more like "Reee-AH-lee." Carla stifled a laugh.

"What a coincidence. Are you from Manhattan, Charlotte?"

"No, not originally."

"Really. Where did you grow up?"

"Seattle."

"Seattle?"

"Uh-hm. Have you ever been there?"

"Not without my umbrella," she said, then laughed at her own ridiculous joke. Carla looked over at Rand, who was absorbing the conversation with amusement.

"I love Seattle," he interjected, smiling at Carla. "In fact, I climbed Mt. Rainier back in the summer of eighty-four."

*Carla, you need to know that an August snowfall isn't uncommon at Mt. Rainier's 14,400-foot peak, and Seattle is every bit as rainy as its reputation. From October through May it feels like you're living beneath a damp mop. But during the summer months there is simply no more desirable place on the face of the earth. It is clear and sunny most of the time, with mild humidity. There are gin-clear lakes and streams; the Puget Sound gleams and is surrounded by lush green islands, and snow-capped mountain ranges east and west offer ethereal sunrises and sunsets.*

"And I'll bet it was cold up top," Carla said.

"You bet right." He feigned a shiver. "In fact, there were fires burning out of control in the lower Cascades, so a burn ban was imposed and we couldn't even start a campfire. Those were a couple of pretty cold nights. But when we got back to the city, it was gorgeous. Warm, sunny. I loved it. Even did some sailing."

"Whereabouts? We kept a boat on Lake Union. I grew up sailing on the Puget Sound."

Feeling left out of the conversation, Sylvia interrupted.

"Excuse me, I'm going to get a drink. Anyone need a re-fresher?"

"No, thanks," Rand and Carla answered simultaneously.

"Be right back."

Carla waited till the woman was out of range. "Is she your girlfriend?" she boldly asked.

"No," he said, slightly shaking his head. "We're just good friends." He paused, looked downward, then fixed his eyes on hers.

"Listen, I know this might not be the most appropriate time to ask. But would you like to go out sometime?"

Carla's heart quickened. Before she could answer, and in a gesture that made her laugh, he pulled out a pen and then a ten-dollar bill.

"Here," he said playfully, handing them to her. "Just write your number up top."

Sylvia March watched from across the veranda as Char-lotte wrote something down—on what appeared to be cur-rency, no less—then handed it to Rand along with his pen.

*"Thank you. I'll call you soon."* She could read his lips.

Smiling like an ingenue, Carla lightly nodded her head, bade him farewell, and then left.

*That face . . . how do I know that face?* Sylvia asked her-self. She couldn't imagine, as she only knew two people from Seattle—both men. And according to Rand, Charlotte had been in New York only a short period of time.

He watched her walk away, his mouth curled, his eyes bright. The fact that he was on to someone new always brought a renewed measure of concern to Sylvia. But know-ing his behavior pattern made it easier to dismiss those feel-ings. He would use her just as he'd used countless women before her.

Or would he? There was something different about her, something intangible that put Sylvia on edge.

*Will she break the cycle?* Sylvia wondered, then promptly pushed the thought to the back of her mind as she cut her way back through the crowd to Rand.

"Another anemic?" she asked.

He laughed. "Hard to say. She is pretty, though, isn't she?"

# CHAPTER
# 14

It took Carla two hours to dress for their date. Even when she knew Rand was on his way up to her twenty-fifth-floor apartment, she was still vacillating between sporty gold loop earrings and more conservative pearls.

Faced with a loaner wardrobe brimming with designer clothes, Carla was nervous about the appropriate attire. In spite of being coached on what to wear, she'd spent most of her life in a Catholic school uniform, a martial arts dobok, or a pair of jeans, and possessed no natural sense of fashion.

She'd finally settled on a short, sleeveless dark brown Emmanuel Ungaro dress with a loosely fitted jacket. Thought it was September, it was still quite warm so, wearing no stockings, she slipped into a pair of brown, low-heeled platform-style sandals. With her sun-bronzed arms and legs, and blonde-streaked hair, it all made for a very arresting appearance.

"Gold loops."

She'd never worn pearls before and felt decidedly more comfortable with this pick. The doorbell rang, and while still clasping one earring she headed his way, then stopped abruptly in the foyer. Her heart pounded, and instead of immediately greeting him, she tried composing herself with some slow, rhythmic breathing.

Though the doorbell rang again, followed by a light tap, she continued breathing deeply. Slowly opening her eyes, she rotated her neck, took one more deep breath, then opened the door.

"Hi," she smiled with feigned warmth.

"Hello," he said, his eyes aglow. "Nice to see you."

"Thanks. Come on in." Carla gestured with her hand, while stepping back to fully open the door.

"How are you? You look really pretty," he said.

Carla blushed.

"I'm doing well, thanks."

*Show you are comfortable spending time with him. Invite him to have a glass of wine before you go out.*

"I have a terrific bottle of Pouilly Fuissé. Would you care for a glass?"

"Well, sure. Except we have a small stretch of this gorgeous day left. I thought it might be nice to have pre-dinner cocktails al fresco. What do you think?"

"That's fine with me. Only let me warn you that this bottle might not be here if you ever come back."

He laughed. "That's irrelevant. What's more important is that *you're* here."

"I'm not sure I deserve all these compliments," Carla responded lightly. "But I'll take whatever I can get. Now, if you'll excuse me, I'll get my purse and we can be on our way."

Disappearing into the bedroom, she grabbed her small handbag, then glanced once more in the full-length mirror. She barely recognized herself, but had to admit that the effect was sexy and sophisticated. She turned and glanced over her shoulder, approving of the rear view as well, then nervously smoothed down her dress. Closing her eyes, she took a few more deep, relaxing breaths. *I'll be so glad when this is over,* she thought.

When she returned to the living room, she discovered Rand studying a picture of her faux family on their happy sailing adventure.

"I take it this is your family. Is this your J-105?"

*J-105?* She thought frantically. "Yes, of course," she quickly answered, referring to the 36-foot, $200,000 racing boat being tilled by her counterfeit father.

Rand grinned while placing the gold-leafed frame back on the glass-topped, skirted table. "I have a boat."

"Really?" she answered, fearful that he might drag her into a detailed discussion on sailing.

"Yeah, a Swan-65. I keep it out in the Hamptons, next to my summer house."

"How nice."

"You'll have to see for yourself."

She didn't respond to his implied invitation. "Are we ready?"

"Let's go." He opened the door and waited patiently as she closed it shut. While fussing with the locks, she glanced at him. He seemed so confident and relaxed.

She tossed the keys in her handbag, then smiled sweetly. He responded by gently placing his hand on her back as they walked toward the elevator.

"You look very beautiful," he said. She could tell by his tone that he meant it.


"How did we ever get on this subject?" Carla asked, realizing she was about to lose ground in this verbal battle. She laughed. They were seated outdoors at an Upper West Side café, separated from the endless sidewalk traffic by stand-alone flower boxes doubling as dividers. Sitting at a small, round table with folding metal chairs, they were enjoying the last blush of daylight and a half carafe of white wine. Carla couldn't help but think how masculine and striking he looked in his dark Ray Ban sunglasses while smoking a cigar.

"I believe *you're* the one who first brought it up," Rand said, chuckling back. He'd been preaching on the virtues of a flat tax rate.

"I can't imagine why I would ever do that."

After going toe-to-toe with him on the economic merits of such a radically different tax code, Carla decided enough already. Though she had a degree in economics, he was quite good at poking holes in any theory she presented.

"I can see they taught you well at Harvard Business School."

His face and tone of voice went deadpan. "Who said I went to Harvard Business School?"

*Shit! I can't believe I just did that. Of course he never told me.* Her mind raced furiously through their every conversation. She did not recall him ever telling her that; it was something she'd learned of his profile during training.

Carla let out a muted chuckle. "I'm sorry. Didn't you tell me you went to Harvard Business School? I hope I didn't offend you."

He laughed softly himself. "I did go to Harvard, but I don't remember telling you."

*This is ridiculous. It's like I'm being tested. Why would he keep something like that to himself?*

"That's amazing. I can't imagine I would have said that if you hadn't told me." She looked down into her wineglass, then back up with sincerity. "You're an incredibly smart man. It would have been easy to guess."

She sensed his ego swelling slightly, and used the shift in conversation to excuse herself, hoping that they could drop the subject.

"Be right back," she said, then headed to the ladies' room.

Turning back briefly, she caught a glimpse of him, still wearing a slightly puzzled expression.

She was so distracted by her thoughts that she barely noticed the man sitting alone at the bar, nursing a cocktail and seemingly oblivious to everything. He was large but not heavyset, with dark hair and some obvious acne scars.

As she hurried into the bathroom, she suddenly recalled his face. Eager for another glimpse, on her return trip she discovered him—and any evidence of his drink—gone. It was only when she was back outside and saw Rand's face that it clicked.

*Cameron Bulloch's funeral!* She remembered clearly now. *I saw him at the funeral, and then at the reception. How odd to see him here.*

As she approached Rand, he politely rose from his seat. "I took care of the check and thought we could head on over to Café des Artistes for dinner. Are you ready to leave?"

"Sure," she said casually, masking her curiosity about the man.

*And where the hell is he now?* She wondered, quickly scanning the premises as they departed. He was nowhere in sight.

Carla fired up her computer and prepared her electronic report for Liz Phillips. She decided to keep the Harvard slip to herself for right now. Additionally, she chose not to report sighting that man in the bar, thinking she'd only seen him for a second or two, and couldn't be positive he was the person she'd seen at the funeral.

*Had cocktails and dinner with Emmerson. The evening began with drinks at Café Fiorello across from Lincoln Center, followed by dinner at Café des Artistes. In keeping with your instructions to remain aloof and gradually build up his* trust, I declined an invitation to go to a nightclub with him afterwards.

He is a very smart and engaging man, and an amusing master of trivia. (For example, did you know that Mickey Mouse was the first nonhuman to ever win an Oscar? I learned that as we strolled past the Disney Store en route to dinner!)

With regard to Cameron Bulloch, Rand reiterated how close they'd been in college. Though they were busy with their respective careers, and rarely saw each other, they had stayed in touch by phone. He said Bulloch wasn't serious about anyone, but did mention the name of one woman whom he saw from time to time (the translation was, someone with whom he had casual sex). Her name is Kimberly Prescott. She's a nurse at East Side General and lives in Brooklyn.

Our conversations ranged from the economy to current political events to the Knicks (he's a diehard fan). But most importantly, I was able to bring up the Courtland and Cunningham murders. He bristled at it, revealing that he'd been invited to Courtland's wedding, but declined the invitation because of a business trip. Furthermore, he stated that he'd known her through Malcolm, and that she'd sought some investment advice from him. He claimed to have spoken with her in that regard shortly before her death. Like everyone else, he claimed to be deeply shocked and saddened by the news, stating that this was a particularly difficult time for him as he'd just lost two friends in a matter of months.

Regarding the Cunninghams, he claimed not to have known them, but laughed, even wondered aloud about his own safety because he had Princeton and Harvard in common with the dead man.

He inquired about my background, and his interest in me became heightened when he learned that I'd recently made *money on Intex stock after the company's initial public offering. I told him that I follow technology stocks fairly closely, but with an added dash of luck watched the value of my Intex stock soar. Apparently he made some money on Intex as well, but only a fraction of my supposed $100,000.*

*We also talked briefly about Sylvia March. Apparently they once dated, but broke up over two years ago and now remain close friends. He encouraged me once more to call her with regard to a publishing position. I told him I wasn't in a hurry for full-time employment, and very casually mentioned living off investments and a trust fund, making me free to accept occasional pieces of contractual work until I found just the right position.*

*Though he didn't specify when, he did ask if I'd see him again. Please advise as to the next step. CD.*

Liz Phillips smiled when she read the report. First, because Emmerson lied, claiming not to have known the Cunninghams when phone records clearly indicated otherwise. And also because she was impressed with Carla's savvy and the job she had done thus far.

*I'll have his ass in a sling in no time,* Liz thought smugly as she turned off the highly secure laptop computer.

# CHAPTER
# 15

It was shortly before midnight in the tiny New Mexico hamlet of Thoreau when Ken Nickerson opened the rear door and hollered at his barking dog.

"Tugboat, get in here." The aging bulldog looked at his master, looked off in the distance, and barked twice more. Nickerson glanced around his backyard into the darkness: The only threat in sight was a midnight-blue sky heavily laced with stars and a full, radiant moon.

"Too bad," he muttered. As chief of the local volunteer fire department, he would welcome a few cloudy days. The weather had been hot and dry for a month, and as always, he worried about brushfires. He was short-staffed right now, and had been on call himself twenty-four hours a day for the past three weeks.

Tugboat finally retreated, huffing toward him up a short flight of wooden steps. Nickerson finally heard what he'd stayed up so late to enjoy. Garth Brooks was on *The Tonight Show* this evening, and had begun belting out a song from his latest CD. Abandoning the dog, Nickerson retreated to the living room and turned up the volume just a notch.

"Damn!" Nickerson exclaimed at the song's conclusion,

wishing the artist would sing another hit. Sure enough, Leno announced that Brooks would sing again.

Ken Nickerson would never see the end of that show.

The earsplitting sound of a collision coming from outside coincided almost precisely with his turning the volume back down. For a moment he was caught in a twilight zone—the violent screech and thunderous clash of crunching metal sounded familiar—but only as something he recognized from the movies and various training videos. He felt his breathing go shallow, fearing that a dozen years of firefighting was insufficient preparation for whatever doom had just occurred.

Shaken, his wife of fifteen years, Karen, rose out of bed and joined him in the living room. The look on her face portrayed everything he felt—dread. Standing quiet and pale in her thin cotton nightdress, drawing her slender arms tightly around herself, she watched as he grabbed his radio, then commanded help.

"Metro Dispatch, this is Chief 101. Be advised that we have a possible train collision or derailment. Please notify state police and page out Thoreau. I don't care where anybody is, or what they are doing. I need every qualified person to get over to the tracks, now!" he shouted to the dispatcher. Karen quickly disappeared into the bedroom, seconds later returning with his shoes.

"Thanks, babe," he said while quickly putting them on. Standing up, he strapped on his radio belt. Both of them listened intently to the Metro dispatcher's urgent call for help over the radio's crackling airwaves.

"God, I just hope it's not a passenger train," he exclaimed. He kissed Karen lightly on the mouth, then bolted out the door.

Fortunately for Nickerson, he lived just around the corner from the fire station, but discovered mixed luck upon

arrival, as the first person at the station was a rookie volunteer. Bobby Walker was a recent high school graduate
who worked full time in the local sawmill and, as often as
possible, at the firehouse. He'd only completed his training
two months ago. But, hoping to become assistant chief, he
had made himself readily available during Nickerson's
current labor shortage. He had wasted no time climbing
into his bunker gear and revving up the pumper truck, and
was all ready to go when Nickerson arrived.

"Shit," Nickerson muttered beneath his breath, hoping at
least one other veteran would arrive before they pulled out.
No such luck. As the station was not manned during late
hours, and radio dispatch was the only means of gathering
the troops, Nickerson prayed the other folks he relied on
would arrive at the scene shortly thereafter.

Bobby offered to drive, and as Nickerson jumped into
his own bunker gear he inwardly disagreed, thinking the
kid wasn't ready yet. But what the hell? he concluded.
Now was as good a time as any for Bobby to learn.

"What are you waiting for?" he asked, now fully attired
and climbing into the passenger side.

The young man's mouth curled into a constrained smile
as he scrambled back inside the truck, checked his systems, and turned on the siren. Within thirty seconds the
two-man team raced toward the disaster. From a quarter
mile away they could see the mangled wreckage of a
twenty-five-car freight train. The first three cars were off
the track but still standing; a dozen cars behind them lay
like lame horses, while the balance of the cars were still on
the rails.

"Thank God it's not a passenger train," Nickerson said
as they approached. At least they wouldn't be dealing with
scores of deaths or injuries. His relief on that count was

very short-lived, however, as he quickly realized that the entire town was at a deadly risk.

"What is it? What is it! My God! My eyes. They're burning!" the freshman firefighter cried.

Within an instant of drawing his next breath, Nickerson knew exactly what demon they were dealing with.

"Jesus Christ! There's an ammonia leak. Pull over!" he shouted. "Pull over!"

Bobby brought the rescue rig to an abrupt halt, blinking hard and fast over his suddenly burning eyes.

"Don your SCBA!" Nickerson demanded. The young man immediately reached for the breathing apparatus and protective hear, and handed a tank to his commander.

Nickerson wasted no time whipping on his gear, then grabbed a powerful flashlight and a pair of binoculars out of a bin. Every rail tanker was required by law to display a metal placard on each side of the car declaring the contents within. With the aid of the light and high-powered glasses, Nickerson hoped to confirm what substance he already suspected they were dealing with. Though Thoreau's fire station was not specifically equipped to deal with hazardous materials, Nickerson certainly had enough training and awareness to know the various chemicals and what immediate, if limited, action they should take.

He turned to Bobby. "Dispatch Metro and advise them that we have a major incident—a train derailment. I need all roads shut down in every direction coming in for at least one mile, and a townwide evacuation. We need statewide assistance and a HAZMAT team here stat. You got it?"

"Yes, sir," the young man responded, giving a thumbs up as Nickerson exited the truck.

"Shit," Nickerson declared to himself, after climbing out of the vehicle. With his limited breathing apparatus, there was no way he could get near enough the wreckage to pull out any survivors, and he just hoped those capable could flee the scene on foot.

As he neared the train wreckage, he could see a billowy white cloud drifting toward them. Ammonia led the list of poisonous and corrosive substances—especially anhydrous ammonia, the most widely used soil fertilizer. A vast and intricate transportation network, involving trucks, trains, ships, and pipelines shipped millions of tons of the product throughout the world. Transported mostly as a liquefied, compressed gas in insulated tank cars, in an uncontrolled leak it became a deadly and visible low-floating cloud the moment it hit the atmosphere. A water-free and pungent chemical, it would literally suck the moisture right out of a victim's skin, eyes, and lungs, causing asphyxiation to anyone unfortunate enough to be caught in its drift. He knew they could spray down the vapor cloud, but without the sophisticated clothing and proper breathing equipment necessary to do battle, it was a deadly proposition. So, until Gallup's HAZMAT team could arrive from thirty miles away, the best they could do was evacuate Thoreau's residents and detour all nonemergency traffic heading around the town.

Turning on the strong beam of light and peering through his goggles into the binoculars, he began edging toward the train, looking for the placard. Just as he assumed, the symbol on top of the overturned vehicle indicated the presence of the liquified gas.

Feeling relieved to know at least that much, he inched forward again to see what the next car contained. If not for the overpowering smell of the ammonia and his self-contained breathing apparatus, he would have smelled the leaking propane from the adjacent fallen tank.

Bobby had just connected with Metro from the confines

of the truck when *Whaaammmmm!* came the sound of the flash fire that spread toward him with the fury of hell.

"Oh, my God, oh, my God," Bobby screamed, watching in horror as Ken Nickerson's illuminated frame was thrown several yards away. Without hesitation, Bobby dropped the radio, jumped from the vehicle, and ran straight into the fire. Within seconds he reached his fallen colleague. There was no time to assess injuries. With every ounce of strength he could muster, he rolled the man over and began dragging him out of the flames, watching in horror as the reflective striping on his own bunker gear began to smolder and melt. He did not stop until he was in what he considered to be a safe zone, nearly three hundred yards away.

He was about to check Nickerson's vital signs when the bell on his tank began ringing an ominous alarm, warning him that his air supply was about to give out. His face and ears burning, Bobby gently lowered the chief to the ground, and was dashing toward the truck for their spare supplies and emergency medical kit when the third calamity of the night occurred. The tinder-dry brush beneath the truck suddenly burst into flames, within seconds engulfing him and the entire rig in a horrendous fireball.

Roman Petrovsky sat in his dimly lit office, dragging on a filterless cigarette and staring at the paperwork before him. It was well past closing time at the HTP Chemical Plant in Vacherie, Louisiana. And with the exception of a few night watchmen, he was alone.

It had been business as usual today, throughout which the plant steadily churned out tons of product, while various trains and delivery trucks and their containers pulled in and out.

His thoughts turned to Natasha Sorokin. He was thankful that she'd gotten blown away in the bank heist. From practically the first week they'd met, she'd pestered him, after he'd regrettably expressed a fleeting sexual interest in her. Why he was ever interested in her bony ass to begin with he couldn't comprehend. He'd never had difficulty garnering attention from women—particularly women far more attractive and voluptuous. But she had been playful and available at a moment when he was feeling horny. Because of her carefree demeanor, she didn't strike him as the kind of person who would turn a one-night stand into a deadly fixation. Their involvement, however, led not only to her own death, but that of Candace Rutland, Mitchell and Sydney Cunningham, and then his former deputy, Gordy—his once-trusted lieutenant. In retrospect, he regretted not killing the woman himself much earlier, which would have prevented the crap in Manhattan from happening.

The phone rang. Roman glanced up at the wall clock, and then double-checked his watch. It was nearly one a.m. *Who in the hell would be calling,* he wondered.

A representative of Union Pacific Railroad alerted him that an HTP Chemicals freight car had been involved in a major accident in New Mexico. HAZMAT teams were already responding to the spill and subsequent explosion. Already two firefighters and three crewmen were known dead.

Roman's back arched. "What happened?"

"It's too soon to tell, sir," the man said. "But one early report said it appeared the tracks might have been sabotaged."

Roman managed to stay calm, and assured the man HTP would take full responsibility for any clean-up efforts and resulting investigation.

He immediately placed two phone calls. The first was to

an expert contractor on HAZMAT spills who would dispatch his own team of specialists to the site to assist in the cleanup and inevitable investigation. They would also provide Thoreau's residents with any other support they needed.

He lit a cigarette, then placed the second call to Rand Emmerson.

There was simply no giving in, and he'd had enough. If he had to, he was going to Moscow to kill Boris Arkady himself.

He didn't know which was softer—Callie Anderson's bed or her backside. After making love to the woman, he had snuggled up behind her and drifted off happily to sleep when he heard the trill of his cell phone from inside his suit jacket.

"What the fuck?" Rand exclaimed. At first believing it might be Sylvia enticing him to some late-night party, he ignored it. But the ringing persisted even beyond Sylvia's range of stubbornness.

"Ignore it," Callie said sleepily, burrowing her rear into him.

"I can't," he said, jumping out of bed. "What?" he screamed into the device.

For the next two minutes he listened, his face stone cold.

"What do you want me to do?" he asked, emotionless. "I'll do whatever you want," he stated, then snapped the cell phone shut.

Callie sat up in bed, dejection on her face. "You're not leaving, are you?"

"I have to," he said, reaching for his trousers.

"Why?"

He looked at her harshly. "It has nothing to do with you. It's a business matter."

"When will you be back?"

"I don't know."

She threw herself back down on the pillow, pulling the sheet up around herself.

"Will you call me?"

"Of course I will."

"Today?"

"Of course."

She smiled.

He'd forgotten her number already.

# CHAPTER
# 16

"What's up?" said Rand, answering the phone. He knew from his caller ID that it was Sylvia.

She chortled. "And good morning to you, too."

"Okay. Morning. What's up?"

Her mood was starkly different than last week when she'd first learned of the train wreck. She'd gone berserk, screaming at him until he couldn't take it anymore, and he finally slugged her. Afterward she calmed down enough to listen. He knew he could trust her, but that she would require some extra attention for a while.

"Just checking in. Wondered if you might not want to catch a flick with me sometime this weekend?"

"Sure. Maybe."

Sylvia scratched her forehead, knowing that statement meant he was keeping his options open.

"Well, let me just put it this way. I don't have plans on Sunday afternoon. Would you like to go to the movies with me?"

"Sounds good."

"Are you going to John Ashley's party tonight?"

"I was planning on it."

"With a date?"

"Don't know yet. I asked Natalie McBride to go with me

to see Cassandra Wilson at Lincoln Center tonight. But she
might have to go out of town. I'm waiting to hear back from
her."

"I love Cassandra Wilson. If she bails on you, call me."

"All right. Otherwise, I'll see you at John's."

"Keep me posted."


More than a week had passed without a call from Rand.
Liz Phillips, who had previously advised against calling
Sylvia March as the next possible step, was now leaning in
that direction. "Give it one more day," her e-mail missive
had advised.

Now bored beyond belief, Carla waited till it was well
past nine o'clock before donning her jogging attire. It was
perfect September weather, with crisp mornings, hot afternoons, and cool evenings.

Walking through the lobby of the elegant Manhattan
apartment house, Carla stepped outside into the sixty-degree
temperature, stretched her legs against the building's exte-
rior, and then began to jog over to Central Park.

*What a relief,* she thought, both physically and emotionally.
She entered the park near the Seventy-second Street entrance, and made her way down the winding road toward the
lake. Gaining momentum with each step, she felt grateful
for the warm slashes of sunshine and pleasing scenery. The
trees were newly edged in hues of red and golden yellow,
while occasional bursts of migrating birds fluttered rest-
lessly about in high branches. Avoiding the route closest to
Rand's apartment building, she instead chose a northern direction, heading upward toward the Jacqueline Onassis
Reservoir. Jogging past the Metropolitan Museum of Art,
she dashed up the steps leading to the fenced body of water
and began running in a counter-clockwise direction.

There were few people running at this hour, which suited

her just fine, as she wasn't crowded by other joggers and slow-moving pedestrians. She was passing the first bend in the reservoir's perimeter when she first spotted him.

He was jogging clockwise and wearing glasses, which made for delayed recognition. But ten yards beyond him, Carla knew there was no mistaking what she'd seen. Abruptly stopping in her tracks, she turned and retreated, following a safe distance behind him, anxious to find out just where he might go.

*It's him, I know it's him!* she thought. It was the man from the bar, the same one who'd been to Bulloch's funeral. His long legs were thick and strong, and his momentum was steady. Carla kept a short pace behind him, slowing down when he stopped, stretched, and then gulped water from a drinking fountain.

Thinking at first not to approach him, she instead slowed down, easing her way up toward the fountain.

He slowly raised his head, and then turned, almost as if he knew it was she standing there. Like a gentleman he moved aside so that she could take a drink.

"Thanks," she grinned, bending forward while never taking her eyes off of him.

He did not speak. Instead, he began jogging down the steps leading back toward the main road through Central Park.

"Hey!" Carla audaciously shouted. "Just a second. Don't I know you?"

Oddly, he turned to face her while continuing to jog— only backward. Looking straight at her, he remained speechless.

"I think we've met," she stated, still standing at the top of the stairs. He smiled, then ran away.

"Shit," she muttered. "Who is he?"

\* \* \*

Walking into the door of her apartment, her face flushed
and her body sweaty, Carla was surprised to see the blinking
red light on her answering machine. There were only two
people who would possibly call her—either Liz Phillips or
Rand Emmerson.

"Charlotte, hi. This is Rand. Rand Emmerson. Listen, I'm
sorry it's taken me so long to get back to you. All I can say
is, I've been swamped at work." He paused, then added,
"First, I should tell you that I really enjoyed our evening out.
And then, I know it's kind of short notice, but I have tickets
to a jazz performance at Lincoln Center this evening, and I
was hoping you could join me. Please give me a call at
work," he said, concluding with his phone number.

Not wanting to appear anxious, she took a long, relaxing
shower, and then got dressed. It was near lunchtime before
she finally picked up the phone.

"Rand Emmerson, please," she asked of his secretary.

"May I tell him who's calling?"

"Charlotte Desmond, returning his call."

"Thank you. Hold please."

Only a few seconds passed.

"Charlotte. Good to hear from you. How are you?"

"Fine, thanks. And yourself?"

"Well, like I said, things have been crazy. But that's not
for you to worry about. Listen, I know it's late notice. But
are you free this evening? I have two tickets to see Cassandra Wilson at Lincoln Center, and I would really love it if
you could join me."

*Who's Cassandra Wilson?* Carla wondered.

"Sounds great. Only what time? Because I have a late afternoon appointment that could spill over into early
evening."

"The show starts at eight o'clock. If you're up for it, I
could meet you there."

"Okay."

"Great. I'll meet you out in front of Alice Tully Hall at about seven-forty-five. How's that?"

"Good," she said sweetly. "I'll see you then."

She hung up, then grabbed her wallet. There was a record store just across the street, and she wanted to check out Cassandra Wilson.

Only when she got downstairs was her verve replaced by a sliver of paranoia. Before exiting the building, she peered outside to see if the man was watching—and waiting.


Kimberly Prescott wasn't quite finished taping the IV into the youngster's arm when she heard her name being paged. "What in the world?" she muttered. She smiled at the boy, and then his mother.

"Kimberly Prescott," she heard once again, "please phone the operator."

"There," she said, securely taping the catheter. She checked his temperature before finally leaving the room and finding an in-house phone.

"This is Kimberly Prescott," she told the operator, then paused, listening. "What!" she said incredulously. "Okay, tell her I'm on my way down."

Stopping by the nurses' station, she informed the head nurse that a New York City police officer was waiting in the lobby to see her. The woman excused her, ribbing her about any perceived offenses the younger nurse might have committed. Kimberly laughed back, but inside felt growing tension. What was this all about?

Once in the lobby she was greeted by a friendly looking woman.

"Kimberly Prescott?" she said. "Hi. My name is Liz Phillips. I'm with the New York City Police Department."

Kimberly's concern showed clearly. "There's no need to be nervous. I'm here on routine business."

"About what?"

"Cameron Bulloch."

Kimberly's eyes widened in apprehension. "I'm not sure how I can help you, but I'll try."

"Is there some place we can go to talk?"

"The cafeteria?"

"That's fine."

They had started in that direction when suddenly Kimberly stopped. "No, actually I don't want to go there. Follow me." Phillips retreated down the main hallway with the nurse, then turned left down a dead-end passage leading to a set of oak double doors. It was the hospital's chapel. Kimberly gently pushed open one of the doors and, finding the sanctuary empty, walked inside and sat in a rear pew. Phillips slid in beside her.

"I'm sorry," said Kimberly. "I was afraid I might cry, and I didn't want to sit in the cafeteria where the whole world can see me."

"That's understandable."

"How did you know?"

"Know what?"

"Know about Cameron?" She hesitated and looked down. "How did you know about Cameron and me?"

"Your name was in his address book," Phillips lied.

"Really?"

Phillips nodded yes. Kimberly looked downward again, giving Phillips a chance to study her. She had thick, jet-black hair that she wore pulled back, and a nicely shaped oval face, with violet eyes and a rosebud mouth. She was very pretty and also overweight. She wore acrylic nails painted pink with two thin white diagonal stripes across each one; something clearly declassé within Cameron's crowd. She also wore a golden thumb ring on her right hand. Though nervous, she came across as genuine and sweet.

"When was the last time you saw him?"

Kimberly bit her lower lip. Phillips was prepared to hand her a tissue when the young woman looked up and said, "I spent the night at his apartment two nights before he died."

Phillips stayed calm. "Were you two intimately involved?"

Kimberly shut her eyes, nodding her head yes.

"For how long?"

"At least eight months. Actually, we'd been friends for a little while before that. I met him a year ago when I was doing per diem work on one of the medical floors. Pediatrics hired me full time last May, but we'd already been seeing each other before then."

"Were you doing drugs with him?"

"Absolutely not."

"Hmmm," said Phillips, noting the question struck a nerve. "Did you ever met any of his family or friends?"

Kimberly looked away from Phillips, ashamed. "No, not really."

"What do you mean?"

Tears welled up in her eyes. "You know what really stinks?"

"Hmmm?"

"I loved that guy so much. We had such a great time just hanging out together. But"—she released a huge sigh—"I guess I wasn't his type. Or more likely the type his parents and friends had in mind for him. You know, stick thin, well bred—whatever that's supposed to mean—and filthy rich.

"Anyway, we had this . . . chemistry, I guess. Who can explain it? I was trying to get a full-time job and didn't want to jeopardize my chances, and he obviously didn't want a public relationship with a nurse. A fat, nobody nurse. So we kept it to ourselves."

Phillips listened patiently.

"It started out that I helped him with a couple of really difficult patients. Then one day he actually had time for a lunch break, so we went together. It was fun. And the next thing I know . . ."

"A relationship," Phillips interjected. "Only he was probably too screwed up to realize what a truly good thing he had in you."

"Thanks," said Kimberly softly.

"Kimberly, I need to ask you, though. Did you know about his drug use?"

The nurse hesitated, then finally nodded.

"What can you tell me about it?"

"Coke. He loved his cocaine. I had no idea, however, that he'd started doing smack. What an idiot." With that, tears began to fall freely. "God, I still can't believe he's dead."

Phillips offered a light pat of reassurance to Kimberly's arm. It was a dangerous line to cross with any witness, showing too much sympathy. Yet she didn't want to appear heartless. When Kimberly finally stopped crying, Phillips proceeded.

"Were you doing the drugs with him?"

"No, I said. Absolutely, positively not. But I think one of the reasons he felt so comfortable with me was that I didn't put any pressure on him. In fact, the only time we had a fight was when I suggested that what he was doing was risky, I mean, considering he was a doctor and all. He told me to 'mind my own f'ing business' and stormed out of my apartment. I didn't hear from him for at least six weeks after that, and I never brought it up again."

"How often did you see him?"

"You can say it. How often did we sleep together? A cou-

ple times a month. I mean, sometimes we'd bump into each
other at the hospital. But outside of that, he was always on
call and pretty busy working really long hours . . . and . . .
and the truth is . . . well . . . he just didn't want to make the
time. I don't know. When I look back, the whole thing was
pretty screwed up. I really liked the guy. But he couldn't
handle it. I mean, not the fun. The fact that I wasn't his supposed type."

She began to cry again. Phillips reached inside her purse
for a fresh tissue, then handed it to the grateful woman.

"Why does any of this matter? I mean, what exactly is it
you want from me?" Kimberly asked tearfully.

"To tell you the truth, it does matter. It matters that given
his insecurities you were able to care. And it also matters
that someone like you might be able to save someone else's
life."

"How?"

"Kimberly, do you have any idea where he was buying his
dope?"

She bit her lip again, avoiding eye contact.

"We have a good guess. We're looking for confirmation."

Kimberly nervously tightened her ponytail. "How would
I know? I already told you I don't do drugs. That was his
business. I mean, what if I knew and I told you? I'm not saying that I do. But if I did and I told you, would I be in some
kind of trouble?"

"No. But like I said, you might prevent this kind of
tragedy from happening to someone else. Don't you think if
Cameron were alive—"

"Stop it!" Kimberly cut her off. "Don't even go down that
road with me, because it's total crap. You know as well as I
do that even if you shut down one dealer, the next day someone else will open up shop. Besides, if Cameron were alive
today, and knew what fate he faced, he'd probably still do

the same thing. In fact, he must have known better than anybody. He might have been an idiot, but he wasn't stupid. He was a damned doctor, after all."

She got up from the pew and looked at her watch. "I have to get back to work. I don't know anything that could help you. I didn't know he was doing heroin. I don't know where he got his dope. The only thing I know is that he's dead. I'm sorry, but I've got to go."

Phillips arose and stepped back to let the woman pass by. But not without making one final stab.

"Kimberly, I know you're upset. And I know you still love him. That will never change. But think about it. And think about it hard. You might not have been able to change a thing in his life, but you might be able to make a difference in the life of someone else." She reached into her pocket and pulled out a business card, then handed it over. "Call me if you want."

She watched as the crestfallen nurse left the chapel, and then sat back down.

*How pathetic,* she thought about Kimberly's doomed relationship, then ran through the entire conversation once more in her head. *Funny how she said, "The next day someone else will open up shop."*

# CHAPTER
## 17

Again, Carla spent an excessive amount of time grooming herself for Rand, this time while listening to Cassandra Wilson's latest CD; something that turned out to be a happy acquisition. Never one for jazz, Carla discovered she liked the singer's rich and wide-ranging voice.

Her new bedroom had begun to resemble her own room back in Queens—clothes haphazardly strewn about on the floor and dangling from various pieces of furniture. Discarding a two-piece Calvin Klein suit, Carla slipped into a black Giorgio Armani pantsuit. Rummaging through the boxes of shoes in her walk-in closet, she discovered a pair of black Fortuna Valentina shoes with stiletto heels. Slipping into them and then posturing in front of the full-length mirror, she smiled. The suit was chic, the shoes hot fun.

"This is dangerous," she said, glancing at the rear view. Beginning to develop some fashion confidence, Carla realized she not only liked how she looked, she liked how she felt. Until now she had never understood how women could waste so much time and money on clothes, jewelry, and makeup. But now, tailoring herself as Charlotte Desmond evoked in Carla something she'd never experienced before—a feeling of sexiness that made her feel both powerful and playful.

Trying on a variety of earrings, she momentarily decided on the gold loops she'd worn last week, as they went well with her ensemble. But realizing it was probably gauche to be seen wearing the same of anything twice—particularly on successive occasions—she abandoned them and opted for a pair of diamond studs.

"Oh, God, what a mess!" she exclaimed, first glancing at the clock, which read 7:40 P.M., and then at the clutter she'd created. Grateful that no one would be seeing her room, she shut the bedroom door, snatched her purse and keys from the foyer table, and began making her way across the street to Lincoln Center.

He was easy to spot, leaning against a pillar outside the famed performance hall. He appeared to be relaxed, wearing his trademark Ray-Bans and a loose-fitting gray double-breasted suit, while smoking a cigar. Wandering toward him, she could tell that behind his dark shades he was watching her, as through another drag of his cigar his face broke into a faint smile.

"Hello," she said demurely.

"Mmm," he murmured, then leaned over and kissed her cheek. "Very good to see you. How'd your meeting go?"

"Pretty well, thanks. I was able to wrap it up earlier than I expected," she said.

*Remember to occasionally give subtle compliments, indicating that you notice the smaller details in his life. If he got a haircut, mention it. Interesting socks, say so. An imaginative tie, bring it up. Men appreciate that kind of attention.*

"By the way, I like your tie. It's sharp."

"You do, huh? Chosen especially for you," he said lightly.

"Oh, come on. Really?"

"Really. Listen, we don't have much time, but would you like a glass of wine before the show starts?"

"No thanks."

Stubbing out his cigar on a concrete column, and then placing the stump in his suit jacket, he gently grabbed her arm and escorted her inside. As opposed to their previous date, when such a gesture made her nervous, Carla found surprising warmth from his touch.

"That was amazing. How do you know them?" Carla asked as they headed to TriBeCa in a taxi. Following the show, Rand had taken her backstage to meet not only Cassandra Wilson but Wynton Marsalis, the band leader and artistic director of Jazz at Lincoln Center.

"I just do," he grinned smugly.

"Perhaps I ought to be asking how do they know *you*?"

"Now you're learning."

Carla had met famous musicians at the Met through her mother. But those introductions were always formal and brief. Both Wilson and Marsalis, however, warmly greeted Emmerson, with Marsalis mentioning a previous conversation the two had had. Rand, a frustrated musician, obviously relished the connection but handled himself coolly, as if such encounters were common. One of the managers, who also recognized Rand, had invited them to a post-show party in midtown. Rand extended their regrets, stating that they had previous plans.

"Why didn't you want to go to the party?" Carla asked.

"Because I'm taking you to another party. Friend of mine from Princeton is having a few people over tonight." His voice grew cocky. "And, I want to show you off."

Carla scanned the party crowd and knew that if she weren't Rand's date she would have felt helplessly out of place. It wasn't as if she'd never been to a party. She'd simply never been to a party with this many beautiful and sophisticated people. It was unimaginable that any of those gathered would, in reality, care for a local girl from Queens. A chic crowd—she couldn't help but notice that no one was overweight, everyone seemed well prepared with a quip, and the atmosphere was thick with conceit.

"I'd like you to meet Charlotte Desmond." Rand spoke above the noise. He was talking to a strikingly familiar man.

"Nice to meet you. Malcolm Rutland," he said. He smiled benignly, then took a sip of champagne.

*My God! For a man who has recently and tragically lost his wife, he doesn't seem very despondent.*

"Nice to meet you, Malcolm." He was as good-looking in person as he was in all the news clips she'd seen of him.

"Rand tells me you're from Seattle."

*So he's been talking about me.*

"I have some friends there," Malcolm continued.

*Charlotte Desmond, the daughter of Walter Desmond, an entrepreneur, was raised with a sister and brother in Seattle's exclusive Highlands community.*

"Really? Who are they?"

"Bader. Brett and Marda Bader."

"I don't know them," she said with forced calm while lightly shaking her head. "Will you both excuse me? I'm going to get a glass of champagne. Rand, would you like one?"

"No, thanks," he said, then smiled warmly.

"I'll be back in a minute," she told him, then headed toward the bar. Once obtaining her champagne, she turned around and through the crowd could see that Sylvia March had joined them; her arm was across Malcolm's shoulder and she was laughing amiably, while the two men smiled broadly. She looked beautiful this evening, too. In the sea of black attire, Sylvia stood out in a cream-colored pantsuit that made her appear taller and nicely complemented her blonde hair. And in her high heels, she stood at least an inch taller than Malcolm.

*They seem awfully close and comfortable.*

"Pardon me," said a man with a pleasant British accent.

"Oh, sure," Carla responded, making way for him as he cut through to the bar to get himself a drink. Shortly after, he moved up beside her.

"Cheers," he said, unexpectedly clinking his glass against hers.

Carla laughed at his presumptuousness. "Cheers," she responded blithely.

"My name is Crawford Tuttle," he said. "And you are?"

*An undercover cop,* Carla thought sarcastically.

"Charlotte Desmond. Nice to meet you. Anything in particular we're celebrating?" she asked, slightly tilting her glass toward him.

"Whatever you'd care to celebrate," he said lightheartedly. There was an appealing warmth and gentleness in his demeanor. Carla sensed that, like her, he didn't really know many people here and felt grateful for their encounter.

"To new friends," she said.

"Sounds good." He said, tapping her glass once more then sipped from his flute.

"Are you from England?"

"What makes you say that?" he responded playfully.

She laughed lightly. "Just a guess."

"A rather good one. I'm from London."

"Are you visiting?"

"No, actually, I just moved here."

"Really? So did I. How do you know this crowd of people?"

"John Ashley and I are chums from school. He spent a year at Oxford the same time I was there."

"That's nice you've stayed in touch," she said. "Where are you living now?"

"I'm renting a loft in SoHo. It's not far from where I'm presently working."

"What kind of work do you do?"

"Publishing. I'm an editor."

*I don't believe this!* "Oh, you work in publishing." She said nonchalantly, then took a large sip of her champagne.

"Yes, indeed. And you? You say you just moved here, too. Where were you living?"

"You won't believe this. I was living near *London's* Soho."

"Indeed!" he said with surprise. "So did I. Where was your flat?"

*This simply cannot be happening!* Common sense told her to get away as quickly as possible, and while deliberating how to excuse herself, she felt an arm slip around her waist. She startled at the touch.

"What's wrong with you?" It was Rand. He laughed, his caramel-colored eyes smiling.

"Oh, hi. It's you."

"Expecting someone else to squeeze you?" He didn't wait for her answer. Instead, he turned and extended his hand to Crawford. "Hi, Rand Emmerson."

"Crawford Tuttle. Nice to meet you."

"Oh, you're John's friend from London. Right?"

"Yes. I understand that Charlotte just moved here from London herself."

Carla wanted to disintegrate with anxiety.

"Yeah. How about that. Had you two met before?"

"No. But as a matter of fact," Crawford stated, "it turns out we both lived in Soho."

Carla was about to take a sip of her champagne, when by

sheer luck a female guest bumped into her from behind, causing Carla to spill the contents of the flute on herself.

"Oh, my God!" the woman slightly slurred, realizing what she'd done. "What a mess. Stay here, I'll be right back with a towel."

"It's okay, really," said Carla politely. She looked at Rand. "If you'll excuse me, I'm going to find the bathroom."

"There's a powder room in the hallway. But why don't you go down the hall and use the one in John's master bedroom. I'm sure he won't mind."

"Thanks. I'll see you shortly." She turned to Crawford and smiled, mostly with relief. "Nice to meet you."

"Likewise," he said warmly.

Carla was surprised to find the bedroom empty, and welcomed the respite from the crowd. She opened the door to a walk-in closet first, and then upon opening the second door found herself in the first section of the master bathroom. It contained a large Jacuzzi tub, a black marble-topped vanity, and had an antique Spanish rug on the tile floor. Grabbing a hand towel, she spot-cleaned her suit. Assuming she was alone, Carla then pushed open the next door leading to the john. It opened right into someone standing on the other side.

"Oh, my God! Excuse me!" Carla exclaimed, then promptly shut the door.

"Charlotte?"

"Sylvia?"

Sylvia opened the door just enough to stick her head out. She bore the silliest grin. "I'm sorry, do you want to use the bathroom?"

"That's okay, I can wait."

"Come here, I want to show you something."

Carla simply couldn't imagine. "What?" she said skeptically.

Sylvia opened the door all the way, dragged her in, then shut and locked the door.

"I should have done that in the first place," she said, then sniffed. "Here, want some?"

Carla contained her incredulity. There was a small rectangular mirror on the back of the toilet, on top of which were three healthy lines of cocaine.

"One for me, one for you, one for me. Unless of course you'd like that to be one for you, one for me, one for you. I'm not greedy. Here." She held up the tray as if offering hors d'oeuvres.

"Oh, no, thanks. Actually, I came into the bathroom to clean off the champagne someone just spilled on me."

"No, thanks?" said Sylvia, ignoring her plight. "You've got to be kidding. Don't tell me you're one of those goody-two-shoes?"

"Actually, no. I used it from time to time in college. But I'm one of those people who usually can't get enough of a good thing."

Sylvia let out an obnoxious laugh. "Then why are you hanging around Emmerson?"

"That's kind of cruel," Carla said, then laughed back. "I thought you two were good friends."

"I'm joking. Trust me. If I didn't love him so much as my friend, I wouldn't get away with saying half the things I do. You know," she said, then stopped talking for a moment to inhale a line. "Speaking of confusing. I keep thinking I recognize you from somewhere. How could that be? At the risk of sounding crass, I know you come from money, which means maybe we met on some exotic vacation our parents took when we were children or something. Hey I know, where did you go to camp?"

"Camp?"

"You know. Summer camp?"

"When?"

"Last year."

"Camp! Last year?"

"You're not that naive, are you? When you were a kid, of course." She let out another annoying laugh. Carla joined in with her.

"I never went to camp."

"You never went to camp? How odd. If you'd grown up in Manhattan, your parents would have packed you up the first summer you could hold a crayon." She heartily inhaled the second line. "Sure I can't talk you into this third line? It's really good stuff."

Carla chuckled, while shaking her head no. "Thanks, really. But if I ever want to buy some for myself, where would I go?"

"Place up on Third. But you can't just go in there and ask for it. You need to know someone. Let me know if you ever decide to go, because I'll introduce you." Carla was stunned by the woman's candor.

She helped herself to the third line, licked her finger, dabbed the remains off the mirror, licked her finger again, then stashed the mirror back in her purse.

"Listen. You should give me your phone number. Maybe we can have lunch together someday."

"I would like that."

"Good. Do you have a pen? Give me your number."

"Sure," Carla smiled as Sylvia handed her a cocktail napkin from beneath her glass of wine. Carla wrote down her number, which Sylvia jammed into a pocket of her suit pants.

"Okay, Charlotte. Bathroom's all yours. And by the way, keep this to yourself," she said, tapping the side of her nose. "Promise?"

\*     \*     \*

"Did you enjoy yourself this evening?" asked Rand once inside Carla's apartment.

"Yes and no."

"What parts yes and what parts no?" Without waiting for an invitation he had moved past her and already kicked off his loafers.

"I enjoyed spending time with you. And it was interesting to meet some of your friends. But to tell you the truth, I'm not a big crowd person. I much prefer one on one," she said, speaking from the heart. Immediately, however, she regretted the comment. "Don't get me wrong, I loved meeting your friends. I just met an overwhelming number of people tonight."

"I know what you mean. I actually prefer spending time alone, too. And right now I'm glad for some quiet time with you. Come here."

"What are you doing?" she asked playfully, wondering how to get rid of him.

"Hopefully I'm going to kiss you," he said, moving close and wrapping his arms around her.

He did not hesitate, and he did not give her a chance to say no. Instead he kissed her in the most tantalizing manner.
*Stop right now.*

She closed her eyes as he continued placing soft, warm kisses on her face. It was remarkably nice, and she found him nearly impossible to resist. She had no idea how long they stood in the center of her living room making out. She didn't want him to leave. She definitely didn't want him to stay. But she felt incapable of shutting it down.

"Come on," he said, taking her by the hand and leading her toward the bedroom.
*If he makes a sexual advance, you know what to do.*

"Rand, I need to tell you something," she said softly.

"What? Are you HIV positive or something?"

"No, but it is something you need to know. Something that is very important to me," she said firmly.

His looked was puzzled.

"I'm a virgin."

# CHAPTER
# 18

Carla slept well that night. But when she awoke Saturday morning, her thoughts churned around Rand. She wondered how they might feel about each other under other circumstances. He was smart, fun, sexy, and rich—in essence, very desirable. The memory of his kiss caused an unexpected sexual ache.

"Stop it," she said, chastising herself aloud. Throwing back the covers, she jumped out of bed. Changing into a pair of running shorts and a sweatshirt, it occurred to her while stretching for her morning jog that she needed to e-mail Liz with her report. It would be a long one today.

*I'll do it after my shower.*

It was a gorgeous fall morning. The sun was out, the air was crisp, and it was relatively quiet in Central Park. Carla did a few extra laps around the reservoir before heading home, and was so absorbed in the music on her headset that at first she didn't notice him. He would, in fact, have been very hard to miss.

Parked outside her building was Rand, standing beside one of the most gorgeous motorcycles she'd ever laid eyes on—a top-of-the-line, root beer–colored Harley Davidson. With highly polished chrome and a black leather Road Zeppelin seat, she knew that the Ultra Classic Electra Glide cost considerably more than her annual salary.

He barely appeared the same man she'd seen six hours before. In place of the expensive Italian-made suit were faded denims with a sizable hole over the right knee, along with a white T-shirt under a short black leather coat. He wore black, thick-soled Dr. Martens, and as always, the Ray-Bans. He was munching on a muffin, a Starbucks coffee cup in the other hand.

"You ready?" he asked.

"For what?" she said, then laughed.

"For breakfast." Sitting on the gas tank was another cup of coffee. "Here," he said, then offered it to her. She could tell that behind the glasses he was checking out her legs.

"You are amazing. How did you know I'd be here?"

"You live here, don't you?" He didn't wait for her reply. "I wanted to surprise you. Your doorman told me you'd gone for a jog. I figured you'd be back soon enough."

*So much for security,* she thought, then took the coffee.

"Pick your poison," he said, producing an array of sweeteners from his pocket.

"No, thanks. It's fine just the way it is."

"Good. I hope this is, too," he said, reaching into his other pocket, pulling out a bagel.

"How in the world did you manage to get two cups of coffee here on your motorcycle?"

"I balanced them on the gas tank. You should have seen me cutting through traffic on Broadway."

"You did not!"

"In case you haven't noticed, there's a Starbucks on the corner. I parked the bike and walked over. Come here," he said.

She edged a little closer. "Why? I'm all sweaty."

"So?" He leaned over, then gave her a kiss, causing an unexpected tingle to run through her body.

"You up for a ride?"

"Right now? Like this?"

"No. Go change your clothes, then come on."

"I need to take a shower."

"Make it a bird bath." He looked absolutely adorable in his jeans. "Come on," he said, leading the way into her building.

There was no doubt she would join him. But Carla knew it was imperative that she let Liz Phillips know her plans first.

"Where were you planning on taking us?" she inquired.

"It's a surprise."

"I'm not big on surprises."

"You're a woman, aren't you?"

"Last I checked."

"Then you love surprises."

They boarded the elevator. "Rand. I have some business to take care of before I can leave."

"Why do I get the impression you don't want to be with me?" he said sarcastically.

"That's not true at all!"

He laughed. "I'm still trying to get over last night."

The elevator door opened onto her floor. "Get over last night? What's to get over?"

"Your virginity," he whispered close to her ear.

She blushed, waiting to respond until they were inside her apartment. "My virginity! Do you have a problem with it?"

He laughed again. "Of course not. It's just that—"

"What? You don't meet many virgins anymore?"

"No, not at all. And I'm sorry," he said, then drew her in for another unexpected kiss. It was short, but sweet and tender, renewing in her that same electric charge she'd felt last night.

"Let me go change," she said, gently breaking away. "How long do you think we'll be gone?"

"Long as you want."

Carla looked at her watch. It was 8:15 A.M. She had till noon to fire off her report to Phillips. Thinking it unwise to attempt it with Rand nearby, she took a quick shower while he watched TV, then changed into her own T-shirt, jeans, and leather jacket ensemble.

He laughed out loud at the sight of her.

"We look like twins. Tell me, are you wearing boxers or briefs?"

She blushed.

"All right, all right. We won't even go there."

They headed downstairs and he handed her an extra helmet. Adjusting her hair, and then fastening the helmet tight, she climbed on behind him, gently gripping his waist.

"I don't bite, you know." She held tighter.

With its fuel injected engine, firing up the bike was a cinch. Carla rhapsodically soaked up its roar and vibration. He pulled out of the driveway, carefully maneuvered his way through traffic, then made his way to the Long Island Expressway.

It was an absolutely glorious day for such an adventure. With every whip of the wind and thrust of the engine, Carla became more relaxed. For the next hour she leaned into Rand's back, her arms fully and comfortably around his waist.

Until the engine began to sputter. It started out with the pop of a backfire, and spiraled into reduced delivery of power. She could feel the palpable tension in his body. He was obviously trying to get the bike off the main highway before it faltered altogether.

The bike misfired again, startling them both. "Shit," he
stated. "I wonder what it is?" They were now traveling at
half the speed as a minute before.

"Keep going," she suggested. "I think we can make it to
this exit."

He wasn't enthused with her input, instead muttering
something beneath his breath. Spotting a convenience store
just off the exit, she breathed a sigh of relief. The bike carried them to the parking lot before giving up completely,
after which Rand glided for a final fifteen yards toward a
pay phone.

"What the hell? It's a brand-new bike." He tried starting
it up again, but was met with failure.

"Hop off," he said, striding to the pay phone.

"Don't you want to look it over first?" Carla suggested.
"To see if you can spot any problems yourself?"

"Charlotte, I am mechanically impaired. Why don't you
just go inside and grab a couple of sodas while I place this
call?"

She winced at his condescending tone. He was obviously
flustered and perhaps embarrassed. She climbed off and
watched as he began placing a call. Instead of getting
drinks, though, she squatted down and began visually inspecting the engine.

Her own motorcycle would choke from time to time,
which she knew precisely how to fix. But this one had a
fuel-injected engine, which made its choking an improbable
cause of their trouble. It didn't take her long, however, to
discover the problem. She could clearly see a loose fastener
on one of the plug wires, which meant the spark wasn't fully
hitting the cylinder. Since the surrounding metal was hot,
she moved her hand delicately toward the apparatus and, as
carefully as she could, reattached the device.

She stood up, prepared to start the engine, only to discover Rand staring perplexedly at her from the opposite side of the bike.

"Oh, my gosh," she stammered. "I didn't see you!"

"What are you doing?"

She gulped hard, then forced a grin. "Fixing your motorcycle."

"Oh, and you're suddenly an expert? What the hell do you know about mechanics?"

She swallowed hard again. "Well—not much. It's just that—well, I think I spotted your problem. You might want to try starting the bike again."

"What did you do?" he asked angrily.

"I found a loose plug wire. It's easy to miss." He appeared unconvinced. "Really. I only know this because my brother has a bike, a Harley, and the exact same thing happened once when I was with him." Carla backed away a couple of steps.

He didn't say anything more as he remounted the bike. And as though nothing had ever happened, the bike started, its engine fully firing up. He promptly turned it off, gave it a moment to cool down, then tried again. It worked. He turned it off once more, then climbed off the vehicle and marched back over to the pay phone, where he canceled his distress call, then headed back toward her.

"You still want that soda?" she asked cautiously, unable to decipher his mood.

"No," he answered firmly. Instead, he walked over to her side of the bike, and without warning kissed her yet again.

"Is this how you pay all your mechanics?"

"No. Some get much better treatment than this," he wise-cracked, gently kissing her forehead. "Would you mind showing me exactly what it was you did, just in case it ever happens again?"

"No problem." Freeing herself from his embrace, she positioned herself beside the engine and pointed out the problem.

"Amazing," he said, this time wrapping an arm around her shoulder and giving her a light squeeze as they stood up. "My treat. You want a soda?"

"Sure," she smiled, heaving a huge sigh as he disappeared.

She tried calling his cell phone at least six times, each time learning the phone was not on. She tried calling his apartment an equal number of times, leaving messages on two occasions. She even tried his office.

"Where is he?" Sylvia thought angrily. In spite of needing to finish some errands, she stayed home, her agitation increasing with each unanswered call from Rand.

She tried reading a magazine to distract herself. It was useless. She reorganized her closet, but each outfit seemed to remind her of a time spent with him. Worse, she hadn't made plans for the evening, and would be stuck home tonight wondering what in the hell he was up to. At least she would see him tomorrow afternoon for their movie date.

"I'll bet he spent the night with Charlotte!" She was afraid her instincts about Charlotte Desmond were right. There was something different about her. Something, she worried, that he found very appealing. And still, she could not get the nagging thought out of her head that somehow they'd previously met.

Deciding she wanted an excuse to call Charlotte, she remembered their tentative lunch plans.

"Oh, shit," Sylvia exclaimed, realizing she'd left Charlotte's number in her pants pocket, which she'd dropped off at the dry cleaners that morning.

She tried directory information, but her number was unlisted. Quickly grabbing her jacket and purse, she dashed out of her building and across the street to the cleaners. The owner, a short, swarthy man, smiled at her with his large gap-toothed grin.

"George, I need help," she said urgently.

"It's too late, Ms. March. I can't get anything cleaned today."

"No, no. That's not what I need. I left something in one of my pants pockets. Can you please get the cream-colored slacks that I left?"

"I already checked the pockets."

"What?"

"I always do."

"Are you looking for money?" she asked harshly.

He was not pleased. "No. Some people leave tissue and other crap in their pockets that gets torn up during cleaning."

"So you checked my pockets, then?"

"Yeah."

"I'm looking for a cocktail napkin with a phone number on it."

"I threw it away."

"Why?"

"I thought it was trash."

"Where is it?"

"In the trash."

"Where is your trash?"

"It's out back."

She let out a disgusted sigh. "Go get it."

"Go get it yourself," he said brusquely.

"Goddamn you. You make a fortune off my dry cleaning. Go get the fucking trash and help me find that phone number."

The man had no interest in accommodating her, but he also wanted her out of his face. Without speaking, he went to the back alley and retrieved three large plastic bags.

"Oh, that's a big help," she said as he dropped them in front of her. "I'd suggest you start digging."

"Did anyone ever tell you that you're an asshole?"

"How dare you!"

"It's true. And basically the only thing you get from an asshole is shit. Start digging yourself," he said, then smiled politely at a customer who walked in behind her.

After ringing a couple of times, an answering machine picked up. "Hello. This is Charlotte. Please leave a message, and I'll call you as soon as possible."

"Charlotte, hi. This is Sylvia March. Rand mentioned you were looking for a job in publishing, and there's an opening at Gilbert Brown. Please give me a call. Even if you're not interested in a position, I would still love a chance to have lunch sometime. Talk with you soon," she said sweetly after giving her number, then hung up.

There was almost always an opening at Gilbert Brown, particularly for entry-level editors, so she certainly hadn't lied. Feeling somewhat relieved, but still edgy, she opened up her refrigerator, then poured herself a glass of Chardonnay, easily gulping it down. But it wasn't enough. And though it was barely late afternoon, and she usually only indulged in the evening, she pulled out a vial of coke and inhaled two lines, at last feeling better.

The intoxicating smell of salt air invigorated Carla in the deepest and most unexpected way. Though she loved the ocean, typically she disliked the damp air and sand in everything that came with beach living. Perhaps, she thought, if she'd ever stayed in a luxury beachfront house like this one, she might have learned to like it. They were standing on the rear deck of his two-story property.

"What do you think of my hideaway?" Rand asked.

It was a four-thousand-square-foot home situated on two lush green acres with the Atlantic Ocean on one side and Mecox Bay where he docked his sixty-five-foot yacht on the other. The weathered clapboard Nantucket Colonial, with its bright white trim and gabled roof, exuded warmth and charm in spite of its size.

"This is some surprise."

"Do you like it?"

"Of course. It's just that I'm shocked it's not glass block. I thought you preferred a more contemporary style."

"I prefer a bargain better. A former client of mine became involved in a palimony suit and let me have it for far less than market value to spite his ex-girlfriend."

"What did she get?"

"The kid."

"A better bargain, if you ask me."

He did not reply, but responded by gently squeezing her waist, then kissing her lightly on the temple.

"When I think of palimony suits I think of celebrities. Was it anyone I might know?"

"Moses Stein."

"Moses Stein is one of your clients!"

"Was. Kind of hard to do business from jail."

Stein was a notorious Wall Street raider who had made hundreds of millions on high-risk securities, then later landed in prison for insider trading.

"And you were his broker?"

"Yeah, hard to believe. Just commodities. I had nothing to do with his other transactions."

"Still, he's a shrewd businessman. You must be good at what you do." She paused, her thoughts quickly flowing. *This place must be worth millions,* Carla thought, looking out at the expansive lawn and heated pool.

"How long have you owned it?"

"About three years."

"Do you come down frequently?"

"In the summer, yes. It all depends in the winter. There's a lot going on in the city. But sometimes, like today, I'll spend two hours driving here just to spend an hour soaking up the air. I love this place." He looked out at his boat. "It's a great day for a sail. What do you say?"

*We kept a boat on Lake Union. I grew up sailing on the Puget Sound.* She recalled the lie she'd told him after Cameron Bulloch's funeral.

"Not today, thanks. I really need to watch my time."

"And what do you have going on that's so important?" he asked sardonically.

"Business."

"Business can wait today."

"Oh, really? And should I forward my bills to you?"

"Hardly. I am, after all, speaking to someone who made some sizable pocket change off Intex stock. That alone should keep you going for a while."

"Smart aleck. So what if that's true? I still have contractual obligations to meet. I'm in the process of editing a book right now, and promised my client I'd have it back by Monday."

"There's always tomorrow."

"You're impossible."

"You're no fun," he said lightly.

"You have no idea."

"Idea of what?"

"Idea how much fun I can be." With that she kicked off her boots, stripped off her socks, and threw her jacket down on the deck. "Let the games begin," she provoked him, then dashed across his lush green lawn to the shore.

Running as fast as she possibly could, and with Rand still in his Dr. Martens chasing her, she beat him to the shoreline by at least twenty yards. She was running along the water's edge when she saw him quickly abandon his boots after his first step on the sand. Seeing his renewed mad dash her way, she stopped long enough to taunt him, then launched another all-out run. He was on top of her in seconds. Grabbing her from behind, he wrapped his arms around her waist and swung her toward the water.

"It's probably sixty degrees at the most," he said laughingly. "Are you ready for a swim?"

"No, don't," she screamed playfully. "I can't swim."

"Baloney," he said, cradling her above a low-breaking wave.

"Please, please, no," Carla cried.

He swung her around a couple of times. "Here's a new one. Date discus throwing. I wonder how far she can fly?"

"Let me down. Please let me down!"

"Oh, no. The fun has just begun." He stopped his rotations, then swung her up over his shoulder.

"Let me down, you ogre," she cried, playfully whacking him on the back.

"Ogre!" He let out a throaty growl, then gently bit her in the butt. "Ogres eat people, don't they?" Turning her around, he carefully dropped her onto the sand. Then lying down on top of her, he pinned her arms out to the side and began licking her face.

"Hmm, tastes good."

Carla laughed hysterically. "Stop it," she cried, turning her head from side to side. He started sucking on her neck.

"Oh, no you don't. No hickeys!"

He stopped. "Are you calling me a hickey now?" he said with a devilish grin.

"I'm telling you no hickeys on my neck! Or anywhere else for that matter!"

He lifted her shirt just above her navel and began sucking there.

"Oh, my God. You're impossible!"

"No, I'm not," he said, then ever so gently moved up and delivered three intoxicating kisses on her mouth. Impulsively, Carla closed her eyes and kissed him back, immersing herself in the growing sexual tension. She found a delicious warmth in being held so close against the brisk sea air, and though her intuition warned her she was in the hands of a master at seduction, the desire for him and for an even deeper closeness was gaining furiously inside her. Each of his sensuous kisses seemed to strip away another layer of Charlotte's veneer, leaving Carla to abandon all pretenses and fully embrace this man and the moment. Rand rolled over on the sand, gently pulling Carla on top of him, prompting her to deliver her own succession of kisses to his neck and face.

*Stop this!* She tried telling herself. *Stop it now!*

She could not. No one had ever held her with this kind of tenderness. He ran his hands affectionately down her back, then pulled her in even closer. Only then, when she felt his hardness, did she begin to snap out of it.

*"With all due respect, Lizzie, why a woman? And why Carla? I mean, she's smart, attractive, and tough. But she's not tough enough yet. Think about it. Why not send in one of the boys? Even someone nearer his age?"* Her father's words rang in her ears. She suddenly sat upright, staring quizzically at the man beneath her.

*"Two reasons. From the sketchy information I've gathered about Rand Emmerson, he's quite a womanizer. The male friends are more of a constant, but the women come and go. I think Carla would possess a greater chance of getting near him."*

"Rand," she said, her voice slightly cracking. "What time is it?"

He laughed. "I don't believe this! We have the whole beach—the whole world—to ourselves. And you want to know what time it is? It's time to relax, Charlotte Desmond," he said, running a hand very softly through her hair.

"Come here." He pulled her close again, kissed her tenderly on her earlobe, then made room for her to put her head on his shoulder. "Just think. We could stay here till the stars come out."

Carla snuggled up beside him. She wanted to be firm with him about going home. But his warm touch and loving mood made such a break impossible at the moment. She looked up at the sky, imagining the glimmering stars.

*I simply cannot imagine this man having anything to do with murder,* she thought, slipping her hand into his.

They did not leave the Hamptons that night.

And by dawn there would be three angry people looking for Rand Emmerson: Liz Phillips, Sylvia March, and, after a botched assassination attempt on his life, the ruthless Russian crime lord Boris Arkady.

# CHAPTER
# 19

Upon entering the apartment, Carla realized she hadn't even opened the shades from the previous day. Though it was sunny outside, the living room was cool and darkened.

She kicked off her boots, then began heading toward her bedroom to take a shower.

"Where have you been?" The voice was low and steady.

Carla felt her heart leap into her throat. It was Liz Phillips.

"Jesus Christ. You just scared the shit out of me," Carla said, abruptly turning around. An ironic sense of anger surged through her over this unexpected intrusion into her domain.

"Where have you been?" Phillips asked again. She was sitting in a club chair in a corner of the living room, one leg casually crossed over the other, a pillow in her lap. She must have been there for a while. In the darkened room it was difficult to see the anger etched in her face. But it was clear in her voice.

"Out in the Hamptons."

"Did you have fun?" she said sarcastically.

Carla contemplated what to say and for the moment remained silent.

"I asked you a question."

"Commander Phillips, I am sorry I've been out of touch. I've been with Rand all weekend," she confessed. "There was not a safe moment to contact you."

"Not one minute when you could have excused yourself to use a pay phone?"

"No," Carla said, immediately realizing there had been several such chances.

"Did you sleep with him?"

"What do you mean?"

"You know exactly what I mean."

"No. I did not have sex with him."

"But you spent the night with him."

"Yes."

"Why?"

"We took a motorcycle ride out to his house in East Hampton yesterday. We spent a lot of time talking. It turned dark before we thought about going home. Neither of us wanted to ride on his motorcycle at night, so we decided to wait till morning. I slept on the sofa—in my clothes."

Phillips sighed wearily. "Sit down," she commanded.

Carla welcomed the chance to relax her trembling legs. *Oh, God,* she thought. *I've really screwed up. I'm probably going to get thrown off the case. Maybe even off the force.*

"You know," Carla began, "you're assuming the worst. And I can understand why. But you might just want to hear what happened first."

Phillips let out a short cynical laugh. "I'm all ears."

Carla took a deep breath. And then for the next fifteen minutes detailed for the commander all that had happened in the past forty-eight hours. Even in the dark, she could see the furrowed look on the woman's face ease with each new revelation about Rand.

"He bought the house in Waterville from Moses Stein in 1996 for three million dollars—cash. Worth double that today. He's got over two hundred feet of waterfront on the ocean, with an equal amount on Mecox Bay. The boat, a Swan-65 called the *Reciprocity,* was registered in his name around the same time.

"Also, he told me that up to and through undergraduate school his father paid for everything. In fact, he'd given Rand anything he'd ever wanted. But just before Rand was set to leave for graduate school, his father cut him off— cold turkey—saying that he considered hunger to be the greatest source of achievement. He told Rand to find a way to succeed on his own, further adding he should not expect any red carpet treatment on Wall Street once he graduated."

Liz listened keenly.

"Rand told me that it was probably one of the best and worst things that ever happened to him. At first he only half believed his father. He managed to arrange financial aid to pay for tuition. But it wasn't so easy changing his lifestyle. He apparently racked up a lot of bills, thinking his father would bail him out. It didn't happen."

Liz finally spoke. "What is their relationship like today?"

"They are estranged. Rand hasn't spoken to him since his first year at Harvard, and said he won't until he succeeds him."

"In what way?"

"Financially."

"Is Rand still in debt?"

"He claims not."

"Did he mention involvement with drugs at all?"

"No. In fact, he doesn't use drugs himself. But he obviously doesn't condemn anyone who uses them."

"Then, why did Sylvia ask you to 'keep it to yourself,' as you said after your encounter in the bathroom?"

"Who knows."

"You say she mentioned a place up on Third Avenue where she buys her coke. No other details?"

"No. She just told me that if I ever wanted to buy some to let her know."

"I don't want you to go that route."

Carla let out a slight sigh of relief, inferring from Phillips's last statement that she would remain on the job.

"Listen, Commander Phillips. You have to understand. I really did not have a clean opportunity to call you."

"I understand," Phillips responded.

"There's something else I've been meaning to tell you. I think I'm being followed." She went on to describe the man she'd seen twice since Cameron Bulloch's funeral.

"Shit!" exclaimed Phillips.

"What?"

"You are being followed. But obviously not very well."

"Why? What do you mean?"

"Ray Connelly, the well-built man with some acne scarring. He's with us."

Carla was incredulous. "Was he with us out in the Hamptons?"

"No, he wasn't in the Hamptons. If he'd followed you there, I wouldn't be here right now. I would have known where in the hell you were. Carla, I'm sorry I didn't tell you earlier that you had a 'ghost' following you. But you have to understand, it was only to protect you."

"Did my father put you up to it?" Carla asked with perceptible indignation.

"No. And don't be so hard on him. You should know," she added somewhat softly, "that he regrets like hell not sticking around to see you being privately sworn in."

Carla fought back sudden tears. She had somewhat empathized with Rand's story of his father's betrayal, as she too felt a need to prove her own success. Unlike Rand, however, she missed her father deeply. He had always been one of her best friends.

Liz broke into her thoughts. "I made the decision to have you followed, Carla. Given the nature of what I've put you up to, I thought it was a wise thing to do."

"How is it he wasn't in the Hamptons?"

"He'd slipped into a restaurant to use the john shortly after you two disappeared upstairs. He wasn't gone long. But it was long enough to lose you."

"Don't you think I can hold my own?"

"I'm more convinced of that now."

"Will I still be followed?"

Phillips quickly reappraised the matter. No coverage was out of the question. But she worried the natural flow of things would be disrupted if Carla knew she was being followed.

"Carla, tell me something. Are you attracted to him?"

Carla reflected for a moment. "Yes and no. I've never gone out with anyone like him before. But I'm realistic about it. He's attracted to Charlotte Desmond and not Carla Jennings."

"Has he tried to have sex with you?"

"Yes."

Liz sighed. "How did you handle it?"

"Just like you told me."

"You told him you were a virgin?"

Carla nodded her head yes.

"Did that work?"

"Yes and no. In some ways I think it makes me more alluring."

Liz sat back in her chair, and while looking upward remained momentarily quiet. After sorting out her thoughts, she spoke very deliberately.

"What's your gut instinct right now? Do you think he had

anything to do with the murders of the Cunninghams and
Candace Rutland?"

Carla also deliberated before answering. "It's possible.
Anything is possible. But I just can't imagine anyone with
his warmth could be so cold."

# CHAPTER
## 20

"You have got to be kidding! I would have given anything to see that!" Sylvia responded with feigned amusement over Carla's tale of fixing Rand's motorcycle. Sylvia had already heard Rand's version, but pretended not to know any details. They were seated at the Park Avenue Café, each enjoying a chicken Caesar salad while sharing a carafe of white wine. Continued shopping along Madison Avenue would follow, in spite of the fact that Carla had already spent fifteen hundred NYPD dollars on two cashmere sweaters at a swank boutique. Of course, she would return them later.

"I can't imagine how you knew what to do. I mean," she said, holding her well-manicured hand up to her chest, "I can barely plug in my blow dryer."

*Yeah, right,* thought Carla, then stated demurely, "I was pretty nervous. After all, I don't know much about motorcycles. What if I just made the problem worse? But my brother's Harley did the same thing when we last went out for a ride. So it was easy spotting the loose connection on Rand's bike."

"Loose connection!" Sylvia laughed. "You say that with such authority."

"What do you mean?" Carla asked, slightly cocking her head.

Carla's directness caught Sylvia momentarily off-guard, and she flashed a more genuine smile as she tried explaining.

"Oh, gosh, if it had been me, and I was even capable of spotting the problem," she said, confidingly, "I would have never been smart enough to define it as a loose connection. I probably would have said something like, 'It looks like the thingy-ma-bob is off the whose-e-what.' "

Carla looked her squarely in the eye and laughed, which made Sylvia feel mildly self-conscious. Sylvia had tried muting the thought that she somehow knew Charlotte, as it seemed unlikely they'd ever met. But a flash of vague recognition suddenly crossed her mind again.

*How odd,* she thought. *I remember those deep-set dimples.*

She suddenly felt downcast about this charming creature sitting across from her. Regardless of the fact that she was quite beautiful, she possessed an assuredness lacking in many of the women whom Rand had dated. And she wasn't nearly so eager to please or impress Sylvia as the others, who all relished an opportunity to learn some of his secrets and bolster themselves through her. But so far Charlotte had revealed little. Sylvia simply didn't sense that Charlotte had lost her head over Rand, news she would normally welcome, as it usually marked the beginning of the end with him. Charlotte, she decided, meant trouble. Not only was she physically attractive, but from what Rand reported, quite wealthy. Combined with her confidence and seeming indifference, it made for precisely the type of woman with whom he might fall in love.

Furthermore, when Charlotte finally called her back, Sylvia was surprised to discover that she had no interest in any position at Gilbert Brown. Instead, she told Sylvia, she'd found some freelance work, and wasn't in any hurry to find full-time employment. After learning Charlotte had previously worked at the venerable St. Dunstan's Press in London, Sylvia felt somewhat foolish for having offered up an entry-level editorial position. This was obviously a very bright and well-connected woman, and someone not needing her help.

Sylvia's cell phone began ringing, prompting her to open her black Moschino handbag to retrieve her Star TAC.

"Hel-oooo," she said, smiled broadly, then glanced at Carla. "What an absolute coincidence. I'm having lunch with one Charlotte Desmond as we speak. Would you care to join us?"

Carla shifted in her seat, smiled slightly, then sipped her wine.

"What? Stuffy Park Avenue denizens and Madison Avenue shops bore you? I can't imagine." Sylvia nibbled at her salad. "Why would I know where he is? I haven't spoken to Serge in weeks." She listened. "You'd like to speak to Charlotte? Here." Her contrived friendliness vanished as she handed over the phone. She was still somewhat sore at him for standing her up the previous Sunday for their movie date.

"Hello," said Carla.

"Do not believe anything she tells you—about me, that is. It's all lies." He laughed.

"Don't flatter yourself. Your name has hardly come up."

"I find that extremely hard to believe. Well, then, you should be careful what *you* tell *her*," he said. "She's the town crier."

"I find that hard to believe," she said, her voice edged in sarcasm.

"Listen, while I have you on the phone, can I talk you into dinner on Friday night?"

"That might work."

"It might? Or it will?"

She laughed. "Actually, yes. And since I'm out shopping already, any suggestions as to what I might buy?"

"Buy one of each."

"One of each what?"

"One of everything. Then you'll always be prepared."

"For what?"

"Anything and everything."

"Boy, you're feisty today."

"Is that a problem?"

"No." She laughed.

"So, you game? Friday night?"

"Absolutely."

"Great. I'll call you later, and we can settle the specifics. And listen. There is a really hot dress in the window at Shanghai Tang. Love to see you in it."

"We'll see."

"Don't disappoint me."

"Why don't I just surprise you?"

"I like that better. 'Bye for now."

" 'Bye," said Carla, then handed the phone to Sylvia.

"Rand," said Sylvia into the mouthpiece. There was no answer. "I think he hung up. That creep." She put the device away, miffed that he hadn't spoken with her again and jealous of their banter. "Surprise him with what?"

"A dress from Shanghai Tang," she replied about the expensive Chinese import store.

Sylvia picked up the carafe and refilled her glass, not bothering to offer any. Her whole countenance had shifted from upbeat to dispirited. Carla watched as Sylvia downed her wine in practically two gulps, then poured herself another.

"Would you like some more?" she asked at last.

"No, thanks. I'm fine," said Carla, watching as Sylvia poured herself the remains.

"He is such a creep," Sylvia muttered again.

"What do you mean?"

Sylvia scowled. "Listen, I've known him for a long time." She stopped to collect her thoughts, then finally met Carla's curious expression. "And even though we're very good buddies, I still think it's rude when he hangs up on me like that. That's all."

Carla sensed Sylvia's sudden dismay was less over his callousness—she was probably used to that—and more over Carla's favorable status. Concerned that Sylvia might insist on discussing her anger, Carla changed the subject.

"Who is Serge?" she asked nonchalantly.

"Serge?" Sylvia looked momentarily perplexed, then recalled she'd just mentioned his name. "Oh, yeah, Serge. Serge Fedorov. You haven't met him?"

"No," Carla casually shook her head. "Is he one of Rand's clients?"

"Hardly." She let out a cynical laugh. "He's a friend of Rand's from Harvard. They do some business together now."

"Commodities?"

"Oh, I suppose in a sense."

"You mean Serge is also a commodities broker?"

"No, no. They refer business to each other, that's all."

"Is he a stockbroker or something?"

"No. He's just . . . I don't know. He's just Serge. I don't get too much into it." She polished off her wine, then looked at her watch. "Does it really matter?"

"No." Carla smiled.

"Are you ready for more shopping?"

"Of course, aren't you?"

Sylvia felt emotionally strained and now a bit drunk. "Absolutely!" she lied, then motioned for the waiter to bring them the check. "You like him, don't you?"

"Who?"

"Who else? Rand," Sylvia said, with all the sincerity of a Linda Tripp.

"Why do you say that? I mean, I like him as a friend. But I barely know him."

"That's what they all say."

"What do you mean, 'they'?"

"Oh, all the women that have come and gone in his life. They all start by pretending that they're not in love. But they're pretty hopeless. Charlotte, I've been around him long enough to see the pattern."

"Sylvia, what exactly are you saying? Are you suggesting that I'm in love with him?"

"No. But you could be. He makes it easy, you know. He's also a notorious heartbreaker."

"I thought you were his good friend. Why would you do this to him?"

"Oh, I don't know. And you're right. It's not fair for me to talk about him behind his back. It's just that I like you, Charlotte. You seem like a really nice person, and I don't want to see you get hurt. Just keep your options open, that's all."

"Well, I appreciate the heads up then." Carla smiled affably.

The waiter delivered the check, which Sylvia promptly paid for them both.

"Let's go shopping, girlfriend!"

"I'm ready," Carla said, retrieving her Louis Vuitton handbag.

"Charlotte, I'm so glad we're doing this today," said Sylvia through a contrived smile.

"Me, too," Carla said through her own calculated grin. "Me, too."

Frank Kelley loved the sound of a baseball bat cracking a home run hit. He took a sip of his beer and smiled. The Yankees were rallying in the ninth. As the fans cheered, he turned down the radio, refocusing his attention on his computer, which, along with a soft, gurgling aquarium, illuminated his den.

He'd been surfing the Internet for over an hour, looking up everything possible in relation to fertilizers in Louisiana. It was the second time this week he'd searched, the first time coming up with over 300,000 hits. Tonight he tried fertilizers and New Orleans, stirring up a nearly equal number of hits. It was like being a tourist on a glass-bottomed boat, just bobbing on information waves until something notable passed by. From what he could gather so far, Red's friend could just as well be selling lawn fertilizers as he could be teaching at an agricultural extension program.

The crowd let forth another boisterous cheer, prompting Kelley to turn up the volume and listen to the game for a moment. It was the bottom of the ninth, the Yanks down by one, the bases were loaded, and Tino Martinez was at the plate, having already sucked up strike one.

"Strike two!" the announcer said.

"C'mon!" Kelley called. "Hit the damned ball."

He could hear what sounded like a hit, followed by "Foul ball." He swallowed the remains of his beer.

"Shit," muttered Kelley. He stood up to relieve some tension in his neck, his head jerking sideways a few times. *I would have been a great baseball manager,* he thought wistfully.

"Steeeriiike three!"

"Ah, go to hell," Kelley groused at the umpire. Four to three, Orioles. Yankees lose, again.

Kelley used the john, got another beer, and then looked at the clock. It was 10:35 P.M. He thought about turning off the computer, but it had taken him an hour to get online tonight, and he didn't want to lose his connection. So instead he surfed through Louisiana and fertilizers a bit longer. Still, nothing jumped out at him.

"How about an electronic trip to Russia?" he mused.

FERTILIZERS RUSSIA he typed. Expecting another lengthy range of hits to choose from, he relaxed and slugged back some beer. What appeared next, however, surprised him so much that he promptly put down the bottle. There were only a few hits. Even so, it would be another four hours before he turned off his computer.

The following day, Liz Phillips called him into her office and handed him a slip of paper with the name Sergei Fedorov on it.

"Do me a favor. Contact the INS on this guy. Find out what they've got on him."

"Another Russian, heh?" He started to tell Liz what he'd found on the computer last night, but hesitated. He didn't want to waste her time until he was more certain about the leads he'd discovered.

"Hey, Kelley," said one of the secretaries at the Investigative Division of the Immigration and Naturalization Service. Her friendliness surprised him, since most of the clerks here could double as guards at a maximum security prison. He smiled but said nothing, only strolling onward to the gray metal desk of his friend, Barry Robertson.

Robertson's head was bent forward, and he was furiously erasing something. Kelley slid up behind him, then realizing what his friend was up to, and having already completed the same crossword puzzle that morning, offered some unsolicited help. "Thirteen down, six letters, clue: scavenger; answer: magpie."

Robertson glared up at him.

"What!" Kelley exclaimed. "I was just trying to help."

"Yeah, right. And now you want *me* to help *you*, right?"

"No, really. I'm just a nice guy who thought you wouldn't mind some friendly advice."

"Sit down." Robertson grinned. "What can I do for you?"

Barry Robertson and Frank Kelley had started their respective law enforcement careers around the same time, and initially met when Kelley's first investigation involved a double homicide committed by an illegal immigrant. Special Agent Barry Robertson, something of a rookie himself, helped Kelley to profile the man. It was a new experience for both officers, but something that would eventually turn them into longtime friends.

"I'm not sure, really. Remember Red?"

"Oh, sure. The Russian?"

"Yeah, I got another one I need you to check out."

"Another dead Russian?"

"No." Kelley laughed. "At least as far as I know." He handed Robertson a slip of paper with a name on it. "Guy by the name of Sergei Fedorov. Might be in his late twenties, early thirties."

"That it?"

"That's it."

Robertson studied his friend for a minute. He was a different man from when they first met a dozen years ago. Then Kelley was a robust, handsome guy with a crop of thick black hair. But with gray, thinning locks, a slight paunch, and now this tic, Robertson would have never recognized him on the street had he not kept in touch with him.

"Hey, Kelley, I hope you don't mind my getting personal with you. But aren't they doing anything for you?"

"What do you mean?"

"Don't you get tired of that damned tic? Isn't there something you can take?"

"No. And what's worse—it's contagious."

"Get outta here!"

"No kidding. That's how I got it. Some jerk kissed me in the subway."

With that he stood up, leaned over, and kissed his old friend on the top of his head.

"Have a good day," he chided Robertson, and began walking away. "And call me as soon as you know something."

"You jerk!" said Robertson, wiping the perceived contagion off his head with a handkerchief.

"You might try some hydrochloric acid with that," said Kelley, laughing. "Call me when you know something," he repeated, then left.

Later that afternoon Barry Robertson called him.

"He's illegal."

"Really. What have you got?"

"Attended Harvard Business School on a student visa, which has long since expired, and has no other applications on file. If you want, we could send him back home tonight. What's going on with him? Was he friends with Red?"

"Don't know. It's all unclear. He might have been an acquaintance. Listen, do me a favor though. Keep this information to yourself until I have further instructions from Liz Phillips what to do."

"Is he under suspicion for murder?"

"Like I said. I'll call you when I know something."

# CHAPTER
# 21

Returning from a late lunch, Liz Phillips checked her voice mail. There were several messages, including one from Kimberly Prescott.

"I get off work at four p.m. There's something I want to show you. Please meet me in the hospital lobby." That was it.

It was already 3:35 P.M., and Phillips had a half dozen things to do in the next couple of hours. She thought to call the hospital and have the nurse paged, but then decided against it. Instead she rearranged her schedule and then jumped on the number six train heading uptown. She was seven minutes late, and upon dashing into the lobby she discovered Prescott was nowhere in sight.

"Dammit," she uttered. She was about to have Kimberly paged when she spotted her exiting a nearby elevator. She sported a well-worn jean jacket over her uniform. She was also wearing dark, round sunglasses, and over her shoulder she carried a blue nylon backpack.

"Hi," she said, approaching Phillips. "Glad to see you."

"Thanks. Do you want to go somewhere to talk?"

"No. I want to take you somewhere. Just come with me, please."

They left the building, and Prescott quickly hailed a taxi.

"After you," she said, waiting till Phillips climbed in, then instructed the driver. "Seventy-eighth and Third, please."

Phillips's mind ran quickly through the possibilities of what Prescott might be doing. What happened next was entirely unexpected.

"Far right side," she told the driver. He slowed down and then stopped as instructed. Prescott handed him a five-dollar bill for a four-dollar fare, then stepped out of the car. Phillips quickly jumped out behind the woman, who was two paces ahead of her on the sidewalk already. Prescott stopped two doors away from the Candy Connection—a hole-in-the-wall candy shop—and then turned.

"Do not stand directly in front of the store. Get as close as you can and just watch."

Prescott then entered the store, biding her time looking at all the different candies in the Plexiglas bins while another customer received service. After that patron left, and with her back to Phillips, she spoke to the clerk. Moments later she left the store. Phillips followed behind for two blocks until Prescott let her catch up. She opened her knapsack to reveal a glassine bag of coke.

"I hope you're not going to bust me," said Prescott, still walking.

"You've got to be kidding. That easy, huh?"

"That easy." Stopping short, she turned and faced Phillips, tears now rimming her eyes. "You know, you were right. And the only reason I just stuck my ass on the line like this with you is to hopefully prevent another tragedy like this from occurring again. At least in my life."

The tears began sliding down her cheeks. "He used me. That bastard just used me. He was afraid of getting caught. Worried what it might do to his career, you see. So he sent me." She reached in her pocket and pulled out a balled-up napkin, into which she blew her nose.

"You know, I really believed he liked me. And maybe in the beginning he did. But in reality, he never cared about me. The only thing he cared about were his goddamned drugs and getting laid every once in a while. I was so stupid, *so stupid,*" she lamented. "I bought his drugs for him and then let him fuck me, too. Pretty smart, huh? Oh, God," she sobbed.

Phillips tucked the contraband inside her purse. "Listen, Kimberly, I promise you're not going to be arrested. But I need your help, and we need to talk."

It took a few moments before Kimberly gathered her wits, finally suggesting a walk in Central Park. It took them ten minutes to get there, walking in silence as they did. At last they reached the concrete boat pond, where children and adults alike were amusing themselves racing miniature electronic yachts. Approaching the old brick boathouse, Phillips bought them each a soda and pretzel before heading to a nearby bench.

"Kimberly, you made a very courageous decision today. Thank you. Tell me something, though. How long had you been buying his dope?"

Kimberly took a bite of her oversized pretzel before speaking. "Six months, at least," she said, chewing.

"And was it always from that same location?"

"Yeah."

"Hmmm. Tell me what happens in there."

"Well, there's a system, you see. You have to know someone—one of their reliable customers—before they'll do business with you. Cameron knew the right people."

"Did he ever buy dope himself?"

"Sometimes. But he'd mostly come to depend on me."

"Do you know who those 'right people' were for him?"

She shook her head while swallowing a sip of soda.

"Kimberly, do you realize that you could have spent the

rest of your life in jail if you'd ever been busted doing this? That's a pretty steep penalty for some watered-down love."

"Shows you how steep my stupidity was."

"Do they only deal in small quantities?"

"Yeah. It's a boutique operation, and the people buying it are pretty much recreational cocaine users on the Upper East Side."

"Kimberly, did you *ever* meet any of Cameron's friends?" Phillips had asked the question before, but had a hunch the answer this time would be different.

"Once, when a small group of his friends had some casual dinner party. Naturally he wanted me to pick up his dope first, which I did. Anyway, I got to this party, and it was apparent in no time that I didn't fit in with this crowd. I could tell Cameron was really uncomfortable too, 'cause he barely spoke to me. It was the only time *I* ever got mad at *him*. I left the party early and didn't return any of his phone calls for a week. Basically," she said, looking downward, "I wasn't as mad as I was really hurt."

"Then what happened?"

"He came over to my apartment, and we made up. But he never invited me out with his friends again."

"Kimberly, is this the only store you know of selling drugs like this?"

"Yeah, I suppose. I mean, that was the only one I ever went to."

"Do you know how long it's been in operation?"

"Nope."

"Any idea who owns it?"

"No, quite honestly, I don't. Cameron might have known, but he was pretty closemouthed about it if he did."

"Weren't you ever afraid of being caught?"

"Yeah, but not as much as I was afraid of losing him. That's what's so screwed up about it."

Sliding down on the bench so that her head rested on the back, she actually appeared to relax. She sank her hands into her pockets, then crossed her feet. However, when she finally spoke, her voice was edged with bitterness. "Do you think he would have ever come to visit me in jail?"

Phillips swallowed the last of her soda and then pitched the empty can into a nearby bin.

"Nice toss."

"Thanks. Kimberly, you want to know something? In my previous incarnation I was a street cop in the Bronx." Phillips let out one of her light but contagious laughs. "Believe me, honey, there ain't nothing I ain't seen."

"I can imagine," Kimberly conceded with a slight grin.

"Anyway. There are some big misconceptions about poverty and wealth. The first is that being poor means being miserable, and the second is that money makes you happy. Wrong. It's true that there are a lot of unhappy poor people. And a lot of very happy rich folks. But some of the kindest and most genuinely happy people I've met are the poorest, and some of the most wretched and miserable were rich beyond belief."

"Yeah, so?"

"Yeah, so stick with me. What I've also witnessed in both cases is a distorted reality. The poor don't think they'll ever make it; the rich think they'll never lose. Because of their money and being always treated with deference, they become insular. They tend to lack empathy.

"What I'm getting at, Kimberly, is, don't be so hard on yourself. And get over the demented notion that Cameron Bulloch had what it took to make you happy. He might have had money and pedigree, but he didn't have class. In reality he was a drug-addicted, emotionally abusive man. I think what happened with you is that at some level you felt sorry for him, actually believed you could heal him, be his savior, and live happily ever after. Believe me, that only happens in fairy tales. So stop feeling sorry for yourself. You might have bought him the drugs. But he's the idiot who did them."

Kimberly removed her glasses and then wiped her eyes and nose.

"Kimberly, you've got so much going for you. More than he ever did, trust me."

"I don't want anything more to do with this," she said abruptly.

"With what?"

"With you. With any of this. I want to forget about it."

"Well, I'm not surprised."

"Good. Because you and I are finished. You know his drug source. Do with it what you want. But from now on, keep me out of it. You promise?"

Phillips did not immediately respond. "You promise you'll never buy drugs again?" she finally said, looking at her hard.

"Trust me," Prescott said firmly. Then gathering her well-worn backpack, she rose off the green wooden bench and walked away.

# CHAPTER
## 22

Jack Jennings had certainly lost his temper with his children before, and had used a switch for discipline from time to time. But looking over at Robbie, sitting on a bench in their neighborhood's police precinct, made him realize that for the first time as a parent he was at a loss over what to do.

His youngest son had been picked up for shoplifting. If that wasn't bad enough, he'd done so while skipping school—after forging his father's name on a note excusing him from class to go see the family doctor. He wasn't alone in this misadventure. Two other classmates had been picked up with him, their combined absences prompting one suspicious teacher to alert the principal. He then put in a call to Jack and the other parents, which Jack considered humiliating enough. None of his kids had ever been truants. An hour later, however, came even worse embarrassment as Jack got a call from the precinct captain. They'd been busted at Circuit City trying to pilfer a miniature boom box. Though Robbie hadn't been caught with the merchandise, he'd been caught with the fledgling outlaw, and for the moment he was down as his accomplice.

Jack looked at the arresting officer and asked, "What about the charges?"

"The store manager wants to teach them all a lesson."

"Can they prove Robbie had anything to do with it?"

"Jack, c'mon. You know better. He helped."

Jack rubbed the back of his hand across his forehead. "You know, I couldn't tell you how many parents I've counseled over the years about this kind of thing. Easy to be an expert when you don't know what you're talking about. None of my others ever did it."

"You mean they never got caught."

"Probably more like it. What the hell did I know?"

"Anything else going on in the kid's life? Grades okay?"

"Yeah, he pulls steady Bs, occasional As. Been a little tougher lately, but I think it's the curriculum."

"You sure? Any sign of drug use? This shoplifting is sometimes an indicator of that, you know."

"Mike, dammit. What do I know? Right now I'd like to beat the shit out of him. What good is that going to do? Listen, let me sign the papers and get the heck out of here. I think what we need most is a heart-to-heart."

"Why do I have a feeling that's what you told all the other parents to do?"

"Because it sounded like good advice."

Bobby shuffled over to the booth and grinned as she handed Jack and the youngest Jennings some Blue Bay Diner menus.

"A little late for lunch and too early for dinner. What's up? You want a milkshake or something?"

"Bobby, we missed lunch today. I'll have a cup of coffee and a tuna sandwich. Robbie, what about you, son? You want a burger and fries?"

He barely looked up. "Yeah," he said somberly. "With a chocolate shake."

Bobby hadn't seen him in so long she barely recognized him. He'd grown at least one foot, his skin was mildly broken out, and his voice seemed to crack with every other syllable. Still, she could see that he possessed that delectable Jennings charm. "You want the works with that burger?" she asked.

"Yeah," he said, still not making eye contact.

Jack scratched his chin, then unrolled his utensils from the paper napkin and began playing nervously with his fork and knife. "You doing okay, son?"

"Yeah," he said grimly.

"Just 'yeah.' Anything you want to talk about?"

"No."

Jack bit his lower lip, trying to contain a sigh.

What came next was unexpected, but welcome. "Dad. I'm sorry."

"Yeah, me too. You're in a bit of a pickle, kid. And I'm not sure if there's anything I can do to help you out."

Robbie shook his head. "It sucks. I'm so embarrassed."

"Yeah, that pretty much sums it up."

Big tears filled the young man's eyes. He fought them desperately, but to no avail. "It's all my fault," he said, then unrolled his own set of utensils and blew his nose with the napkin.

"I'm not sure I follow you, son."

"I wish I'd never been born."

"What in God's green earth are you talking about?"

"Mom would still be alive if it weren't for me!" he snapped back.

"Now, wait a minute, Rob. That's the craziest thing you ever said. Of course that's not true."

"It is, Dad. It is. I heard her say it to Aunt Peg one time. She said she was going to have a hysterectomy, and then got pregnant with me. If she'd never gotten pregnant, she would have had the hysterectomy and never died of cancer."

"Oh, Mary, Mother of God," said Jack, reaching across

the table for his son's hand. "Robbie, nothing could be further from the truth. As God is my witness, you were the only one we planned. She used to joke all the time about getting a hysterectomy, but she never meant it. You gotta believe me. No child was ever more desired than you. We loved the family we had so much, and we knew because we were getting on in age that if we wanted another baby it better be soon. We made love like a couple of teenagers for your sake." He balled up the napkin sitting in front of him and dabbed the tears welling in his own eyes. "You miss your mom, don't ya?"

Robbie could barely speak, instead nodding yes.

"Me, too, son. Me, too." It took Jack a moment more to collect himself. "You're missing Carla too, aren't ya?"

Forgoing his napkin for a sleeve, Robbie wiped his nose and nodded. "Yeah."

Jack let out a huge sigh. "Me, too."

"Where in the hell is she, Dad?" Robbie blurted. "I mean, why doesn't she ever call? It's not like we hate her, or something. You know what I think? I think Carla wouldn't have been so unhappy if she hadn't spent so much time taking care of me."

"Robbie, that is simply not true. First of all, Carla was not unhappy. She was just unsure. And furthermore, she never had what she considered to be a hard time with you. She made a conscious decision to stick around and help raise you, and you're a better person because of it. And just because she took off like she did doesn't mean you're to blame. Did you ever stop to think it might just be the best thing that ever happened to her?"

Robbie's mouth twisted as he looked out the window.

"Let me tell you something, son. You're going through a lot of changes right now. Changes you'd be dealing with regardless of Carla—or your mother. Your brothers all went through it; Carla went through it. It's a part of growing up. And they all survived. So will you. But you better remember two things to keep you steady through it all. First, whether you can help it or not, you're going to get emotional. Sometimes you'll feel angry and sometimes hurt. But those emotions—real as they seem—are temporary, so don't let them run your life. It's important to try to take an extra minute to think about what you're going to say or do when anger or hurt are talking, 'cause they love nothing more than to run you into the ground and embarrass you to death.

"And the second thing is, don't think for one minute that you are not loved—or wanted. Or that you were the cause of any doom and gloom. I cherish you, son. I look at you and see the greatest benefit of having had your mother as my wife."

Robbie nodded.

"And there's one last thing," Jack added. "I guarantee you that your sister is happier than she's ever been."

# CHAPTER
## 23

"Send him up," said Carla over the house phone to her door-man. He had called to say that her Chinese food had arrived. The doorbell rang while she was in her bedroom digging out cash from her wallet. *That was fast,* she thought. The door-bell rang again.

"I'll be right there," she hollered.

Wearing gray sweats and socks, her hair pulled back in a ponytail, she slid across the foyer's marble entry and quickly unlocked the deadbolt. Opening the door, she shrieked at the sight before her.

The man was hidden behind an enormous arrangement of bright and fragrant flowers. There were peach gladiolas, pink stargazer lilies, white miniature roses, purple al-stomera, and broad ferns fanning out from an oversized vase, all of which concealed his face.

"What is this?" she said incredulously.

"A table arrangement to complement your dinner," he said, and with his other hand raised a brown paper bag con-taining her food. Carla laughed, as she immediately recog-nized the voice.

*Does this guy ever call ahead?*

"Rand Emmerson, I ought to shoot you!"

"You might have a better shot if you took these flowers first. Can you help me out? They're kind of heavy."

Carla, smiling broadly, shook her head in wonderment, then relieved him of the Chinese food. "Come on in."

"Where would you like these, ma'am?"

"The kitchen, right now," she said, leading the way.

"The kitchen?"

"For now. I'll find a better spot later," she said somewhat indifferently.

"I hope you like them," he said, with a hint of self-awareness.

"I love them," she said, offering reassurance. In fact, she'd never received such a king-size flower arrangement before. An old boyfriend once brought her a bunch of daffodils from a street vendor, something she'd thought was sweet and romantic.

"How in the world did you manage to coordinate this?"

"Serendipity. I was going to have these delivered. Then I thought, that's crazy, because then he gets to see you and I don't. So I brought them over myself. I just happened to walk in the door at the same time your dinner arrived, and the doorman agreed to let me bring them up with your food."

Carla masked her annoyance over the doorman's false assumption that it was okay to send Rand up unannounced.

"You paid for my dinner?"

"Of course. My treat."

"That was sweet. Thank you. Are you hungry?"

"That all depends. What did you get?"

Carla laughed as she began pulling out plates and utensils.

"General Tso's chicken, egg rolls, and some wonton soup."

"Then, I'll stay."

"What if I said Szechuan beef?"

"I would have stayed. Sweet and sour pork—I'd be out the door."

Through his smile, Carla could see that he was studying her face, and she suddenly realized she was wearing no makeup. She felt naked and exposed without her powdery armor.

His smile expanded. "You know something, Charlotte Desmond, you are a very beautiful woman."

Carla blushed deeply, and turned her face away from him as she began fussing with the flowers and the food.

"Come here," he said, then without waiting for a response moved up and wrapped his arms around her waist from behind her, then kissed her on the ear.

Any common sense telling her to break away was suddenly muted by an unexpected flash of desire. There was something richly sexual in Rand Emmerson's touch, and the warmth of his body against hers, the mixture of strength and tenderness in his hands, the subtle scent of his cologne, and the lingering effect of his delicate kiss left her feeling limp. Instead of enforcing distance, she relished the measure of affection, momentarily allowing him to cradle her.

He kissed her on the other ear, sending a surprising rush of hot blood coursing through her body. She stood in place. Unable to look at him, unwilling to move, she did not know what to do.

He resolved that for her. "The dim sum is pretty good," he whispered in her ear, kissed it once again, then backed away while lightly patting her on the behind. She felt like her head was floating while her feet remained fixed in lead blocks.

"Where's the wine?" he asked, nonchalantly opening the refrigerator. "Do you ever go to the store?" He exclaimed. "Practically all you have is milk!"

"To go with my Frosted Mini Wheats."

"You and those damned Mini Wheats. What happened to

that bottle of Pouilly Fuissé you offered me on our first date?"

"I drank it."

"By yourself—I hope."

An impish grin consumed her face, causing her deep-set dimples to nearly fold in on themselves. He playfully dipped a finger in one of them, causing her to laugh.

"Is that a yes or a no?" he said, holding his finger in place. "Oh, my God, your face is turning crimson. Charlotte Desmond, you're either a drunk or a cheat. Which one?"

"What if I said a cheatin' drunk?"

"Then I'd say you're my kind of girl!"

He kissed her again, and with every ounce of strength she could muster, Carla tried not to kiss him back. But it was hopeless. His mouth felt warm and sensuous, and again every nerve in her body tingled with excitement.

*Why is he doing this to me? Why is he here?*

He pecked her gently on her neck, then once more on the mouth, leaving her feeling, for the first time in her life, physically out of control.

She took a deep breath, and then another, and finally opened her eyes wide, meeting Rand's sultry gaze.

"Wow, you sure know how to tease a girl, don't you?"

"Who said I was teasing?"

She grabbed his hand and gave it an affectionate squeeze. "Listen, the Pouilly Fuissé is gone. But how about some bubbly?"

She reopened the refrigerator and pulled out a large bottle of carbonated water.

"Now who's the tease?"

"Actually, I do have some wine. The problem is, I've got work to do this evening. I have a project deadline to meet tomorrow, and I can't very well finish it if I'm drunk."

"Does that mean you're throwing me out?"

"Not this minute. But still, we can't visit long."

He tried hard not to show any sense of rejection. Usually after such displays of affection, he'd have to beg a woman for permission to leave.

"That's fine," he said complacently. "I knew I shouldn't have just barged in on you. But I've been thinking about you all day, and like I said, I didn't think it fair the florist should see you and not I."

"These flowers are beautiful. Thank you." She chuckled. "You cannot imagine how surprised I was at the sight of them."

*Shocked is more like it,* she thought. By now she'd loaded up two plates with the Chinese food and set them down on a small table in her kitchen.

"You know what I love about Chinese food?" he said after swallowing the first mouthful.

"Well, I know it's not sweet and sour pork. What?"

"I love that they give you enough to feed a family of eight. They must think Americans have bottomless pits for stomachs."

Carla smiled and nodded in agreement while sipping her wonton soup.

"Listen," he went on. "I had asked you about dinner this Friday night. A bunch of us are going to Pacifica. Do you know about it?"

"Nope. Can't say that I do."

"To tell you the truth, I'd be surprised if you did, since you're still fairly new here. It's in a Holiday Inn down in Chinatown, kind of off the beaten path. But they probably have some of the most authentic Chinese food you've ever tasted. Terrific braised shark fins."

"Braised shark fins? I can hardly wait."

"Trust me, you'll enjoy it."

"I'm game. By the way, I enjoyed myself with Sylvia the other day. She seems like a really nice person."

Rand let out a low, cynical laugh.

"What?" Carla prompted him.

"Don't get me wrong. She is a nice person. When she wants to be."

"I thought you two were such good friends. How could you say such a thing?"

"Because I know her, and I can. Trust me. The only reason she's interested in you is because of me."

Carla tried hard not to show what she already suspected.

"God, Rand. That kind of hurts. I mean, I would hope she's not so duplicitous. I enjoyed talking with her, and it seemed she liked me too."

"I understand, and that's probably true. But just be careful what you say around her. Especially," he added with a wink, "if you don't want it getting back to me."

"Did she tell you anything I said so far?"

"Actually, no. Which is kind of surprising."

"Maybe I didn't say anything that bears repeating."

"Now, that kind of hurts. You mean you didn't tell her how desperately in love you are with me? That you would die without me?"

"Oh, my God!" Carla said, her face a mixture of admonishment and amusement. "Truly," she added. "I'm surprised to hear you talk about her this way. I mean, after all, you two are business partners, aren't you?"

His face suddenly turned blank. "She told you we were business partners?"

*Play it cool.*

"Well, sort of, I suppose. She didn't say specifically what business, or specifically business partners. I think she said you shared some investments. That's kind of the same thing, isn't it?"

He chortled, then put down his fork and folded his hands while leaning his elbows on the table. She could see she'd struck some kind of nerve.

"You're right. Actually, you and Sylvia are both right. I helped her get into commodity investments. That's a bit more factual."

"Oh," Carla said with contrived innocence. "So how'd she do? I presume all right. After all, you're her broker, right?"

"I am. And she's done quite well."

*Look for opportunities to present yourself as a potential investor. Remember, commodities are the riskiest investment of all. You must have money to lose.*

"That's good to know. Actually, I've been thinking of investing in commodities myself."

"Why?"

"Why not?"

"Charlotte, there are a lot more sound investments out there."

"I understand."

"Have you ever invested in commodities before?"

"No."

"Listen, I know from one of our previous conversations that you play the stocks. It sounds like you've done okay from that. Stick with it."

"You mean you wouldn't want my business?"

"Charlotte, I don't mean to be rude. But the people with whom I do business can afford to invest and lose one hundred thousand in a day."

She raised her eyebrows as she looked at him, artfully playing up the silence. He carefully studied her face, then took a swig of his water, next chomping down on an ice cube.

"Go on," she said determinedly.

"Charlotte, I handle the really high rollers. That's all. The only reason I've done any business with Sylvia is because she's a good friend from way back. But her investments are small time for me, like pimples to a dermatologist."

Carla laughed, then took the last bite from her plate. "Do you want some more?" she said, then stood up.

"No, I'm fine."

"Just suppose—and this is only hypothetical, mind you—but just suppose that I had that kind of money to invest."

"Even then, Charlotte, it's still risky. You might lose it and then, well, I might lose you."

"True. But then I might double my money."

"True. Then I'd never get rid of you!"

"Oh, thanks a lot," she said, playfully whacking his arm. "Would that be so bad?"

"No," he said, gently grabbing her hand and drawing her close. "What I'm trying to tell you is that it's not in my nature to mix business with pleasure."

"Fine," she said, pulling away. "I'll take my business somewhere else."

"And not your pleasure, I hope." Contrary to the look in his eyes when speaking of Sylvia, he now seemed amused. She squeezed his shoulder as she walked toward the counter to refill her plate.

"Listen, at the risk of sounding boastful, I want to tell you something. I cannot afford to lose one hundred thousand dollars every day. But I do have a pretty healthy trust fund, some of which I wouldn't mind gambling. It's not inconceivable that I could risk one hundred thousand dollars— perhaps more." She said it so convincing, she almost believed it herself.

"I wondered how you could afford to live this lifestyle on such a meager salary," he mused.

"Well, mostly because I'm good at grocery shopping."

"You never buy them."

"Precisely."

"But you then spend even more money on eating out."

"Oh, no I don't," she said coquettishly.

"Oh, I see, and you just wait for fools like me to show up and pay for your dinner."

"Well, I wouldn't have put it quite like that."

"No, of course not. But you know what? It was worth it. And it will be worth treating you to dinner on Friday night. You can go, can't you?"

"Absolutely. Especially after spending all that money on Madison Avenue the other day for your benefit, I'd better." She ate a couple of mouthfuls out of a container, then scrapped the rest. "What time is it?" she asked.

"Eight-thirty," he said, glancing at his watch.

"Egads. I've got to get back to work."

"As if that's necessary," he said with bemusement.

"Well, I might be able to eliminate the need altogether if I strike it rich with commodities."

He rose from his seat, placed his dish on the sleek granite countertop, then pulled her close, kissing her once more. "You," he said, "are a rare commodity." He could feel her tension transition into warm supplication.

"I will see you Friday, eight o'clock," he added.

"Friday, eight," she murmured while kissing him back, then watched with unforeseen heaviness as he left.

She had no idea how to begin her report to Liz Phillips.

Frank Kelley discovered an intriguing thing while searching the Internet: a Russian running a fertilizer plant in Louisiana.

"Robertson, this is Kelley. I've got another one I need you to check out."

"Dead or alive?" said the INS agent.

"Don't know. But it's another Russian. Fellow by the name of Roman Petrovsky."

"What do you know about him?"

"Not much—yet."

"How do you spell it?"

Kelley spelled out the name. "Thanks, bud. Call me when you know something."

It didn't take long. Kelley learned that Petrovsky had arrived in the States from Odessa three years ago on a legal visa allowing entry by a limited number of skilled foreign workers.

Having narrowed his search to fertilizers and Russia, Kelley discovered a plant in Odessa that produced anhydrous ammonia. Then searching the same product in the United States, he came across a small mountain of information, and in it noticed a *New York Times* article describing the recently derailed train in New Mexico carrying anhydrous ammonia. HTP Chemicals in Vacherie, Louisiana, was mentioned. The manager: Roman Petrovsky.

Further researching HTP Chemicals, he came across a tombstone ad hailing the financing of the company. It was placed by Southern Capital, a Charlotte, North Carolina, bank, in a financial periodical designed to promote the bank's successful capitalization of HTP. It was their way of saying, "If we did it for them, we can surely do it for you." As the financier, they'd arranged a twelve-million-dollar loan for the purchase of HTP Chemicals.

Posing as a potential investor in a fertilizer plant, Kelley called Southern Capital and asked to speak to someone involved with the previous financing of HTP Chemicals, and was referred to an account manager named Lenny Dilworth.

It took a few days to hear back from him, but it was worth the wait. Lenny was a glib good ole boy. Though it had been a few years since the transaction, he recalled the diligence conducted and even the names of a few players. He was quite open about HTP's success, how the company had grown and even prepaid the loan. In fact, he added, he had heard they were looking to expand. He suggested that if Kelley was looking for an investment, he should start there.

"It's unbelievable," he said. "They turned that second-rate, rundown plant into one of the highest-grossing businesses in that region. A true diamond in the rough. It was one of the best risks we ever took."

Kelley asked Dilworth for the names of any principles.

"Yeah, there was some young kid, commodities broker, Emmerson, I think. He knew anhydrous ammonia was about to be listed as a product for trade at the Chicago Mercantile Exchange. In analyzing the product, he saw the potential for growth and profit. Figuring they could corner a portion of the market, they went bottom-fishing for a company that manufactured it, and discovered HTP. It was a small, family-run operation. He got a small pool of investors together and then financed the rest through us."

"Who else?" Kelley asked.

"Let me think. Cunningham. Mitchell Cunningham. He's in New York. I don't suppose he'd be too hard to find."

*No,* Kelley thought. *I know exactly where he's buried.*

# CHAPTER
## 24

Though she'd eaten scallops before, Carla had never had the imported, dried variety served a la Pacifica with hairy sea moss and black mushrooms. The pungent, briny dish, Carla learned, was a staple of the Chinese New Year, supposedly bringing prosperity. Rand ate generous portions of the platter. He also introduced her to the previously mentioned braised shark fins, and an astounding assortment of dim sum. Most of the group, she observed, washed down dinner with multiple martinis. That fit in fine with her agenda, as she slowly nursed one of her own.

*Keep it simple and tasteful. No frozen drinks. No beer, no heavy cordials. Stick with white wine, scotch on the rocks, or martinis.*

To the uninitiated, the exotic menu was intimidating. On her own Carla wouldn't have had the slightest idea where to begin, as her adventures with Chinese food usually began with an egg roll and ended with a mild chicken dish. Much to her surprise, however, she enjoyed Pacifica's wondrous fare.

She also, surprisingly, enjoyed the company. Expecting a group of uptight, narrow-minded socialites, she was delighted to discover a small group of highly engaging people with whom she could relax. Even Sylvia—whose wicked

sense of humor occasionally unnerved Carla—was a lively
raconteur.

As it was a Friday night, and 12:30 A.M. when dinner concluded—still early according to all—a group decision was
made to go club hopping. They started at the Roxy, over on
West Eighteenth Street, with its two floors of music and
hardcore dancing.

It came as no surprise to Carla that Rand knew the doorman, who smiled at him and allowed them to bypass the
block-long line. The loud and popular club had a dense
throng of people and a positively charged atmosphere. The
group split up, leaving Rand with her, as he seemed intent
on safeguarding Carla against male intruders. She was not at
all displeased with his behavior. As they jostled their way toward the dance floor, Rand took her by the hand, cutting his
way through the crowd while likewise protecting her.

Once on the dance floor, she closed her eyes while moving to the music, a song by INXS. Finally looking at Rand,
she saw him dancing a breath away, watching her with deep
intensity.

*God, is he sexy,* she thought. In spite of being with a
group of people all night long, he'd never left her side. In
fact, he'd been particularly attentive during dinner, twice
slipping his hand affectionately into hers—something not
unnoticed by Sylvia. The first time he did it, Sylvia was in
the middle of telling a story, which she managed to finish
while staring strangely at him. It made Carla feel deeply
self-conscious, which she presently felt dancing so close to
Rand.

Feeling the need for a breather, Carla excused herself to
go to the ladies' room, and returned to see Rand standing
near the bar talking to a stranger, or at least a stranger to her.
Rand didn't say anything as she arrived. Instead, he unexpectedly kissed her forehead, conveying pleasure to see her.

"Charlotte, I'd like you to meet my friend, Sergei Fe-dorov."

He was an average-sized man with a boyish face framed by thick, dark hair. His skin was pale, his lips were thick and moist, and his eyes, though a dull shade of green, had a gleam in them.

Slightly lowering his head, his eyes fixed squarely on hers, Serge took hold of Carla's right hand and teasingly kissed each knuckle. She laughed, then smirked after the second kiss. But following the fourth such wet caress, Carla withdrew her hand.

"Charlotte," he said softly, picking up her hand again, his eyes steadily focused on her.

"All right, Serge, that's enough," Rand butted in. The two men cracked up, making Carla realize this was obviously part of his shtick.

Still holding her hand, Serge asked very seductively, "Where have you been hiding?"

"Excuse me?" She blushed. "Me?"

"Charlotte, ignore him," Rand said, at last grabbing her hand away from his. "He's not as harmless as he seems. Here," he said, reaching over to the bar. "I got you a mar-tini."

*Pace yourself.*

"Cheers," he said, tapping his glass against hers.

"Cheers," she responded warmly.

She had just taken a sip when—of all things—she spotted her brother Tommy. He was standing less than twenty feet away. Her breathing went shallow, and the drink burned her throat, causing her to choke.

"Are you all right?" Rand asked with concern.

Carla tried speaking, but couldn't. She immediately turned her back on Rand so that Tommy wouldn't see her.

*What the hell is he doing here?* She wondered. *Oh, leave*

*it to him! He could turn up anywhere. I've got to get out of
here before he sees me.*

She angled herself for another glance, and saw him talking to an attractive young woman. Fortunately, he hadn't noticed Carla, and even if he did she wondered if he'd even
recognize her. Still, she didn't want to take any chances.

"I'm fine," she said, her voice cracking.

"Do you want some water?"

"No. Actually, I'd like to leave."

"And go where?" Rand asked, obviously perplexed.

"I don't know," she offered truthfully, "maybe go some-
place a little quieter."

"First let me get you some water," he said, then moved
closer to the bar. That's when Tommy saw her. She could tell
by the look on his face that he recognized her, too. She
moved forward a few inches, standing next to Rand, then
peeked behind his shoulder. Tommy was headed her way.

"Rand, I'm sorry," she interjected, "I think I really need
some fresh air."

He looked disapprovingly at her. "Sure," he said, "first let
me tell the others." He belted back his martini. "Serge, you
want to join us?"

Serge nodded, then threw back his own vodka martini,
slamming the glass down on the bar.

"I'll meet you outside," she said and, without waiting for
Rand, cut through the dense crowd and left the club. She
knew her behavior would be seen as rude and erratic. But
the bigger danger was that any minute Tommy might be
upon her.

Though it was only five minutes, it seemed like an eternity before the group rejoined her on the street. Sylvia was
the first to make her exasperation known.

"Charlotte, any idea where we might go next?" she said
mockingly.

She barely heard Sylvia, as in horror she saw a man exiting the back of a dark four-door sedan. He was carrying a gun. Stopping in the street and raising the weapon, he appeared to be aiming it at Rand, who was standing beside her.

"Rand!" she screamed, dive-bombing on top of him before the man could fire. As they hit the ground, pandemonium broke out. A shot was fired, then another, followed by shrill and horrifying screams. Carla saw people ducking all around them.

Rand tried getting up, but she pushed him back down. He forcibly shoved her aside, which was when Carla saw the absolute terror etched in his face.

"Charlotte, run," he screamed, then scrambled upward and ran madly down the street, turning at the first corner. Carla chased after him, but could barely keep up—he was like a man possessed.

"Rand, wait," she hollered.

He did not stop. Pure adrenaline pushed her to the limit until she caught up with him.

"Dammit, stop!" She grabbed the back of his jacket. "What the hell is going on?"

"I don't know. I don't know!" he cried frantically. "Let's just get the hell out of here."

They began running again, this time into the subway, taking the steps three at a time. He jumped the turnstile, leaving Carla standing behind. She could hear the train coming. At the same time she saw the station clerk watching her hawklike from inside the token booth. It was then that Carla heard the pounding noise coming down the stairs. It was another man, large and fierce looking, his eyes bearing down on her with laser-like intensity.

She looked for Rand. He had run toward the end of the platform and was nowhere in sight. Panicking as the man reached the last step, she did exactly what her instinct suggested. She whip-turned around, and with the force of a jackhammer, landed a sidekick square in the man's jaw. He fell hard to the ground, and without hesitation, Carla jumped the turnstile just as the train approached. Running the length of the platform, she joined Rand in the very last car.

She sat exhausted in Rand's lobby, immobile, just waiting. She'd been there for five hours and would stay for another five if that's what it took to see him.

The events of the evening revolved repeatedly in Sylvia's mind. Charlotte's demand to leave. Charlotte jumping on top of Rand. Charlotte running away with Rand. Rand nowhere to be found. *Someone tried to kill Rand. It's no safer here,* she thought, but she needed him so badly she couldn't help herself. She was limp with fatigue awaiting his arrival in one of the lobby's chairs.

Another hour passed, and she had just dozed off when he brushed by her, touching her foot but not speaking to her. She rose out of the chair and followed him to the elevator bank, remaining speechless as they rode to the twenty-ninth floor together. He said nothing even after they entered his apartment, remaining silent while tending to mundane things. Sylvia promptly went to the wall-sized window overlooking Central Park and stared outside.

"Where have you been?" she said softly.

"Where do you think?" he stated flatly.

"They tried to kill you." She turned to watch him, unable to comprehend his mood. He stopped sorting his mail, then finally met her look.

"They missed."

"With a little help."

"Are you sorry?" he said bitingly. "Or are you sorry they didn't get her?"

Exasperation consumed her. "You are so fucking selfish. Is that all you ever think about, yourself?"

"Myself? Someone took aim at me last night, and *I'm* selfish? You know what this is really about, Sylvia. It's about Charlotte, isn't it? You're not here out of genuine concern for me. Charlotte saved my life, and not you, and you can't stand it, can you?"

"Fuck you," she said.

"Keep your voice down."

She glowered at him.

"What do you want me to do, Sylvia? For whatever reason, Charlotte saw it coming and risked her life for me."

"They're going to kill us all."

She slumped down into his contemporary black leather sofa, then placed her head on a pillow and began to cry.

"Sylvia, I'm sorry," he whispered, kneeling down beside her. He took her hand and kissed it, and then wiped away her tears with the back of his hand.

"Rand, I'm so scared."

"I know. But Roman assured me that it was under control."

"How, Rand, how? The police will start investigating this incident. What are they going to find?"

"Trust me. They won't find a thing."

"When will this end? Will it ever end?" She was still crying.

"Sylvia, trust me. The end is in sight, I promise," he said, his voice betraying his own deep anguish. Neither of them knew that the assassin Roman had hired in Moscow to kill Boris Arkady had failed. And that Arkady, who was directly behind the murders of Candace Courtland Rutland and Mitchell and Sydney Cunningham, was literally out to kill the competition in an intense battle of wills concerning HTP Chemicals' profits from importing and selling cocaine.

"Rand," she said softly. "Will you please hold me? Just hold me." He looked away for a moment. The thought of holding Charlotte all night was still fresh in his mind.

"Come here," he said, standing up and opening his arms.

"No," she implored, "come here." With that she pulled him down on the sofa, forcing him on top of her. "Please, just hold me. Make me feel like everything is going to be all right."

"Scoot over," he said, then rolled behind her, wrapping an arm around her waist. She immediately burrowed her backside into him, then cried a while longer. Gently stroking her hair and rubbing her arm, he could feel her calm down, then eventually go to sleep. When at last it seemed safe, he climbed off the sofa and dialed the phone, waiting for Roman to answer.

# CHAPTER
## 25

"Jack, she broke his fucking jaw."

"Are you surprised? She's a black belt in Hapkido, Lizzie. What did you expect? She didn't know he was a damned detective. Christ, it's amazing no one got killed. We may not be so lucky the next time," Jack Jennings said angrily.

Liz all but ignored his last comment. "He spent the night at her apartment."

"Who?"

"Who do you think? Emmerson."

"What happened?"

"Nothing, according to Carla. But it's not the first time. They seemed to be developing a stronger interest in each other before this incident occurred. Supposedly Rand clung to her all night after the attempt on his life."

"Goddammit, Liz! You've known my feelings from the start—I didn't want her there in the first place, and now that it's clear how dangerous this is, I really don't. Why in the hell isn't her apartment wired yet? The hell with that," he added. "Just get her out, now."

"Jack, I can't, not yet. Think about it. Emmerson can explain things any damned way he pleases—it was a random, drive-by shooting; he did casual business with people who were murdered; he paid cash for his properties because of his income and bonuses. His friends do drugs, not him. There's nothing yet to indict him!"

"I don't care. You know as well as I do, dammit, that Carla's life is in jeopardy anytime she's near him. I noticed that jackass detective that got his jaw smashed didn't do any bullet dodging for my daughter. You said it yourself, Liz. Emmerson could be as harmless as a tadpole or as ruthless as a shark. I think by now we know which species we're dealing with, and for the record, I'm telling you I want her out of there. Not to mention the fact that he's developed a romantic interest in her, and on that account alone she may find herself swimming over her head—with a goddamned shark!"

Liz readily met his angry eyes. "Are you ready for the real kicker?" she asked.

"I can hardly wait," he said, scowling.

"Your son, Tommy, was there. Apparently he recognized Carla and was cutting his way through the crowd toward her when she abruptly left the bar, forcing Rand and his friends outside."

"Always the last to know," he said wearily, the dreary day outside matching his mood. "He never mentioned it. But if he managed to spot her, then God only knows who else might identify her."

Liz had turned in her chair and began tapping her pencil on the armrest in rhythm with the rain. She was beginning to feel almost as if she was in over her own head. She had deliberately pulled in the reins on the task force, asking them to slow down aspects of the investigation while her undercover agent gathered more information. With few exceptions no one knew about the fresh-faced rookie at the heart of this probe. Best of all, the mayor knew nothing, only presuming that he'd intimidated her into leaving Rand alone. And while she knew at any minute this entire gamble could fail, she also knew that staying the course with Carla was the best possible means of gathering the most incriminating evidence.

Jack interrupted her thoughts. "Liz, c'mon. You've got three people murdered that knew him and one dead drug-addicted Russian who happened to call him not long before she died. What are you waiting for?"

"Jack, I'm sorry. I know it's hard. I want to keep Carla on the job another two weeks. If by then we don't have our smoking gun, she's out of there."

Thoughts of Charlotte Desmond obsessed Sylvia March. It just didn't add up. How did someone so seemingly feminine suddenly throw herself on top of Rand and save his life? How did the same person who needed a breath of fresh air ten minutes earlier at the Roxy not get freaked out and fall apart at the first sound of gunfire? Sylvia still shuddered at the memory of it all and the thought that her own life was imperiled.

And that face. The distant chord of familiarity kept striking at Sylvia. How could she have possibly known her? All through their shopping expedition, and later during dinner at la Pacifica she kept wondering the same thing, but repeatedly dismissed it. It seemed impossible that they could have ever met.

Just yesterday she had called St. Dunstan's Press in London seeking a reference on Charlotte's behalf. They confirmed she'd worked there for two years, providing a glowing report on her abilities. She checked with the University of Michigan—she'd graduated with honors. She searched the Internet for any possible tidbits, but came up cold.

One thought, however, kept surfacing in her mind. A concept she tried to disregard but that became increasingly attractive. She had already scoped out Charlotte's address in her pre-war, high-rise building. There were doormen in the lobby, but Sylvia was certain she could slip past them and get into Charlotte's apartment. It would take careful planning, but it could be done.

Gathering her purse, she left her office and informed her assistant that she was heading uptown for a doctor's appointment. "I'm not sure when I'll be back," she informed the young man.

"Tootle-oo," he responded, happy to see her leave for a while.

Grabbing the next taxi, she gave him instructions to take her to the Upper West Side, where she asked to be left off near Lincoln Center. Unbothered by the rain, she popped open her umbrella and strolled casually along Columbus Avenue, at last spotting what she needed.

Pushing open the door to the locksmith's shop, she smiled sweetly at the young man behind the counter. "What a day!" she said. "Should I leave my umbrella outside? It's dripping wet."

"No, no." He smiled back. "You can leave it on the floor over there. How can I help you?"

"Oh, I just need to get a few extras made."

"Let me see what you've got."

She pulled out her keys. "I misplaced these the other day, and it gave me quite a scare since I don't have a replacement set."

"Which ones do you need?" he asked. He was a handsome and friendly Israeli.

"Actually, I'd like to get all of them copied."

He carefully examined each key. "You have car keys, house keys, and what's this?"

"Oh, that's my desk key. Copy that one, too."

"No problem. It's going to take me a while."

"That's fine. I have some shopping to do. Can you get them done in say, an hour?"

"No problem. I'll start right now."

"Terrific. What's your name, by the way?"

"Gideon."

"Gideon. What a great name," she said. "I'll see you back here in a little while."

He smiled as she picked up her umbrella and walked out the door.

She gave him two hours to do the job. When she returned, her arms were heavy with shopping bags.

"Hi, Gideon."

"Was there a clearance sale somewhere?" he joked.

"I wish! Listen, I have a big favor to ask you. I need to run a few more errands. Do you mind if I just leave these bags with you for a little while?"

"No problem. And your keys are ready whenever you are."

"Terrific. I'll be back," she said, departing the store once again.

*Perfect,* she thought. *He can see that I trust him.*

She entered a coffee shop, ordered a latte, then read a newspaper and a tattered *Cosmopolitan* magazine someone had left behind. Her horoscope from the sexy rag told her that romance featured prominently this month—she had reason to hope. After an hour passed, she headed back to the locksmith.

"Well, at least it's not raining anymore," she said lightly upon entering the shop.

"You're empty-handed! What's wrong? Your money is only good when it rains?"

"You're so funny. I couldn't find what I was looking for," she said sweetly.

"Here are your keys."

"Oh, thanks. What do I owe you?"

"Eighteen dollars."

"Eighteen dollars! Gideon, I almost need a loan for that!"

"I'm sorry. I don't make the prices."

"I'm only teasing. Listen, do you have a business card just in case these don't work?"

"Absolutely," he said, handing her one.

"Oh, I see you're available twenty-four hours a day. That's good to know. I've locked myself out on more than one occasion. You know us women—always changing our purses and forgetting our keys. What's worse," she added, "I cannot leave a set of my keys with the building superintendent. There's been a rash of burglaries in my building, and the tenants all think it's an inside job."

"Really? Which building do you live in?"

She quickly offered Carla's address. He nodded, as if he knew which one.

"In fact, my apartment was one of seven that got hit last year. It was awful. There was no sign of forced entry. It seems the doormen and maintenance men are all in cahoots with each other. They know when you're not home, and have keys to almost all apartments. I just couldn't believe it," she added, beginning to impress herself with this tale. "I had taken that day off, and left for the grocery store. I was gone less than an hour and came home to discover everything in my apartment had been turned upside down."

"Really. Did the police do anything?"

"Nothing. What could they do? Whoever did it was careful not to leave any fingerprints. And, of course, no one sees the person. Which means they probably have a scout working in the building—someone no one would suspect."

"What did they take?"

"Jewelry. I was so upset. A couple of valuable heirloom pieces from my grandmother were stolen." She looked downward and shook her head in disgust. "It wasn't the money so much as the sentiment. They stole some very precious memories."

"Did you have your locks changed?"

"Of course. But the building supervisor said we were required to leave a set of keys with him." She chuckled, then half whispered. "So you know what I did? I gave that guy a set of dummy keys. I sure hope I never get locked out again!"

"Well, don't worry. I would help you. Just keep my card. Call me anytime."

"Thanks, Gideon. I mean, hopefully that won't happen. But you never know."

It took nearly three days for Carla to feel like herself again—whatever that meant nowadays. And today, with the gloomy weather, Carla was satisfied to stay inside. The apartment was dark, except for a few aromatic candles she'd lit to help calm her frayed nerves. She lay on the floor, her head on her hands, thinking through it all.

Certainly she'd been exposed to gunfire before, having accompanied her father to the practice range on numerous occasions. She'd even learned how to clean and load a gun. But the reverberations she felt from her last night out with Rand were more than from the bullets fired. She could have died. He could have died. It was amazing that no one had been killed. And then there was the detective's jaw she smashed.

*Why in the hell did Phillips lie to me? She told me I wasn't going to have a tag. Don't they trust me?*

Liz Phillips had reassured her when she came to her apartment for a debriefing that, yes, they did trust her. But it was the investigation itself that was considered untrustworthy. She'd pressed Carla hard for every detail of the evening, and Carla told her everything she could remember—everything she wanted to tell. Except how she really felt—her mixed-up emotions about Rand.

He'd exposed an unexpected neediness to her that evening, asserting he didn't know why anyone would take a shot at him, his mood alternating between macho bravado and controlled terror. He'd insisted on going to her apartment when they left the subway, stealing nervous glances all around as they hurried to her building. Once inside, he turned on the television, looking for any news of the event, then stretched out on the sofa, falling asleep in a blink. Carla used that opportunity to change out of her slacks and sweater and into a comfortable pair of sweats. But exiting the bathroom, she was shocked to discover that he'd abandoned the sofa for her bed.

"Come here," he'd said softly in his baritone voice.

"What are you doing?"

"Nothing, trust me. Charlotte, I just need to hug you."

*Oh, God help me,* she'd thought, at the same time she moved closer to him. She stared at him for a moment. Why did she feel sorry for him? Why did she feel any need to reassure him that everything was okay? Perhaps because she needed the reassurance herself. In the darkness, she sat on the edge of the bed, then ran a hand through his wavy hair. He pulled her hand to his mouth, tenderly kissing her palm.

"Thank you," he said, conveying his gratitude. She remained silent. She was trembling.

Amidst all the fear and confusion, she knew one thing clearly: At the heart of this duplicity was a young woman out on her own for the first time. She was experiencing life in the fast lane and then—worst of all—a dangerous desire for this man. Her life had always been so predictable. She always knew what was expected of her, how to feel, how to behave. But her life now was filled with uncertainty, volatil-

ity, and now an intense sexual craving that she'd never felt
before.

As he kissed her hand again, she began to cry. The fear,
the tension, the desire—all finding release in the hand of the
enemy. He pulled her close, soothing and cradling her as he
stroked her hair. Neither one spoke. They just lay together,
each tortured by their own secrets; each absorbing the
other's anguish.

They did not make love. They did not have to.

At last Carla drifted off to sleep, awaking a few hours
later as the first sliver of daylight crept into her bedroom.
Realizing that she was still cradled in his arms, she barely
opened her eyes. Instead she listened to his soft breathing,
now in rhythm with her own, then fell back into a deep
sleep. When finally she awoke, there was a piercing ray of
sun in her eyes. She squinted, looked upward, then gasped
at the sight before her.

Illuminated, and seemingly grave with omen, were her
mother's rosary beads she'd left dangling on her bedpost.

# CHAPTER
## 26

"What are you up to tonight?" Sylvia inquired.

"Actually, it's kind of a quiet night."

"Really? Are you staying in?"

"No, not that quiet. I'm taking Charlotte out to dinner. It's our anniversary."

"Your what?" she responded incredulously.

"It's been six weeks since our first date."

"I think I'm going to gag. Since when did you start celebrating anniversaries with any of your girlfriends?"

"Since I met Charlotte."

"What does she have to say about this?"

"Nothing. I don't even know if she's aware of it. I thought I would remind her at dinner."

"I see. So it took a near-death experience for you to finally start treating a woman with respect."

"Well, maybe if you dodged a bullet for me, you might get lucky—again."

"You are such a jerk, and that was such a low blow."

"Thank you. What are you up to tonight?"

"I'm not sure. I'm supposed to get together with a friend, and we were thinking about going to a movie."

"Male or female?"

"None of your beeswax."

"Give me a break. It's okay for you to pry into my life, but you can't even tell me who you're going to the movies with. On your own again?"

"Screw you," she said, then laughed. The truth was, she didn't have a date, and was hoping that he and Charlotte were going out.

"Where are you going to dinner?"

"I'm going to let her choose."

"That ought to be interesting. What time are you guys going out?"

"You're starting to sound like my mother. What do you care?"

"I don't know." She laughed. "Maybe because sometimes I feel like your mother. I mean, who else looks out for you the way I do?"

"I'm picking her up at eight-thirty. Any particular time you'd like me home?"

"No, dear. Just enjoy yourselves. I'll be sure to leave the light on."


When Sylvia paged Gideon, it was 8:45 P.M. She figured Charlotte and Rand were now settled into the restaurant, and knowing him, it would be at least two more hours before they left.

"Hello," she said sweetly, answering her cell phone. "Oh, hi, Gideon. I'm so glad it's you that got my page. How are you?"

"I'm doing great, thanks. Let me guess. You switched handbags."

Sylvia let out one of her throaty laughs. "I'm so embarrassed. And wouldn't you know, the extra set of keys are in my apartment, too! I'm such a fool."

"Where are you?"

"I'm in the building's lobby. But listen, I don't want the

doormen or the supervisor to know about this. Then they'll insist on my giving them a set of keys. So," she said, "when you get here, just be very discreet. Wait until you see the doorman is busy with someone else, then just slip in and head up to the twenty-fifth floor."

"What if they stop me?"

"Well, then, I'll vouch for you. But it would make my life a lot easier, or rather safer, if they don't. Can you come now?"

"I'll be there in a half hour."

"Great. I'll meet you outside my apartment, number 2535."

Sylvia March hurried out of her apartment, then hailed a taxi to take her to Charlotte's Upper West Side address.

"Oh, my gosh, Gideon, I'm so happy to see you," Sylvia enthused outside 2535. "Did anyone give you a hard time?"

"No, it was a piece of cake. Though, I'm not sure this will be so easy," he said as he bent down to examine the two locks on the door. "These are pretty hardcore dead bolts."

"Wouldn't you know it," Sylvia said. "I don't suppose you brought a blowtorch with you?"

Gideon laughed. "I'm sure we can discreetly blow a hole in your door." He opened up his tool kit and began fumbling for the proper pick.

"Listen, just in case someone comes along, can you stop what you're doing?"

He looked at her rather suspiciously. "You do live here, don't you?" he asked, his tone playful, the question serious.

"Gideon, how could you even ask me such a question? Of course I live here. I'll be happy to show you my ID once we get inside."

"Okay. If you say so. Just checking."

"Trust me. If I say so, then I mean it. I just don't want this reported back to the super."

Gideon shrugged, but smiled, then promptly went to work.


"You guys are laughing now," said Commander Mike Kapowski, rattling the king-size bottle of artificial Viagra tablets someone had given him. "But I'll be smiling—for a long, long time!"

Coarse groans erupted among the guests gathered this evening for his retirement party.

"In other words, you'll still be smiling when they bury you!" cracked Jack Jennings Sr.

"At least I'll die happy!" quipped Kapowski, smiling earnestly at his friend and colleague. He and Jennings had served as the NYPD's co-commanders of Manhattan for more than twelve years now, with Jennings presiding over the southern half while Kapowski supervised the north. They'd been through some equally tough times through the years, developing deep respect for one another along the way.

They were gathered in a back room of an expensive Upper East Side steak house. There had been a more modestly priced party for well-wishing staff members two days before at a downtown hotel. But this was Mike's private party, a small gathering of his favorite fellow cops. It was an all-male group this evening, enjoying thick steaks, hearty wine, and fine cigars. Occasionally the conversation turned lewd, but mostly these old-timers reminisced about their early days on the force, and about the exclusive boys club it used to be.

Jack smiled inwardly during the conversation, thinking of his daughter and how the times had really changed. Women had filled only clerical roles when he first joined the force.

A few years later they had broken into the ranks as meter maids, but it remained a predominantly Irish white male bastion for quite a while after that. One of the true trailblazers had been Liz Phillips, and though she commanded respect from all those gathered this evening, she would never be a member of this club.

Jennings took another sip of his wine, put his cigar down in an ashtray, then politely excused himself for the men's room. Perhaps if he hadn't been thinking of her, on the way back he might have just passed his daughter by.

Inside the restaurant he spotted Carla seated very intimately next to Rand Emmerson. Though their backs were to him, their heads were turned toward one another, showing their profiles. They leaned in close to each other while speaking, then kissed tenderly.

He felt sick to his stomach. He had never seen Carla behave this way with a man before—especially in public. Certainly he'd witnessed her being affectionate with a couple of boyfriends. But her previous behavior seemed benign compared to this.

She kissed him gently once more, than began pushing out her chair. Rand rose from his seat and helped her out, waiting till she disappeared before sitting again. It was an opulent restaurant, with hunter green carpet, crisp white linen tablecloths, fresh flowers, and softly burning candles—a very romantic setting. Jack quickly ducked back inside the men's room for cover.

*"They seemed to be developing a stronger interest in each other before this incident occurred. Supposedly Rand clung to her all night after the attempt on his life."*

Jack's heart raced. He stood on the other side of the bathroom door, holding it open just a crack, waiting for her to leave the ladies' room. Finally, she emerged, appearing confident and glamorous. Jack waited till she passed before he slipped out, catching up with her before she left the hallway.

There was another small private and empty dining room off to their right. Jack grabbed his daughter and pushed her into it, quickly shutting the door and leaving them standing in darkness.

"Carla—" he spoke, but before he could finish she had kneed him in the groin, then slammed a fist into his jaw. Fortunately in the darkness her upper aim was slightly off, but Jack immediately doubled over in pain from the lower hit.

"Jesus, Carla, are you trying to kill me?" he moaned.

"Oh, my God," she barely whispered. "Dad, is that you?"

"Yes!" he said through clenched teeth.

She began fumbling for a light switch.

"Don't!" he warned her.

"What is going on here? What are you doing?"

"I was about to ask you the same thing," he said angrily.

"What do you mean? What are you talking about?"

Jack felt considerable pain and was breathing hard to fight it. "Get me a chair," he demanded. She groped around in the darkness, grabbed the closest one, then placed it beside his aching body.

"Here," she said.

He sat down, then let out a moan.

"Dad, I'm so sorry. I'm so sorry. I had no idea."

He was still struggling for composure.

Gaining her own sense of control, she startled him a second time with sudden indignance.

"Why the hell did you do that? And what are you doing here?"

He could feel his temper rising dangerously. "I happened to be here for Mike Kapowski's retirement party. And don't you use that tone of voice with me, young lady," he snapped.

"Give me a break, Dad. Young lady? In case you forgot, I'm pulling duty twenty-four hours a day, seven days a week as a cop right now. There's no need to talk to me like a child."

"You've got a lot of nerve, Carla Jennings," he said, his voice rumbling and angry.

"Would you mind explaining this to me? Why the hell are you here? What do you want?"

"I guess it's no longer enough to see your old man, heh? Forget about me, Carla. Forget about the whole lot of us. But remember this. I want you to realize the next time you place your sweet lips on that man's that it's not a cop doing the kissing. It's a beautiful young woman teasing a dangerous man."

She heaved a sigh of exasperation. "Who said he was so dangerous?"

"And you know better? If that's so, then you must be ready to pack it in."

"This case is not solved," she responded sharply. "Why the hell are you doing this to me? Have I ever told you how to do your job?"

"Oh, this is bad," he said, finally straightening up and leaning back on the chair. "What has he done to you? What has this man done to you?"

"What are you implying?"

"I'm implying that you're in deep. You are in way over your head, and you don't even know it."

"That's bullshit."

"Watch your mouth."

"I'll say whatever I damned well please."

After several awkward moments he spoke.

"You may think you can get away with speaking to your father this way. But right now you're talking insubordinately

to the Commander of Manhattan South. I could have you
pulled off this case this instant."

"You wouldn't dare."

He closed his eyes and slowly shook his head.

"You know what? You're right," he said as he slowly rose.
"As far as I'm concerned, young lady, you can follow your
heart wherever that may lead you."

And like the last time she saw him, he abruptly left. Only
this time, he left her alone in the dark.

"Gideon, what's taking so long?"

"I told you, it's the type of lock. It was designed to prevent exactly what we're doing right now."

"Have you ever done a lock like this before?" Sylvia
asked impatiently.

He gave her an annoyed look. "Do you want me to open
this door or not? I can leave right now, you know, and you
can find yourself someone better qualified."

She could tell by his sarcasm that he was perfectly capable of getting the job done, but that it was, true to his word,
a difficult lock. He refocused his attention on the second
dead bolt.

"C'mon, baby," he uttered. "Just two more tumblers to
go."

Sylvia kept glancing at her wristwatch. It had already
taken him twenty-five minutes to get this far, and they'd
been extremely lucky that no one had passed them by in the
hall.

"Good, good," he said, keenly focusing, "one to go, just
one more to go."

Sylvia practically held her breath. Her nerves were so
frayed now, she hoped she could keep her composure. Suddenly she heard the sound of the elevator stopping at the
twenty-fifth floor. She looked at Gideon in a panic.

He, however, smiled calmly. As the door to the elevator opened, so too did the door to Charlotte's apartment.

She bolted inside.

"After you," he said.

"Come in," she said, then quickly shut the door after him, praying that it wasn't Charlotte and Rand coming home unexpectedly. She could hear the voice of a couple, but it wasn't them and it drifted in the opposite direction down the hall.

"How much do I owe you, Gideon?"

"One hundred and fifty."

"One hundred and fifty?" she said. "Between this and having keys made, I'm going to have to file for bankruptcy. My money's in my bedroom," she said. "I'll be right back," and then disappeared into the apartment. Standing out of sight from Gideon, she dug in her pocket for cash and produced two one-hundred-dollar bills, then returned to the entrance foyer.

"Here," she said, "this should cover it."

"Thanks," responded Gideon when he saw the two bills. "Do you want a receipt?"

"No, I don't think so. But I will be sure to keep your phone number handy in case I ever do something so foolish again."

"See you," he said, then gathering his tool kit left the apartment, thinking how strange it was that she never turned on the lights.

She locked the door behind him and then sighed with relief. "Now what?" she muttered, her mind racing over what to do next. If nothing else, Charlotte Desmond had money—and lots of it. The apartment, with its plaster walls and moldings, lofty ceilings, and exclusive address, probably cost her $4,000 per month in rent. Sylvia was also impressed with the richly appointed furnishings.

Choosing for now to work in the dark, Sylvia peered inside the hall closet and discovered coats for every season—including a full-length mink. Turning on the foyer light for a moment, she opened the coat to look for a monogram and quickly discovered the initials C.M.D. embroidered in silk thread on an inside panel.

"I wonder what the *M* is for? Probably something unique and exciting like Mary."

Finding nothing else of interest, she turned off the light, closed the door, and headed to the bedroom.

She laughed at the sight of clothes strewn about. "Maid on vacation?"

She opened up the walk-in closet and turned on the light, discovering slightly more order in here than in the bedroom itself. Looking through the garments, Sylvia discovered only designer labels and some outfits still bearing tags. Picking up one sleeve of a jacket, she saw that it cost $1200, which didn't faze her as she paid similar prices for her own clothing.

Careful to leave everything in place, she moved through the bedroom, opening dresser drawers. There was nothing exciting, nothing revealing. She was also finding nothing else bearing Charlotte's name. There appeared to be no mail, no bills, no personal files, no other clutter that would bring to light what Charlotte Desmond was all about. There was one photo of her on the dresser with a handsome couple, presumably her parents. She moved into the second bedroom, and discovered a desk with a computer on it.

"Bingo. The editor at work," she exclaimed. Sitting down, she turned on the lamp and noticed that other than a pad of paper and a ballpoint pen the desk was clutter free. She opened the drawers and found nothing—not even a pencil. There were no editorial projects on the desk, no reference books on the shelves.

"This is really strange," she said, and then bravely booted up the computer.

"You're sure I can't get you anything?" said Rand with concern.

"No," said Carla dismally. "It must have been something I ate. I'm sure I'll be fine tomorrow."

Rand had promptly offered to leave after she rejoined him at the table. It was obvious from the streaks of mascara that she'd been crying, though she insisted that it was because she'd been vomiting, which was why she'd been gone so long. She'd originally excused herself because of her growing upset stomach, and got sick just after she'd made it to the bathroom.

She still appeared shaken and disturbed, and nothing he said or did seemed to comfort her—she simply wanted to be left alone.

"I'm really worried about you," he said as he ran a soothing hand through her hair. "Can I call you later to see how you're doing?"

"Sure." She tried smiling back at him. Putting her key in her door, she turned. "Thanks for the start of a terrific evening." She opened the door. "I would invite you in, but I'm feeling really crummy, and I just want to go to sleep."

Sylvia March gasped as she heard the door open. She looked at her watch. It was only ten o'clock. What the hell were they doing back so soon? She panicked, trying clumsily to turn off the computer. She hadn't even had a chance to browse through any of Charlotte's electronic files. Finally turning off the light and the device, she retreated inside the closet, praying there would be no reason for them to come in here, and furthermore that Rand would not be spending the night. She could hear his voice for a moment longer, and then nothing after Charlotte shut the front door.

*He left! She actually got rid of him! What the hell?*

She heard keys being plunked down on the marble-topped console in the foyer, and then the sound of Charlotte shuffling into the bedroom. For a moment it sounded as if she were crying.

It seemed like forever before there was absolute silence again. Believing she couldn't stand it in there a moment longer, Sylvia cautiously peered out the door, waiting several seconds longer before leaving the closet altogether. Tiptoeing down the hall, she paused just before Charlotte's bedroom, grateful for the gentle sound of her snoring. Oddly, she couldn't resist a peek, wanting to see for herself whether or not Charlotte was alone.

Indeed she was. Still in her clothes, curled up slightly, she was sound asleep.

Sylvia slithered out of the apartment, softly closing the door behind her, completely perplexed by this woman.

# CHAPTER
## 27

"What's up?" Liz Phillips asked as Frank Kelley entered her office.

"One Russian in the Bayou."

"Really?"

He handed her a stack of papers, including a copy of the *New York Times* story.

"Lead story, jump page, third paragraph. Roman Petrovsky. Manager of HTP Chemicals. He's from Odessa, and HTP Chemicals produces fertilizers."

He could see the excitement grow in her eyes as she read through the article. "The New Mexico train wreck was sabotage, eh? What else do you know?"

Kelley went on to share what Barry Robertson and Lenny Dilworth had told him about Roman, Rand, Mitchell Cunningham, and HTP Chemicals.

"You thinking what I'm thinking?" she finally asked.

"Large-scale drug distribution?"

"And big-time turf war," she added.

The moment he left, she hailed Cliff Blackman into her office to share the latest developments with him. Blackman listened as she spoke, then picked up a rubber band from the top of Phillips's desk and began weaving it around his fingers. Liz became momentarily silent, staring pensively out

the window at the river, her eyes following a slow passing
barge.

"Can I make a suggestion?" he said.

"What?"

"I think it's time we went fishing."

In less than one week they surprised even themselves by
capturing a trophy fish in their snare.


It was not easy getting herself out of bed that morning.
She'd been up partying half the night, and she knew she was
going to be late for work this Monday morning. *Who cares?*
she thought, finally placing her feet on the floor.

"Ewww, God," Sylvia March moaned, lighting a cigarette. Taking several deep drags, she then tossed it into the
toilet. She forced herself to climb into the shower. For fifteen minutes she allowed the hot spikes to massage her
back. It did nothing to cure her hangover, though, and by the
time she finished dressing, she was over two hours late for
work. It was eleven o'clock, and she still had one errand to
run before she went to the office.

She grabbed her purse and moments later was out the
door hailing a taxi. From her Fifty-ninth Street apartment
she would be at the Candy Connection in about ten minutes.

Getting out at Seventy-eighth and Third, she adjusted her
sunglasses, glanced around, and then walked into the store.
As always, Fayed was behind the counter.

"Hey, how's it going?" she said, then smiled.

"Pretty good. And you?" He smiled back. "Excuse me,
just a moment," he said, and began fussing with something
behind the counter. Sylvia thought perhaps he was taking
care of her usual order and left him alone. But a few minutes later he was still ignoring her.

"Uhm, Fayed, are you going to help me?"

"Oh, I'm sorry," he said, looking up with an anxious expression. "Sure, what would you like?"

"You know, the usual."

"That's it?" he said shortly, handing over a plain white bag.

"That's it," she smiled, handing him his cash, then pushed the bag down inside her purse. She bade him farewell, then walked out the door—right into police custody.

"Sylvia, do you realize how clean-cut this case is? We have you on videotape purchasing cocaine. And trust me, I don't care how good your lawyer is, you've committed an A-2 felony. That's a *minimum* of three years and a maximum of life in prison. That's a helluva long time to wait till your next manicure," said Cliff Blackman. Liz Phillips was present, but had remained quiet.

"What is it you want from me?" Sylvia snapped. She was a nervous wreck.

"I just want you to know in advance what you're up against," said Blackman.

"Don't you have bigger crimes to solve?" she said cynically. "I can't imagine why you'd waste so much time on someone like me. I've never even gotten a parking ticket."

One of the staff sergeants suddenly opened the door for George Davidson, March's well-clad, thirty-something lawyer. Sylvia stood up to greet him. "Oh, thank God, you're here," she exclaimed, then embraced him.

He only briefly hugged her back before getting down to business.

"So, tell me what happened," said Davidson, poising an expensive fountain pen on a blank white legal pad.

"Your client's in deep shit," said Blackman.

Davidson glowered. "Thank you for that charming assessment," he said. "Would someone care to start with the facts?"

"No problem," said Blackman. "Watch this."

With that he hit Play on a VCR, allowing Davidson to watch as his client purchased cocaine.

"Maybe you'd like to see it again," said Blackman, watching in amusement as Davidson put down his pen.

"My client has never been in trouble with the law before. She has no record of drug use or abuse. If this ever goes to trial—" He never finished his sentence.

"Mr. Davidson," Liz interrupted, "we have very good reason to believe that your client may know who murdered Candace Courtland Rutland and Mitchell and Sydney Cunningham."

Police work was full of surprises. What followed was one of the finest confessions that Liz Phillips could remember. Sylvia March threw up.

Through the one-way glass, Liz could see that Sylvia was drained. She'd been in police custody for nearly eighteen hours now, spending at least one-third of that time confessing. She was by turns defiant, crying, and exhausted. But one indisputable fact surfaced. Her life as she'd known it was over. And if all that she'd said was true, Rand Emmerson's was as well.

Liz looked over at Cliff Blackman's drawn face. They'd been up through the night, sorting out details, listening repeatedly to key aspects of Sylvia's taped confession. Blackman swallowed the last drops of some cold coffee, then stretched out his legs, casting Liz a concerned look.

What Sylvia told them meshed with information already gathered by Frank Kelley. Rand Emmerson and Roman Petrovsky had developed one of the most far-reaching and swiftest-growing cocaine distributorships in the nation. In the past few years they'd overseen the wholesale distribution of at least several metric tons of cocaine, with a street value of hundreds of millions of dollars. Furthermore, their drug trade linked them indirectly to the murders of the three Manhattan socialites.

"What does Rand Emmerson have to do with this?" Sylvia had asked during the start of the interrogation.

"Do you know him?" Blackman asked again.

"Yes."

"How?"

"God. Who knows? Wait, I think it was second grade. We met playing Pin the Tail on the Donkey at a friend's birthday party."

"Very funny."

"I'm not trying to be funny. We've known each other forever," she replied sarcastically.

"We have reason to believe that he's a drug dealer. If that's true, and you know about it, or are in any way linked to his business, you'd better speak up now. If we learn about your involvement otherwise, then we will tell the prosecution to show you no mercy—which can mean life imprisonment."

"Rand Emmerson has nothing to do with the Candy Connection. He doesn't even do drugs."

"Sylvia," Liz interjected calmly. "Right now we're not interested in the Candy Connection. There is a fertilizer plant in Vacherie, Louisiana, called HTP Chemicals. Rand Emmerson is a principal of that operation, along with Roman Petrovsky. What do you know about HTP Chemicals?"

Whatever manipulative skills Sylvia March thought she possessed vanished in that single question. Silence suddenly replaced insolence.

"What do you know about HTP Chemicals?" Liz repeated.

Sylvia looked down at her tightly clenched hands.

"Do you have any knowledge about HTP Chemicals?" Liz spoke more tersely. Sylvia continued hanging her head. "I'm not going to ask you again. And let me make it clear. If you're not going to cooperate, then neither are we, and any bargaining with us is futile."

Still looking downward, she asked, "Can I please talk with my attorney? Alone?" she added.

Liz looked at Cliff Blackman, who nodded yes, and with the exception of Sylvia and Davidson, the room cleared out.

Liz turned and looked at Sylvia before closing the door. "I'll be back in ten minutes."

Sylvia bit her lower lip. Retreating to the room with the one-way mirror, Liz watched in silence as Sylvia yet again fell into uncontrollable sobs. Davidson stood up, then ran a hand over his tightly coiffed hair before asking her a question. Sylvia said nothing, only nodding her head in response, which prompted the man to look upward at the ceiling with dismay. Half sitting on the table, he placed a reassuring hand on her shoulder, then spoke. She stared up at him, her eyes red with tears, still biting her lip.

"What do I do?" Liz could make out the words. For the next few minutes Sylvia listened intently to what he said. Finally she nodded in agreement. He glanced at the wall clock, sat down, and started making notes while asking her questions. Liz knew that to barge in after the allotted ten minutes might spoil the momentum. And fortunately, while she waited the district attorney finally arrived.

"Thank God you're here," she said to Wesley Lynch. "I think they're ready to fold and I can't complete the deal without you."

Lynch was a notoriously brusque and unsympathetic prosecutor with mayoral aspirations. Liz had briefed him over the phone with the details of the case, prompting him

to drop everything else and head directly to police headquarters.

Davidson looked up as they entered the interrogation
room, and immediately covered his notes. Sylvia squirmed
in her chair as Lynch looked directly into her despairing
eyes.

"My client wants to make a deal," Davidson said.

Lynch and Phillips remained quiet.

"Ms. March is willing to cooperate with your investigation. She believes she can provide you with most of what
you want to know." Davidson pressed on.

"I want to know everything," said Lynch.

"Let me rephrase that. She will tell you everything that
she knows."

"What does she know?"

"She will tell you everything she knows in exchange for
immunity from prosecution and witness protection."

"I want to hear what she has to say before I agree to anything."

"Then there is no deal."

"Mr. Davidson, have you ever told a blackjack dealer
which cards to hand you?"

"I'm not a gambler."

"Bullshit. You're a defense lawyer. And right now I hold
the cards. She shows me her hand first, and then I'll decide
what kind of deal to cut."

"You drive a hard bargain."

"Tell that to the people who were murdered."

"He didn't kill them," Sylvia quietly interjected. Davidson cast her a severe look.

"Who did?" Liz asked.

"I don't know," she said, the tears spilling.

"Sylvia, I'd like to advise you to not say anything yet,"
said Davidson.

"What does it matter?" she blurted. "He didn't kill them. He doesn't know who killed them. Christ, they tried to kill him."

"Who are *they*?" asked Liz.

"Russian mob members." Liz sat upright in her chair.

"Answer me yes or no. Are Rand Emmerson and Roman Petrovsky dealing drugs from HTP Chemicals?"

Sylvia looked Liz square in the eye and nodded her head.

"Are you willing to tell me everything you know about the operation?"

Sylvia began to speak, choked, then finally uttered, "They will kill me."

"No. No, they won't. You work with us, we'll protect you."

"We want full immunity and witness protection," Davidson said.

"I want a full confession first," said Lynch. He looked at Sylvia who nodded yes.

"Then let's get started," he said matter-of-factly, opening his briefcase and pulling out pen and paper.

And for the next six hours she talked.

# CHAPTER
## 28

Rand tried Sylvia's cell phone number several times in vain before picking up Carla for the opening night performance of the Metropolitan Opera. He'd called her office, but was told by her assistant that she'd called late in the afternoon to say she was heading out to her parents' Connecticut country house for some R and R. He said she didn't sound very well, mentioning that she might be coming down with the flu and wanted to be near her mother, who'd extended her own weekend visit there by a couple of days.

Rand knew Sylvia was in good hands with her mother, but felt it was strange that she hadn't called him, especially since they spoke so frequently, and particularly if she wasn't feeling well and decided to leave the city for a few days. He had a nagging feeling that she was upset with him. It wouldn't surprise him in light of his growing fondness for Charlotte. After mentioning their aborted dinner the other night, she'd plied him with questions about Charlotte's well-being, and did he really buy that she was sick or was she perhaps sick of him? He knew Sylvia was jealous and deeply curious as well. But he simply couldn't understand the implication that something was wrong with the relationship and not just with Charlotte that night.

As he and Charlotte settled into their seats inside the ca-

pacious opera house, he reached over and stroked her hand.
"You look stunning this evening."

"Thanks." She smiled in return, releasing her hand from
his touch, then folded her hands on top of her lap. She had
an impulse to tell Rand how her mother had once performed
as a chorus member in *Tosca,* tonight's production, but that
was quickly subdued.

The hall fell silent as the conductor appeared and poised
his baton. For the next hour, until the first intermission,
Carla fortunately forgot about everything other than Tosca's
woeful world.

Jack Jennings Sr. inhaled the cool but pungent air coming
off the Hudson River, sending him back four decades. In his
first week of joining the force, he'd made a vow to himself
to root out the corruption that had eroded an honest man's
living on the waterfront, and made it a part of his routine to
stroll the docks. Over the years he'd kept his ears open, a
policy that had resulted in numerous tips and subsequent
arrests.

He'd been down on the docks less frequently these past
few months, in particular because of the demands back
home. Following Robbie's brief brush with the law and the
revelation of his sadness regarding Donna and Carla, Jack
realized how important his role was in keeping him on the
right track.

As the breeze stiffened, Jack zipped up his jacket. Contrary to his usual custom, he was in plain clothes this
evening, stopping in first to see some of the regulars who
knew him, but otherwise moving about with anonymity. It
was 11:00 P.M. when he finished his two-mile stroll, and he
was just about to approach his car when he heard a heated
argument. Stopping to listen, then moving cautiously around
one of the terminal's corners, he found the source. As it was

dark, he couldn't quite make out their faces, but it was clear
that one of them was a Latin speaking broken English.

"You don't fuck with me," he said.

"You listen to me, you asshole. This is not what I paid for,
and you know it. I want my fucking money back."

"I don't have no money with me. You have to talk with
the man."

"Fuck the man. You're the only one I've dealt with. And
what you sold me is shit. It's total shit. I will not make a
dime off of it."

"Talk to the man."

The accuser cursed violently while hurling a package
down on the ground. He suddenly produced a handgun and
pistol-whipped the other.

"Oh, Mary, Mother of God," Jack muttered under his
breath. Typically he packed a weapon of his own, something
preempted by tonight's spontaneous trip. His options at the
moment were extremely limited, and there was no way he
could call for backup without being noticed. The only two
things he had going for him were his shield and a good deal
of courage.

"Police," he finally bellowed, whipping out his badge
while pressing himself up against the terminal wall. "Drop
the gun."

A burst of gunfire ripped through the air, and he instantly
crouched down. Then he inched his way ahead for a glance
around the corner. In the dark, shimmering shadows, he
could make out the fallen form of one man, while the other
had disappeared. It was impossible to tell if the stricken man
was dead or alive, or in which direction the gunman had
gone. Hoping that someone else had heard the gunfire and
called for help, Jack stood still, watching for signs of motion
by either party. Nothing stirred.

"Are you all right?" he hollered nervously. There was no

answer, and aside from the gunshots still ringing in his ears
and the sounds of the crashing waves against the tidal wall,
he heard nothing. He asked again, still no response. Standing, then peeking again for a better look, he spotted some
faint movement, and his heart sank. He called out again, this
time being met by a moan of agony. There was no way he
could let the young man die alone. Leaving the building's
cover, he began running toward him. He never made it. Another shot was fired, this one right at his heart.


Cavaradossi and Tosca sprang back to life to enjoy thunderous applause. Both Carla and Rand rose for the extended
ovation, swept up by the audience's euphoria over the performance. While clapping, Rand glanced up at the even
more desirable box suites, particularly where he knew his
mother and father were probably seated. Though he talked
with his mother regularly, he hadn't spoken to his father in
years.

"So what did you think?" he asked Carla.

"It was wonderful, absolutely wonderful," she said as
they exited the theater and entered the lobby.

"I'm glad you liked it. I really enjoyed it myself. Listen,
the last I checked they didn't have Frosted Mini Wheats on
the menu, but there is a wonderful French restaurant not far
away that I thought we could try. Are you game?"

"Sure, I would love—"

"Rand." Carla heard the excited voice of a woman. "Darling. What a nice surprise."

"Mother," he said, then pecked her on the cheek.

Her eyes lit up, and in a genteel manner she embraced
him. She was a well-poised and very attractive woman.

He stepped back. "Mother, I'd like you to meet my friend
Charlotte Desmond."

"Pleased to meet you, Charlotte," she said kindly while warmly extending her hand. "Martha Emmerson."

"Thank you. Nice to meet you, Mrs. Emmerson."

"Oh, please, call me Martha. Charlotte," she added with such warmth, "are you from Manhattan?"

"No, ma'am. Seattle."

"Seattle. Why, that's such a lovely spot. Ham and I were out there a few years ago for a business trip—and what a pleasant surprise. I brought rain gear, and it turned out I needed my sunscreen!"

"You must have been there in the summer!"

"Yes, indeed."

"Listen, Mom, I would love to stay and chat, but we have dinner reservations."

"Oh, Rand. Do say hello to your father. He'll be right back, and I'm sure he'd be delighted to meet Charlotte."

"No, Mom, we really have to go. Please just tell him I said hello."

She looked disheartened. "If that's what you'd like. Good night, dear," she said, kissing him lightly once again. As she moved away, an obscure expression crossed Rand's face. He wasn't looking at Carla; rather, when she followed his gaze, she saw he was staring into the face of his double, if not for the white hair.

"Dad," he said politely.

"Nice to see you, son." He exuded none of his wife's warmth. They eyed each other circumspectly.

"Ham, I'd like you to meet Rand's friend, Charlotte Desmond."

"Charlotte," he said politely, offering his hand to shake. "A pleasure." His grip was cool and professional.

"Thank you, sir. It's nice to meet both of you. Did you enjoy the performance?"

"Yes, how about yourself?" he asked matter-of-factly.

"Yes, very much."

"Would you two care to join us for dinner?" Mrs. Em-merson asked.

"No," said Rand firmly. "But thanks, anyway. We have plans. In fact, Charlotte, we're going to be late if we don't leave now. Mom, Dad, nice to see you. Take care."

With that, he whisked Carla away, not bothering to talk with her until they were out near the street.

"Rand, are you all right?" Carla finally asked.

"Yes," he snapped. "Just fine."

"Okay. Just asking."

Competition for a taxi was fierce at the moment, giving rise to further agitation. He let out an exasperated sigh. "Come on," he commanded, taking her by the hand and leading her across the street.

"Can't we just walk there?" Carla suggested.

"No." A few blocks up Broadway he tried in vain to hail a cab, unaware that Carla was keeping a steady eye on crosstown traffic. Suddenly one pulled over across the street, and she could see the passengers climbing out. With-out thinking, she joined her right thumb and middle finger to her mouth and let out a loud shrill whistle. Not only did the taxi driver turn to look, so did several passersby, prompting Ran to turn and upbraid her.

"What was that?"

Carla blushed. "It worked, didn't it?" she said, her impish smile belying her sudden concern. It might have appeared unladylike to him, but it was perfectly natural to her.

As the taxi driver anxiously beeped at them, another pa-tron jumped into the backseat and the car drove away, leav-ing Rand and Carla behind staring curiously at one another.

"Rand, I'm sorry," she said. "I wasn't aware that would offend you." He didn't say anything. "Are you all right?" she asked yet again.

His expression tightened and, his voice low, he finally spoke. "You know what? I really don't want to go out to dinner."

"Rand," she quickly said, "I'm sorry, really. If I—"

He abruptly cut her off. "Stop it. Just stop it." He looked upward and let out a huge sigh.

"But, Rand, if I—"

"Stop beating yourself up. It's not you. It has nothing to do with you. Listen," he said, his tone softening, "I have a better idea. We both like Chinese. So why don't we just go to your apartment and order in?"

She had no desire to entertain him at her apartment. "You're sure that's what you want to do?"

"Absolutely," he said. She acquiesced. Her apartment was only two blocks away, and they walked there slowly.

They entered her building, still holding hands. Just as they were about to board the elevator, Carla turned and then gasped. Liz Phillips was sitting ashen-faced in one of the lobby's wingback chairs. By now Rand had entered the elevator and turned to find Carla looking wide-eyed into the lobby.

"Are you coming?" he said. Carla's heart was pounding while her feet remained frozen in place. She turned to look at Rand, and then back at Liz, who shook her head, indicating Carla should not acknowledge her.

"What's the matter with you?" he said. "You look like you just saw a ghost."

She remained speechless.

"What was it?" he inquired as the door shut.

"I thought I recognized someone, that's all. But I was wrong."

"Hmmm." They rode in silence up to the twenty-fifth floor. Arriving at her apartment, Carla could barely get the key in the door, her hand trembled so much.

*What is she doing here? Good God, is Rand going to be busted tonight? Have they got something on him that I don't know? Why would Liz show up herself if it wasn't something critical?*

Her thoughts ran in dizzying circles as she finally opened the door and then switched on the foyer light.

"Would you excuse me for a second?" she said, and then retreated to her bathroom.

*I need to get back downstairs. I need to know what's going on.*

The uncertainty started closing in on her. If Rand Emmerson was about to be busted, she wanted to know. Thinking through her immediate options, she realized she couldn't listen to her phone messages with him in the apartment. She could get on the computer to check her e-mail, but even that was unrealistic right now. Quickly she made an alternate plan to get to the lobby. She headed back into the living room, only to discover him prone on her sofa, shoes off with feet propped on the armrest, the lights still off.

"Rand?" she said.

"Come here," he responded. She walked nearer, but stopped about two feet away.

"No," he said gently but firmly, "come here."

Moving closer only enabled him to take her by the hand, and once in his grip, to pull her down on top of him.

"What are you doing?"

"Holding you. I just want to hold you."

She lay on top of him, rigid and nervous as hell.

"What's the matter with you?" he said. He gently kissed her forehead. "Just relax," he said, running his fingers through her hair.

She let out a deep sigh. "Listen, I'm kind of hungry. Why don't we go ahead and order?"

"In a minute," he said, his own tension seeming to fade in

their embrace. "The Chinese restaurant isn't going any-where, believe me."

As if by grace the house phone rang.

"What in the wold?" she said, jumping up to retrieve it. "Hello?"

"Carla, just pretend it's the doorman," said Liz Phillips. "Tell Rand that a package was delivered for you here today."

"There's a package for me?"

"Tell him that you need to go downstairs and get it."

"I'll be right down." She hung up the phone.

"Can't it wait?" he said with renewed edginess.

"It'll only take me a minute."

"Don't bother," he said angrily, rising up and slipping into his shoes. "I get the message. I'm going home."

"What message? Can't you just wait?"

He stood, running a hand through his own hair, then re-adjusted his clothing.

"Charlotte, sometimes I just don't understand you."

"Me? You don't understand me?" she said sarcastically.

"What do you mean?"

"What do *I* mean? About twenty minutes ago I thought you were going to leave me stranded on a street corner!"

Now he laughed. "For a minute I thought I would." He sat back down on the sofa, his head hanging down, and hands folded before him.

Finally meeting her eyes, he spoke soberly.

"Charlotte, I suspected my parents might be there this evening, but I fully hoped not to run into them."

"Was it so bad?"

"Yeah. You know I don't have much to do with my father."

"He seemed like a nice guy."

"He's a heartless prick."

"Is that what had you so upset tonight? Running into him?"

He nodded his head.

"I wish I'd known sooner," she said sympathetically.

"Why? It wouldn't have made a difference."

"Well, sure it would." She patted him reassuringly on the back, then laughed. "I might not have been so nice."

He chuckled, then kissed her temple. "I think you're pretty special, Charlotte Desmond."

"Thanks." She lightly kissed him back.

"I'm leaving," he said, "but I'll call you tomorrow. You going to be around?"

"I suppose," she said, moving away.

"Why don't you walk down with me so you can get that package?"

"Fine," she said, then grabbed her keys and escorted him to the lobby.

Walking with him toward the exit, Carla's breath caught. Now sitting in the lobby across from Liz Phillips was Cliff Blackman, wearing the same grim expression.

She smiled wanly at Rand. "Talk with you later," she said, then lightly pecked him on the cheek.

"I'll call you tomorrow," he said, then pushed his way out the revolving door. For several moments Carla remained paralyzed, unable to face the pair behind her. When it was clear that Rand was gone, she finally turned, finding them standing and waiting.

"What the hell is going on?" she whispered.

"Carla, we need to talk with you," Phillips stated softly. "Something terrible has happened."

# CHAPTER
## 29

Carla Jennings's world was shattered.

*"Carla, please sit," said Liz Phillips once the three of them reached her apartment.*

*"No. Just tell me. What is it?"*

*Phillips began to speak, but broke into breath-stealing sobs. Blackman tried to comfort her, but she rejected him.*

*"No," she demanded. "I'll deal with this."*

*"Don't tell me," said Carla, her voice cracking. "Don't tell me."*

*"Carla, I have to. You must listen to me."*

*"Is it my father?"*

*Liz nodded.*

*"Is he all right? Just tell me, is he all right?"*

*Phillips's renewed sobbing said it all. She slowly shook her head. Carla could not even take a breath.*

*"Carla, I'm so sorry to tell you this," said Blackman more stoically. "Your father was shot tonight in the line of duty."*

*She tried to speak. She tried to scream. She could not breathe. She simply passed out.*

When she awoke she was lying on the sofa, clenched by unbearable pain. Phillips's face was frozen; Blackman was on the phone. "Get him over here," she heard him say.

*Get who over? Who are they talking about? How did he
die? Rand. Did Rand have anything to do with this?*

And then her own tears came, a gorge of emotion breaking with violent intensity. *This is not happening. He was
shot? Who shot him? Where's Robbie? Oh, God, Robbie.*

"Where's Robbie?" she cried. "I need to get to Robbie!"
Jumping off the sofa, she ran to the bedroom, tearing at her
evening gown and grabbing for her jeans and a sweater.

"No! Carla!" said Liz from behind. "Stop. Just stop."

"You cannot do this to me," she screamed. "You cannot
do this to him!"

"Carla, wait. Please, just wait. At least for Jack. He's on
his way over."

Carla stopped, falling strangely silent. Phillips watched in
wonder as she slowly moved over to the headboard, and quietly moving aside some pillows, lifted something over the
post. Clutching a pair of rosary beads, she fell to her knees
and began sobbing and praying. Phillips, not a particularly
religious person, knelt down beside her, then placed her arm
around the young woman's shoulder.

"Carla," she whispered tearfully, "I loved him too. He
was a great man."

"She's in the bedroom," said Phillips to Jack Jr. when he
arrived at the apartment less than an hour later. He was in
uniform, his face tormented and tear streaked. He went immediately to the bedroom, knocking gently on the door.
There was no answer. He turned and looked at Cliff, then
knocked again. He pushed the door open into darkness.

"Carla?" he whispered.

"Jack," she murmured. Rising off the bed, she found her
way to him and disintegrated into his arms. For fifteen minutes they held each other, just shaking and weeping, a

brother and sister reunited, two children fused together in pain.

"I'm so glad you're here," she finally said.

"I need to get a look at you," he said, flipping on the switch. Carla blinked her eyes, and Jack let out a short laugh. "For crying out loud, sis, I'm not sure I would have ever recognized you!"

She was still in her evening gown, though it was partly unzipped down the back and hanging halfway off one shoulder. What remained of her makeup was smeared, and her straightened and highlighted page-style locks were mussed.

She chuckled. "Can you believe this? Or my digs? Jack, I'm so glad you're here. I'm coming home," she said, then burst into renewed tears. Jack embraced her yet again, gently rocking her in his strong arms. Finally breaking away, she looked him in the eye.

"Who's with Robbie? Has he been told?"

"Tommy's with him. They're over at Aunt Peg's right now. He's not doing so hot. Nobody is, Carla. It's gonna be rough going for a long time But we'll make it. You know we'll make it."

She nodded her head, and then finally got up to change into her jeans.

"I'm going home with you," she stated.

"Carla—" he started, and then paused.

"What? I'm going home with you. It's that simple."

"No. No it's not."

"What are you talking about? Robbie needs me, and I'm going home."

"No. Not yet."

"Don't tell me what I can't do. I'm going home," she nearly shrieked. Liz Phillips, who had been standing nearby, moved slowly into the bedroom, looking Carla directly in the eye.

"Carla, listen to him. You can't do this, not yet."

"Have you two lost your fucking minds? Jack, you of all people. What is going on here?"

"Carla, we gotta talk," he said. "Please sit down."

"What is wrong with you people? I can take it standing up. Spit it out. What is it?"

Jack ran his hand down the length of his face. "Carla, listen to Liz. Please. Just hear her out."

"Carla, it's about Rand."

A wave of terror coursed through Carla's body. "Did he have something to do with this?"

"No. I already told you, it looks like this was a petty drug deal that went bad. Your father was just in the wrong place at the wrong time trying to do the right thing."

"Then, what is it?"

"We obtained some strong evidence today that links Rand more directly to the Rutland and Cunningham murders."

"Then why don't you arrest him and let me get home to my family?"

"Carla, if it was that easy, I would. But you have to listen to me, and listen carefully. I know you are feeling an extraordinary amount of pain right now. But you also have to understand this. Your job is only half done, and we can't finish it without you."

"What?" she asked. "What are you telling me? That through this insufferable loss I have to put on Charlotte Desmond's happy face and pretend that nothing happened? Don't you see, Commander Phillips, I can't do it. I just can't do it."

Phillips looked imploringly at Carla. "Sylvia March was busted yesterday. She was caught buying cocaine from the same dealer Cameron Bulloch once used."

Panic crossed Carla's face. "Does Rand know this?"

"No. In exchange for her testimony, she's being slipped

into witness protection. As far as Rand and the rest of the world will learn, she died in a car wreck traveling to her parents' country estate." Phillips paused. "He's dealing drugs, Carla. He and a Russian cohort have built up a major cocaine distributorship using a fertilizing business as the front. Sylvia's testimony alone is hearsay, which is why I need your help gathering more evidence."

Carla put her hands on either side of her head and grabbed her hair. "I don't believe this. Any of this!" she exclaimed.

"Calm down, Carla," Jack interjected firmly.

"Dad is dead, Jack. Nothing else matters."

"Bullshit, Carla. *How* he died means everything," he said. "He died in the line of duty. So could you. So could I!" he said, choking on his words. "Every day we put our lives on the line. But you can't give up. Because if you do, then the Rand Emmersons win and everyone else loses."

His eyes and voice softened. "Just remember. Dad will rise in glory, Carla. And those bastards—they will all burn in hell. Carla," he said through his tears, "ask yourself one thing. What would Dad want?"

*"As far as I'm concerned, young lady, you can follow your heart wherever that may lead you."*

She swallowed hard. She had not told Phillips or anyone else of their last encounter, and the thought of having hurt him—emotionally and physically—brought fresh tears.

"He would tell me to follow my heart. And right now my heart is broken."

"Carla, I know it's a tough decision. And you don't need to make it right now. Just think about it, at least tonight," Phillips commented, gently patting her shoulder. "But remember this. Staying the course means staying away. Which also means, I'm very sorry to say, that you cannot attend your father's funeral."

# CHAPTER
## 30

There are no professions more deeply bonded by fraternity than firefighting and police work. And no ceremony is more sacred for firefighters or cops than a funeral for a fallen brother or sister. For a high ranking and beloved officer like Jack Jennings Sr., the funeral Mass was being held in the heart of Manhattan at St. Patrick's Cathedral. It would be officiated by the cardinal, and attended by every conceivable city and state politician, plus nearly one quarter of the force.

For five days Carla agonized over her decision. If she wanted, she could show up and join her family. If Phillips didn't see her, she would know Carla's decision. Liz Phillips had made it clear that she would support her either way. But she also repeatedly asked her to think about it, and think hard.

*"Carla, I know it seems impossible to make a decision like this when you're in such pain. But Jack now knows where you are. I trust him. He can stay in touch with you and tell you how Robbie is doing."*

Carla and Jack consoled one another as much as possible while she remained in the apartment; he had even joined her for dinner last night as she soul searched over what to do.

*"Believe me, Carla, nobody wants you back more than I do. But everyone will understand and be proud of you when*

*you come home. I promise. I know, because I'm exceedingly
proud of you already. But you're a cop now. And when all
this is over, Dad will still be gone and you'll still be a cop.*

*"I want you to think about something else. You worry
about Robbie—don't. He'll be fine. More importantly, demon-
strating for him that you stuck with something in spite of
overwhelming odds, well, in the end it's the best thing you
can do for that kid."*

Though the weather started out overcast, by 9:30 A.M. the
clouds broke, giving way to autumn sunshine. The temperature was cool, however, only around 48 degrees, and a
strong breeze had kicked up. As a sea of blue-uniformed officers began swelling on the street outside of St. Patrick's
Cathedral, Carla finished dressing for the funeral. Turning
off the lights in the apartment, she headed toward the elevator bank, glad for her resolve. She knew it was one decision
she would not regret.

She was not surprised when she arrived at Fifth Avenue to
discover that over ten thousand cops had gathered there
already. But instead of jostling her way through the crowd,
she retreated into a building just catercorner to the cathedral.
Once when they were children, her father had taken the family up to the tenth-floor terrace of the building to watch the
St. Patrick's Day parade. As it was closed to the general
public, and today was a Saturday, Carla knew that the spot
would likely be vacant.

First peering inside the lobby, she saw a weekend security
guard sitting behind the desk. Wearing a baseball cap and
glasses, she brazenly walked in and for the first time ever
flashed her badge.

"I'm with the NYPD," she said.

"How come you're not in uniform outside?"

"Because it's warmer in here," she said, then nervously

laughed. "Listen, I need a favor. I'd like to watch the funeral procession from up on the tenth-floor terrace."

"Can't," he said firmly.

Carla reached inside her jacket and produced a crisp hundred-dollar bill, which she slid in his direction.

"Like I said, can't let you stay out there too long. Follow me," he said, the bill disappearing fast. She followed him up in the elevator, and waited as he unlocked the set of doors that led to the terrace.

"Don't do nothing stupid," he said.

"For God's sake, what do you mean by that?"

"Don't do nothing to get yourself noticed, that's all."

"Promise," she said, grateful at last when he left her alone.

A chill spread through her blood as an eerie silence descended over the area and the officers, from Forty-sixth to Fifty-sixth streets, fell quietly into place, forming a giant blue rectangle along the west side of Fifth Avenue. Before it was even in sight, she could hear the low, forceful drone of the motorcycles leading the funeral cortege, and the strong, compelling beat of a dirge as the bagpipe band—all thirty-six members resplendent in their kilts, busbies, and full-length yellow capes—preceded the slow-moving hearse.

"Detail, atten-hut!" a commander bellowed. The officers stood respectfully fixed in place as the hearse, surrounded by four officers marching on either side, turned the corner and pulled up in front of the church. A long line of limousines followed behind it.

Frocked in flowing capes and full-length white robes, a half-dozen members of the clergy, including the cardinal, came down the cathedral steps to receive the slain officer. As the honor guard withdrew the flag-draped casket from the confines of the hearse, the mayor, police commissioner, and every high-ranking official in the city and the police department quietly exited the limos.

However strong Carla believed her resolve, it suddenly faltered at the sight of her three brothers lining up on the sidewalk to accompany their father on this final journey. From afar she could see Robbie, in his oversized jacket and one-size-too-long pants, trembling with grief. While his brothers stood with stoic respect, his lower lip quivered, and he hung his head and began to cry. So too did Carla, the full realization bearing down on her that she would never lay eyes on her father again.

"Present arms!" the commander ordered, prompting every officer stationed on Fifth Avenue to raise a white-gloved hand in a precise and suspended salute. The bagpipers in their glorious attire came to order, letting forth the mournful, piercing sound of "Amazing Grace." As the honor guard bearing the casket ascended the steps into the cathedral, Robbie, Tommy, and Jack—in full uniform himself—followed directly and slowly behind. The clergy and then officials entered the church, while behind them came the officers in crisp lines of three.

As the procession disappeared, Carla fell to her knees, weeping. Clinging tightly to her mother's rosary beads in one hand, her badge in the other, she prayed to God for strength. Crumbling even further, her thoughts passed like kaleidoscope fragments.

*"It was a clean shot to the heart. He died instantly. Remarkably, the kid who was shot, Manuel Rodriguez, took two hits in the groin and one in the shoulder, and lived long enough to identify his assailant, who was arrested last night. His name is Jake Mundy. He's a small-time dealer with a string of arrests, mostly for petty theft . . ."*

*". . . Carla, we have reason to believe that the man you are investigating may be involved with big-time drug deal-*

*ing. We need you to get close to him, find out who his friends
are, what he's doing with his life . . ."*

*". . . Everyone's different, you know . . . You'd be amazed
at the number of people standing here right now who probably inhaled a line or two before heading out, and you'd
never suspect it."*

She could not hear the service inside, but an hour later the
clergy and troops reappeared, again forming perfect rows
and columns. The pallbearers exited the cathedral, ceremo-
niously stopping in the street just behind the hearse with her
father's casket.

"Present arms," bellowed the commander, and with uncommon precision, thousands upon thousands of white-
gloved hands made a final salute to their fallen comrade,
while a double-echo version of "Taps" filled the chilly air.
Carla rose tall and proud as well, saluting just the same as
five helicopters flew overhead in missing man formation.

"Order arms," came the command, and as every arm
whipped back into place, the casket was slipped into the
hearse, ready to carry Jack Jennings to his final resting place
beside his late, beloved wife.

"Good-bye, Dad," Carla whispered as the door to the
hearse was closed shut. "I love you. And I won't let you
down. I promise."

# CHAPTER
# 31

The smoke from Rand's cigar disintegrated in a blast of cold wind cutting across his apartment building's rooftop. It was 9:00 P.M. and he stood there alone, cloaked in a full-length cashmere coat over sweats, while staring at the stars in the cloudless black sky.

He could not believe that Sylvia was dead.

*Where are you?* he wondered, trying to sort out his thoughts. The realization of his loss had hit him while joining her parents today to scatter her ashes over the Long Island Sound. She'd loved sailing, and had spent many happy hours cruising on her family's boat around the Sound. In recent years she'd frequently joined him on his own boat, often commandeering the wheel while he sat back and relaxed.

He remembered making love to her on his boat and, to his dismay, discovering she was a lousy lover—something that ended any long-term romantic interest in her. She was a sloppy, wet kisser, she moaned too loudly, and she never quite got the hang of a blow job.

But she'd been a loyal and faithful companion. Someone with whom he'd shared his confidences—and someone who had taken his darkest secret to her grave. He was going to miss her.

He knocked a chunky ash off the cigar, then took another drag before settling down in a chaise longue, tucking the coat tightly around himself.

*I hate breaking the news of Sylvia's death to Charlotte, especially considering her own loss.*

He hadn't spoken to her in several days. She'd left a tearful message on his answering machine saying she was returning home indefinitely because her father had died of a sudden stroke. He was perturbed that she'd left no forwarding number or address so that he could at least send flowers. And when he called directory assistance in Seattle he found Walter Desmond's number was unlisted.

*Oh, well. Charlotte might even be relieved,* he thought, thinking how meddlesome Sylvia could be. Cold as it was, he stayed on the roof for the better part of an hour. Flashbacks of Sylvia continued passing through his mind. They'd been through a lot together, and though not always easy to deal with, through it all she'd remained loyal and trustworthy. He recalled after Candace Rutland's murder telling her the truth about HTP Chemicals—that it was a hub for cocaine distribution—and then about the growing turf war with Russian mobsters who had whacked Candace Rutland.

She'd hit him. Repeatedly.

*"You son of a bitch!" she'd screamed. It took several minutes to restrain her. And another half hour before he could carry on a conversation with her.*

*"I'm dead. You're dead. We're all dead. How could you do this?"*

*"I didn't," he'd insisted. "Roman did it."*

*"Come on, Rand. You expect me to believe Roman just 'did it'? This is not like sneezing—as if it just happened."*

*"Sylvia, believe me, I had no idea he'd done this. And they're not going to kill you."*

*"Fuck you. They've already killed Candace."*

*"We fought back."*

*"How?"*

*"We got one of theirs."*

*"What!"*

*"Actually, two of them. Remember Gordy, Roman's assistant? He's the one who returned to Russia then ratted us out."*

*"I cannot fucking believe this. Now you're talking about murder. We could be nailed for murder?"*

*"It happened in Russia. There is no way we can be linked with those deaths."*

*She began sobbing, repeatedly crying out, "How did this happen? How could you do this to me?"*

And then he talked. For the next hour he explained everything. Reminding her how his motivation for joining the brokerage firm Hartson, Devlin and Burns had been grounded in one thing only—making enough money to exceed his father's estimated net worth of a half-billion dollars. But even though he was on the fast track into upper management, and the company paid handsomely, he knew it would never yield the kind of earnings he truly wanted. And so he looked for investment opportunities.

Sylvia was there when he first discovered anhydrous ammonia. The Chicago Mercantile Exchange had closely studied the fertilizer product. It was a globally used item, with ever growing markets. Its price fluctuated according to supply and demand, making the CME believe that it would offer surefire profits as a traded commodity. And so, in the early 1990s, anhydrous ammonia found its place on the exchange along with pork bellies, beef, and other more commonly traded goods.

Rand heavily researched the product himself. The more he learned, the more he believed that he'd profit less from brokering trades and more from owning a production plant of his own. And so he began bottom-fishing for a factory, discovering HTP Chemicals in Vacherie, Louisiana.

He knew nothing about operating such an enterprise. But in sharing his concern with a friend from Harvard Business School, Sergei Fedorov, he discovered Roman Petrovsky.

Roman and Serge knew each other from Odessa. Roman and his father, Viktor Petrovsky, worked in the fertilizer industry together at a plant that also produced anhydrous ammonia. Following the collapse of communism, they had purchased the plant from the government.

Serge introduced Rand to Roman, and for months they discussed via long distance the details of running this type of business. Rand was impressed enough with the man's acumen and level-headedness to ask if he'd be interested in running, perhaps co-owning, a plant in the United States. It wasn't a hard sell, as Roman had expressed an inclination to leave Russia for good.

Rand's biggest hurdle was raising the capital to buy HTP. It was on the block for twenty-five million dollars. Rand knew it could be acquired for twenty, and sought a small pool of solid investors for the down payment, with plans to finance the balance from an investment bank. The first person he consulted about this venture was Mitchell Cunningham.

Cunningham was a legendary figure on Wall Street after making it big on junk bonds. Following an early retirement, he carved out a niche as an independent investor. Rand sought him out, their common denominator being that they were both Princeton undergraduates. After reviewing the facts, Cunningham startled Rand by agreeing to invest two and a half million dollars.

Rand next convinced another Princeton alum, Malcolm Rutland, to invest. Borrowing on Cunningham's instincts,

Rutland parted with two and a half million dollars from his sizable trust fund.

Then Rand hit up Sylvia, who had her own ample trust fund established by her father, the principal stockholder and CEO of an international pharmaceutical company. She was slightly more skeptical than the others, but he knew in the end she'd come through. Eventually she contributed a million dollars. Rand offered a million of his own; Roman Petrovsky contributed a million from the sale of his Russian plant, and Southern Capital Bank financed the remaining twelve million dollars.

It was, as far as everyone knew, a clean investment. And Roman turned out to be a shrewd and capable plant manager. In fact, very shrewd.

As Rand explained to Sylvia that day, HTP Chemicals' success did not stem from the Chicago Mercantile's hype of anhydrous ammonia. As a traded commodity the product sparked but ultimately failed, and not long after its grand introduction, trading of anhydrous ammonia was suspended on the exchange. HTP's true prosperity developed from the bulk shipment and then wholesale distribution of cocaine.

*"Sylvia, I promise you. I had no idea myself. I first learned about it when Roman finally consulted me about money laundering."*

*"What the hell do you know about money laundering?"*

*"Not much. At least not to start, I didn't."*

*"Why didn't you just get out then? Turn him in?"*

*"Because he had thirty-five million dollars earmarked for me."*

*"How kind. And death sentences for everyone else."*

*"There's ten million in it for you."*

*"Are you trying to buy my silence?"*

*"You have no choice."*

*"Rand. We've been friends for a long time. You know I*

love you. And that I would do anything for you. You don't
have to buy my silence."

"You're a good woman, Sylvia March. And you know I
love you too."

He wrapped his arms around her, then held her close,
feeling the excessive tension in her body.

"Come here," he'd said, taking her by the hand and leading her to his bedroom. "You're so tight."

. She didn't resist him. Instead she allowed him to take control as he made her sit on the edge of the bed. He turned off
the lights, lit a couple of candles, then removed her shoes
and swung her legs onto his bed.

"Roll over," he told her, then began softly kneading his
hands into her shoulder blades, down her back, and then
over her buttocks. Working his way back up her spine, he
could hear her begin to moan. He was about to massage
downward again when she suddenly rolled over and placed
his hands on her breasts.

For the next hour they made love, then lay quietly in one
another's arms.

"Sylvia, I don't care what you say. There is ten million
dollars in this for you. You'd be foolish to turn it down."

"Where is it?"

"Costa Rica."

"Costa Rica?"

"We've discovered it's a pretty safe place for offshore
banking and laundering. Besides which, HTP has several
Costa Rican clients that make legitimate purchases of anhydrous ammonia."

"How did Roman ever get started in this?"

"Believe it or not, from his father."

He explained the whole history of events to her. After
the collapse of communism in the former U.S.S.R., Viktor
Petrovsky had turned to an old army buddy named Boris

*Arkady for help in getting money to buy the Russian plant. After serving several years in the Russian Army together, Petrovsky went home, but Arkady stayed, rising to the position of high-level general.*

*"When the Soviet Union fell, Arkady's prosperity rose. He discovered big profits in the illegal trade of arms—particularly in trading arms for drugs with a Colombian cartel.*

*"Petrovsky had heard that Arkady was doing well, and innocently turned to him for help. Arkady realized that the Colombians with whom he was already doing business could benefit from fertilizers, and convinced Petrovsky to do a one-time fertilizer-for-drugs exchange, saying he'd probably make enough money from one deal to buy the plant. Petrovsky exchanged enough fertilizer to satisfy the demands of the transaction. And then sought Roman's help selling the dope. True to Arkady's foresight, the Petrovskys made enough money to buy the plant.*

*"What both Petrovskys thought was a one-shot deal, however, turned into a living hell. Until Viktor's death two years later from a heart attack, they were at Arkady's mercy. He extracted payola and other favors on a whim. Roman felt certain his father would still be alive if not for Arkady, and became so fed up with the man he sold the plant. Shortly afterward I entered the picture, and through me he saw two great opportunities. One, to get out of Russia forever; and two, to grow rich distributing drugs under the cover of anhydrous ammonia. He knew that U.S. Customs and the Coast Guard rarely inspect the containers carrying it because it's so deadly. Investing in HTP and then managing the plant meant—at least Roman thought—that he could conduct his business without interference from Arkady.*

*"After we opened HTP, he went about having several of our tanker cars retrofitted so that one side carries the poisonous gas, while the other half conceals multiple kilos of*

*coke. He recruited a small, tight-knit group of employees to help him out, and before long had a steady and well-run business. We have ships going back and forth to Venezuela and Costa Rica every week, where we have legitimate customers buying anhydrous ammonia. On those return trips, the containers carry the drugs. Once the containers are at the Louisiana plant, targeted trucks and trains carry them to various distribution points around the country. Because anhydrous ammonia is so widely used as a fertilizer and now as a cooling agent in refrigeration systems, delivery of the product to communities large and small goes on unnoticed twenty-four hours a day, seven days a week."*

*"Where did it go wrong?"*

*"In between Roman's legs."*

*"Nice."*

*"I'm not joking. Do you remember that chick that got blown away in the bank heist at Chase Manhattan after she shot the armed guard?"*

*"Yeah."*

*"Her name was Natasha Sorokin. Roman had returned home to visit his mother and ran into her in a bar. Roman had met her before because she was dating one of the drug buyers when he did the first transaction. Anyway, it turns out she wasn't seeing that guy anymore, and that night when Roman saw her they had sex. At least he did. Apparently, for her, it was a mind-fuck. She was obsessed with him after that, and in fact eventually found her way to Louisiana, determined to be with him."*

*"How did she find him there?"*

*"Remember Gordy? He was helping Roman run the plant?"*

*"Sure."*

*"Gordy had traveled back with Roman, and was with him*

*in the bar that night. For some reason he developed an interest in that skinny little bitch, and helped her out."*

*"This is unbelievable."*

*"It gets worse. Roman was shocked when she showed up, and told her to leave. Naturally it was a scene. Besides, she had nowhere else to go. She hung around Vacherie for a few weeks, then finally split, but only after stealing a small stash of dope from his apartment along with his address book. And lucky me—I was the one she called looking for help next. Can you believe that? She hitchhiked to New York and then just called me out of the fucking blue. I put her on hold while I called Roman, who told me to hang up. Which I did. I guess she was pretty fucking desperate, because she ended up trying to rob an armed guard."*

*"Didn't you feel sorry for her?"*

*"Hell no. But apparently Gordy did. It turns out she'd been staying with him the whole time she was in Vacherie. Gordy was pretty broken up by her death, and blamed it on Roman. And then he split. And went straight to Arkady with news of what Roman was up to. He knew Arkady would be furious, and he was, claiming Roman would have never gotten close to the Colombians in the first place if not for him. That's when he began demanding money. And that's when Roman first told him to fuck off."*

*"Why was Candace Rutland murdered?"*

*"Gordy told them everything he knew about our operation—including the names of our American investors. Arkady began threatening to kill us and even our family members if that's what it took to get what he considered to be his rightful share of the profits."*

*"And that's why you're telling me about this. So I can brace myself for being whacked?"*

*"We haven't had a single threat since Gordy and one of Arkady's top lieutenants were murdered."*

*"You had them killed?"*

*"Roman made the arrangements."*

*"Great. So you and I are off the hook."*

*"Sylvia, things calmed down after that. I think Arkady got the message. Besides, the Colombians are not playing favorites. They're happy doing business with Arkady, and they're happy to have a secure source of distribution inside the United States. They've made a killing off of us."*

*"Did you have to put it quite like that?"*

*Rand laughed.*

*"What about Malcolm Rutland? Does he know about this?"*

*"Yes. He won't talk."*

*"What about Mitchell Cunningham?"*

*"He knows. He'd gotten a threat from Arkady shortly before Candace Rutland died and came to me scared shitless and wondering what to do. I'm worried about him, Sylvia. He's extremely upset. Said he just wants out."*

The temperature on Rand's rooftop dropped as the wind picked up. He tightened his coat, took another drag off his cigar, then thought about Cunningham's demise. It was just as well, he'd concluded, as the threat that he'd talk was eliminated.

Still staring at the stars, he remembered how nice it had been holding Sylvia that night. Their lovemaking, for a change, was fairly decent. He would miss her.

It made him wonder if he'd ever have anyone in his life like her again, then renewed thoughts of Charlotte Desmond surfaced.

*A virgin.* He laughed inwardly. *I haven't had a virgin since freshman year in college. This ought to be fun.*

# CHAPTER
## 32

"Tell me honestly, how are you doing?"

"Honestly? I'm exhausted. I cry easily over my father. I miss my brothers. Most of all, I miss being myself," she said.

"I understand," Liz said compassionately. "Carla, I know it's tough. But you did the right thing by sticking it out. I am proud of you. I know your father would be very proud, too."

"Thanks," she said, somberly nodding her head. "Do you want some more?" Carla asked about the chicken divan she'd prepared for their dinner.

"Sure. And some salad, too." Carla dished out extras, then sat back down at the kitchen table.

"Liz, given all that you know about Rand, why can't you just arrest him?"

She'd fully expected this question. She knew that Carla was weary from the entire ordeal. But the next phase in the investigation was crucial, and Liz needed her to hang tough.

"Carla, I wish it was that easy. The problem we're faced with—particularly in a case this complex—is that we have to develop an airtight case. We don't have it yet. We only have a statement from a co-conspirator. No matter if everything Sylvia March told us is true, it won't stand up in court alone."

"But if you know they're dealing drugs from HTP, why not monitor the activities at the plant? Go after them that way?" Carla wondered.

Liz raised an eyebrow. "We're already working with the FBI, DEA, and U.S. Customs on this. They've set up surveillance. Carla, first understand, gathering evidence isn't a tidy, straightforward business. Especially now that every step needs to be carefully monitored. Your apartment will be wired, you need to be wired, Rand's phones and those of HTP are now tapped. U.S. Customs is now quietly tracking all of the containers shipped into and out of HTP to find out where they are going. Again, if what Sylvia told us is true, HTP is one of the prime cocaine distributors in this country. Our goal is to cast as big a net as possible."

"What about the wiretapping? Can't you nail them from phone conversations?"

"Yes, that's probable, but not always possible. Trust me. Their enterprise did not grow by having open conversations on the phone. They're too smart for that. We are, like I said, now eavesdropping on all HTP phone lines and those of Rand Emmerson. We have to wait and see what happens."

"Why didn't you do it before?"

"It's not that simple. First, it's time-consuming and expensive. Someone must monitor the taps twenty-four hours a day. Second, you need a court order and a very good reason to do so. We simply didn't have it up till now. Plus, we had to coordinate with the Feds in Louisiana."

"How am I still needed?" Carla asked.

"This is where it gets tricky."

Carla laughed. "*This* is where it gets tricky?"

"Right!" Liz said, laughing back. "What we learned from Sylvia is that apparently the Colombians with whom Arkady and Rand do business learned about their warfare after the train wreck in New Mexico. The Russians had been operating on poor intelligence and sabotaged the wrong train—which was a lucky break for HTP, since no drugs were found. Still, Roman ordered a hit on Arkady. The Colombians leveled an ultimatum—establish an immediate detente or everyone would be cut off. Arkady's organization, however, with guns to trade possessed sway over the Colombians that Roman didn't have, and still demanded a cut of HTP's business. The Colombians can always find new American distributors, but the weapons they seek are harder to come by. So they asked Roman to compromise, to cut the Russians in on HTP's profits.

"Roman and Rand decided that everyone could profit if they opened up a second plant. By broadening their distribution, they could keep business flowing with the Colombians, provide enough cash to Arkady's organization, and maintain their current profit level.

"There's only one problem. They could buy a second plant with cold cash, but know it would be suspicious. If they went back to Southern Capital for additional financing, they would be subject to due diligence—an auditing process that may reveal their two-tiered accounting system. The only other alternative is to raise the money through private investors—not unlike what Rand did with the purchase of the Louisiana plant—and their deadline is fast approaching. They've secured a contract on a plant in Oklahoma, but still need to raise more legal tender to complete the twenty-three-million-dollar transaction. Sergei Federov, who works as a broker with foreign investors, found three backers for them. But because the rate of return on the authentic investment is only average, luring legitimate private capital hasn't been easy—only eighteen million so far and just a month left to get the job done.

"We want in on their game, Carla. They need another five million, and we want it to come from you."

Again, Carla laughed. "Can I just write them a check?"

"Sure. We'll just take it out of your paycheck." Liz grinned, then took a couple mouthfuls of food before carrying on.

"Carla, you need to tell Rand that with your father's death you've come into a sizable inheritance. Question him. Tell him that you're looking at both traditional and untraditional investment opportunities, and ask him what he recommends."

"Liz, I can't imagine the NYPD has five million in a slush fund to back up my claims."

"No, of course not. But the FBI does."

Carla put her fork down and pinched her forehead. For a short stretch neither one spoke.

Liz finally broke the silence. "What's on your mind?"

"Liz, I'm not going to lie to you. I'm nervous. Rand may be sophisticated and high class, but the reality is he's no better than the low-life bastard who killed my father. To them, the value of life is measured only in dollars.

"What if something goes wrong? What if he discovers the truth about me? I'm dead."

"Carla, I've said it before, and I mean it. If you want out, you can have it. You won't be penalized for it."

"Oh, come on, Liz. Do you think if I wanted out I'd be sitting here right now? Don't you ever get scared? Don't you ever wonder if one of Al DeCarlo's thugs is going to suddenly step out of the darkness?

"Don't you understand, this is a reality check for me. I know tonight I could go back to Queens. I could go through the normal paces at the Academy, then spend time directing traffic while hoping for a promotion, probably ending up with a beat in some Godforsaken, crime-infested neighborhood. My chances of getting hit by a car or stabbed in the throat by some crack-addicted teenager are just as great as ending up dead at the hands of Rand Emmerson. It's just the reality of the work we do, Liz. And so right now, right this minute, all I'm saying is, I'm scared."

Phillips's face lit with a strange grin. At first Carla wondered if she had offended her. But the look in her eyes expressed genuine approval. Oddly, it reminded Carla of Master Tompkins's look after telling her she'd just graduated to the next level belt. It wasn't just the physical discipline that helped her make the grade. Rather, she'd achieved the mental preparedness necessary.

"Congratulations," Phillips spoke softly. "Now you know what it's really like being a cop."

# CHAPTER
## 33

"Charlotte, I am so sorry about your father," said Rand, grateful for a chance to catch up with her at last. "Had he suffered any strokes before?"

"No," Carla said softly. "He was the picture of health. At least for his age. He was only sixty-eight."

"Did he die at home?"

She bit her lower lip, then nodded her head.

"Was your mother home?"

"Uh-hm."

"How is she doing now?"

"All right, I suppose."

"How are you doing?"

"Truthfully, I'm exhausted."

Rand looked at her pensively. They were seated in the Peninsula Hotel's chic and contemporary Adrienne Restaurant. Though she'd seemed happy to see him, he could tell she was preoccupied. She'd only nibbled at her dinner, and had finished only half a glass of wine. He was wondering if this was a good time to tell her about Sylvia, when surprisingly Carla brought up her name.

"You haven't mentioned anything about Sylvia. How is she doing?"

"Charlotte," he said, then gestured for her to give him her

hands. She obliged, looking quizzical. He squeezed her hands. "I'm afraid I have some more bad news for you."

"What?" she said, barely whispering.

"Sylvia is dead."

"Oh, my God!" she said with mock shock. "When? How?" She could see the grief in his face.

"Car wreck. The day after your father died."

"Oh, Rand. I am so sorry. I know you must be devastated. You two were such good friends."

"It's been rough, Charlotte. It was so unexpected."

"What happened?"

"Her car burst into flames after rolling down an embankment. She was heading out to her parents' Connecticut country house in her Porsche. According to police, the road conditions were slick that night and she was speeding. She failed to negotiate a curve and went flying ass over tits into a ravine."

Carla let out an impulsive laugh, then immediately apologized.

"I'm so sorry, really. It's just I'm trying to imagine an official police report stating the subject went flying ass over tits into a ravine."

"You know what I mean," he said with no corresponding levity.

"I do," she said softly, imagining the two men currently listening to her taped conversation chuckling as well. She squeezed his hands. "And I'm very sorry for you. How are her parents doing?"

"Awful. I joined them when they scattered her ashes over the Long Island Sound. It's so hard to believe I will never see her again."

"I simply can't believe this. I'm sorry I missed her funeral and that I wasn't here for you."

*I can't believe you've lost four friends in the span of four months—and all of them are gone because of drugs.*

"Her parents are dedicating the plaza outside her father's office building in her name. There will be a memorial ceremony when that happens. Maybe you can join me then?"

"Well, of course."

Their waiter interrupted their conversation and poured them some more wine. Carla took the opportunity to free her hands from Rand's, then took a sip. "It sounds like her parents have some money."

"That's an understatement. Her father is the CEO of Century Pharmaceuticals."

"Really?" She knew that Century was the world's leading pharmaceutical company.

"Yeah, Sylvia was doing all right with her trust fund."

"I can relate."

"Why do you say that?"

"Well, you already know that I live primarily on my *own* trust fund. And now, since my father passed away, I'm gaining a considerable inheritance. At some point I was hoping to get some investment advice from you."

"I would imagine you have some good ideas of your own. And doesn't your family have a financial adviser or lawyer that recommends how to invest it?"

"Yes, but I've never really liked the man."

"Hmmm." He took a sip of his wine. "I know some people in New York you can consult."

"That's good. If you don't mind, I'd like to get their names and numbers. I'm looking in particular for someone who is savvy about real estate investments."

"What kind of real estate?"

"This might sound crazy, but I'm thinking of buying either apartment buildings or buildings for commercial lease. Income-producing properties."

"You're talking in the plural sense. Just how much are you thinking of investing that way?"

"Probably eight to ten million to start."

He repeated her statement, then laughed. "Most women I've gone out with are looking for a man with eight to ten million to invest!"

"Now look who's talking plural. '*Most* of the *women* I've gone out with'!"

"You know what I mean." She could see from the look on his face that his mind was quick at work. "Where is most of your money invested now?"

"The usual. Stocks, bonds, mutual funds. But I'm interested in examining some more high-risk investments. Why not? I mean, if I can actually afford to lose some money, then why not take a gamble? I know the commodities market is risky. I would invest there, too."

"Have you ever thought about capitalizing a growing business?"

"What kind of business?"

"Well, I'm not sure exactly. This is just a hypothetical question."

"Yes, but my money is not hypothetical. I'm looking for some real direction here."

"I understand. I was just thinking that if you are looking for risk and diversity, you may be willing to do venture capital. Buy into an upstart or growing business."

"Are you talking about a franchise business?"

"Perhaps."

"I wouldn't overlook franchise operations. Do you know much about them?"

"Well, not a franchise business like McDonald's. But I do know about one business venture that has done pretty well. The investors have seen a pretty decent rate of return on their investment, and the owners are thinking of expanding."

"What kind of business is it?"

"Industrial."

"Industrial? What specifically?"

"Honestly, right now it's confidential information. But, why don't I do this? I'll talk with one of the principal investors," he said, diverting her question. "I'll see where his company stands on its expansion plans. If he's interested in talking with you, then maybe I can arrange a meeting. Sound good?"

"Sure. Meanwhile, can you still give me the names of those financial advisers?"

"Okay. And listen," he added, "one more thing. I don't mean to be nosy. But if I'm going to make even a tentative pitch to my friend, do you mind my asking what your current portfolio is worth?"

"About twenty million dollars."

She did not miss the gleam in his eyes.

# CHAPTER
## 34

There was simply nothing that made her feel alive anymore. Two hours after she woke, Sylvia March was still in bed. Except for the garbage collection occurring outside her Milwaukee apartment window and the chittering of a few birds, it was quiet. She didn't bother turning on a television or a radio. There was nothing she cared to learn about the world outside.

She couldn't stand to look at herself in the mirror. Her appearance had been altered so that she looked more like a Midwesterner—in her estimation, unoriginal. Gone were her golden locks, replaced by mousy brown, short hair. Her expensive clothes had been replaced by more pedestrian attire. Clothes from the Gap were the closest thing to designer attire in her new wardrobe. Her apartment was a modest one-bedroom unit on the second floor of a walk-up building. It was furnished in outdated This End Up furniture, and was fairly close to Marquette University. High turnover in the complex meant little interest in the new kid on the block. If anyone asked, she told them she was coming back to school to earn her master's degree in English.

She hated the neighborhood with its beat-up bars, Laundromats, and secondhand shops. She'd done laundry for the first time yesterday, and could barely touch the appliances

for fear of germs. Considering the machines were used
mostly by lowlifes, she felt it inconceivable that her clothes
were actually clean. The only other time she'd stepped into
a Laundromat was to wash her dog's favorite blanket after
he threw up on it during a road trip. She remembered the
jealous looks of the regulars as she parked her Porsche outside, and the amusement of one patron when she asked for
help operating the machine. *I might as well be dead,* she
thought while compulsively searching for dog hairs as she
folded her laundered clothes.

As she lay in bed that morning, certain thoughts kept surfacing. The first, curiosity over how Rand had taken the
news of her death. She missed him. But worse, she was desperately afraid for him, and desperately afraid of him. She
knew the police would eventually nail him, and prayed he
would never learn that it was she who turned him in.

*Why did I do it? Why did I do it?* she inwardly lamented.
*I should have just taken my chances with a trial. There's no
way they would have sent me to prison for life. I probably
wouldn't have served any time at all. I shouldn't have told
them a thing.*

She tossed in bed for a while, imagining how she could
have done things differently, and further wondering why
she'd been targeted at the Candy Connection. If the police
wanted Rand so badly, why didn't they just go after him?

*We learned Cameron Bulloch got his drugs at the Candy
Connection, and have had the place under surveillance
since,* Liz Phillips had told her.

*How did you learn about HTP Chemicals?* Sylvia asked.

*Serendipity,* was all Liz Phillips said.

"Serendipity. Fuck serendipity," Sylvia cried, banging her
fist into a pillow. "Don't tell me about fucking serendipity.
Serendipity was the story of my fucking life!"

She reached over and lit a cigarette, deliberately knocking

the ashes onto the cheap nylon carpet, half wishing the place would catch on fire and consume her with it.

*My God, my parents must be a wreck.* She thought about calling and hanging up just so she could hear their voices, but she knew her phone was tapped and that such a call would be considered a violation of her witness protection conditions. And any violations would be grounds to drag her ass back into Manhattan to stand trial. Which, of course, would be double jeopardy. It would have been one thing to go not breaking her silence. It was something entirely different to squeal and then face trial without any protection.

She stubbed her cigarette into an overflowing ashtray, and then threw back the covers. Her apartment's heat was inadequate against the cold outside. Utilities were included in the rent, and when she called the superintendent to ask that he turn it up a notch, he told her to buy another blanket.

*I wish I were dead,* she thought yet again. It occurred to her that she'd yet to read her obituary in the *New York Times.*

"How exciting!" She laughed cynically. Her clock said it was 10:30 A.M. As it was a weekday, Marquette's library was open and she could go search through back copies of the newspaper.

She took a shower, her thoughts still dwelling on Rand.

*I wonder what he's doing today. By now he must be at work. I wonder what he did last night. Maybe he went out with Charlotte. Charlotte Desmond. How do I know that woman?*

Finally Rand got through to Roman. A potential leak had threatened to shut down the plant, and Roman had been dealing with the problem nearly 'round the clock for two days until it was finally under control. It was almost midnight when at last they chatted.

"What happened?" asked Rand. He actually cared little for the details of plant management.

"Nothing much," Roman responded with typical nonchalance. Ten people could have died from inhaling poisonous fumes, and he would have remained unruffled.

"I think I found an investor for Oklahoma."

"How much?"

"Probably the balance."

"What do you know about him?"

"To start with, it's a her."

"What do you know about her?"

"It's Charlotte."

"Charlotte, eh?" Roman snickered. "Aside from saving your life, how does she qualify?"

"Her old man just died and left her a fortune."

"What kind of fortune?"

"At dinner tonight she mentioned two interesting things. First, she's worth about twenty million dollars. And secondly, she's seeking my investment advice. She said she wants to look into buying commercial real estate. I suggested she think about venture capital, that perhaps she look into investing in a business."

"What do you know about her?"

"What do you mean, what do I know about her?"

"She saved your fucking life. Sylvia March has disappeared. And now Charlotte suddenly has twenty million dollars with an itch to burn it in a real estate investment. Aren't you at all suspicious?"

"Of what?"

"Do I need to spell it out?"

"Roman, what are you suggesting?"

"Did you see the body?"

"Whose body?"

"Sylvia March's body."

"I helped to scatter her ashes over the Long Island Sound."

"Did you see her body?"

"Yes," Rand lied. "What does that have to do with anything?"

"Just checking. What do you know about Charlotte?"

"A lot. What do you need to know?"

"That she's for real."

"You're starting to sound paranoid."

"Aren't you? Have Serge run a background check on her."

"We don't have much time."

Roman let out a laugh. "There's plenty of that in prison, my friend."


It was like sitting down with an old friend. Sylvia March, now known as Molly Moore, took the back copies of the *New York Times* to a reading table. Starting with the front, she began scanning headlines. A major headline in the Metro section that day was about the funeral at St. Patrick's Cathedral of an NYPD commander. She read the front section, and planned to read the rest after jumping to the obituaries.

She gasped at the sight of her smiling, attractive picture in the paper.

SYLVIA CORNWALLIS MARCH, AGE 29, KILLED IN CONNECTICUT CAR CRASH. The article described the full range of achievements in her life, her college graduation, and the cotillion at which she'd made her debut. She could tell her parents had been particularly generous describing her charitable activities; the most she'd done for some of the organizations was helping to organize a fund-raising party. Nonetheless, she came across as intelligent, civic-minded, and altruistic. Tears fell as she read about being survived by her parents and one brother. *No,* she wanted to cry out like a twisted Dorothy in the Land of Oz. *I'm not dead, I'm here. And I'll never leave home again.*

She read the article twice more before resuming her other reading, starting with the obituary of Jack Jennings. Seeing a picture of him, immediately she thought she recognized his face. She read the obit, and saw he was the husband of the late Donna Jennings, who once sang with the chorus of the Metropolitan Opera. She remembered Mrs. Jennings well, as her own mother was the chairperson of the Opera's Volunteer Guild at the time of Donna's death and had arranged for the company's lead soprano to sing at her funeral. Sylvia had even accompanied her mother to the funeral in Queens, but only because they were heading out to the Hamptons immediately afterward and it was on the way.

*How sad,* she thought, remembering that Donna had left behind four children, and now they were without parents. Sylvia read through Commander Jennings's obituary, seeing that he was survived by three sons and one daughter, each one of them named. She then turned back to the front page of the photograph of his family as they saluted his casket.

"Oh, my God!" she nearly shrieked. The three boys were lined up, the daughter nowhere in sight. But there was one son who looked exactly like Charlotte Desmond. He had the same deep-set dimples and finely shaped nose as Charlotte.

"Wait a minute!" she exclaimed. She scanned the entire article to see if another picture existed of Carla Jennings, but found none. It didn't matter. If her memory was right, she remembered meeting Carla at her mother's funeral. And she also remembered that except for gender, she looked exactly like her twin brother, Tommy.

"No fucking way!" she exclaimed, causing a nearby library patron to scowl. She jumped up. Then while standing she furiously turned every last page of the newspaper, looking for additional photos and coverage of Jack Jennings's funeral.

Her adrenaline rushed madly.

*"We learned Cameron Bulloch got his drugs at the Candy Connection, and have had the place under surveillance since."*

*"Sylvia, I'd like you to meet someone. Remember the gal I mentioned who was looking for a job in publishing?"*

*"Charlotte recently met Cameron at East Side General when visiting a sick friend."*

*"Thanks, really. But if I ever decide I want to buy some for myself, where would I go to get it?"*

*"Place up on Third. But you can't just go in there and ask for it. You need to know someone. Let me know if you ever decide to go, because I'll introduce you."*

"It's her. I know it. Charlotte Desmond is Carla Jennings." The realization that Charlotte—or rather Carla—had something to do with her bust made her feel sick. "I'll bet she's a cop. Her brother is, her father was."

She ducked in between two stacks, jammed the newspaper down into her backpack, then went searching for a phone.

Using a pay phone, Sylvia called directory assistance in Queens. Jack Jennings's name and number were listed. Sylvia jotted down the information, including the address, then scrounged for enough change to make the long-distance call.

The number rang several times before a pleasant but husky male voice answered.

"Hello."

She was tongue-tied.

"Hello," he said more loudly.

"Hi," she nervously responded. "I'm looking for Carla. Is she home?"

"Who's calling?"

"A friend of hers from college. Uhm, Mary Knowlton."

"Mary Knowlton. Do I know you?"

"Who's this?"

"Her brother Tommy. You went to Queens College? I thought I knew everyone there."

"Yup, Queens College. Listen, I'm calling to express my condolences. I just got back into town and read the news about your father's death. I'm so sorry."

"Thanks," Tommy said sadly. "It sucks."

"Is Carla home?"

He let out a groan. "No. That's something else that sucks."

"What do you mean?"

"She missed the funeral."

"She missed the funeral! How in the world did that happen?"

"She was about to join the NYPD about four months ago, then had a sudden change of heart. She split on her motorcycle, and we haven't seen or heard from her since."

"She was going to become a cop?"

"Yeah."

"Interesting. And she left no forwarding address whatsoever?"

"None. As far as we know, she has no idea our father died. Who knows if *she's* even alive," he said with muted anger.

*She'll be dead when I get through with her,* thought Sylvia.

"Listen, Tommy. I'm so sorry about everything. When she gets back, just tell her that I called."

"Can I get your number?"

"Oh, she has it. Just tell her that I called."

Sylvia hung up the phone, then promptly headed to the Milwaukee airport.

Rand dropped his mail on the living room coffee table and threw his suit jacket on the floor. He was glad to be home. The contemporary one-bedroom condo, with its floor-to-ceiling windows, had cost him nearly two million dollars, mostly because of the view. The panorama from his perch included the Upper East Side and even Wollman Ice Skating Rink in Central Park. An undiscriminating guest might view the stark interior of his apartment as typical of a bachelor; while a more cultured judge would see the value. A green velvet Art Deco sofa reminiscent of a reupholstered castaway actually cost a cool ten grand. The quirky-legged, glass-topped coffee table cost half that much, while a twenty-thousand-dollar stereo system provided surround sound. The only other embellishments were a large unframed oil painting by Eduardo Bolioli in bold primary colors that was valued at five thousand dollars, and a pricey, glass-front mini refrigerator stocked with vintage wines. He went straight for a bottle of wine before checking his answering machine for messages.

"This ought to be good," he said, then grabbed a large wine goblet from a kitchen cupboard and poured himself a healthy amount. "Definitely worth the wait," he said with satisfaction after taking the first sip. He took another before finally picking up the phone. There was a message from Serge. He called him back.

"What's up, man?" Rand asked.

"I've got most of what you need."

"How does it look?"

"Pretty good. So far everything checks out. She went to Michigan; worked at St. Dunstan's Press, just like she said; her father was a Seattle-based venture capitalist, who according to his obituary died of a stroke. Survivors include his wife, Lois, son, Owen Desmond, and daughter Michelle Desmond, both living in Seattle; and one other daughter, Charlotte Desmond of Manhattan.

"Walter Desmond was a Michigan native, served as a fire inspector in the Air Force before graduating from Northwestern University in 1955. In 1960 he opened a Detroit-based company that sold firefighting equipment and clothing, later obtaining patent rights to several products currently used by firefighters today. In 1979 Desmond sold the company, then relocated to Seattle, where he established Trade Wind Enterprises, a global investment and venture capital firm. From what I could gather, Trade Wind's portfolio is pretty extensive, and according to Dun & Bradstreet, the company is worth about seventy-five million."

"What about her money?"

"At least ten million in liquid assets."

"How liquid?"

"Stocks, bonds, CDs, the usual."

"Wait a fucking minute. You said liquid. I'm talking cash."

"Be patient, my friend. There's five million."

"In cold, hard cash?"

"In cash."

"Why in the hell would anyone have that much money sitting in a regular checking account? Did you get any specifics? Dates of deposits? Any big withdrawals?"

"I don't know."

"First thing in the morning, Serge. I want it done first thing in the fucking morning."

"Don't worry."

"Call me in the morning," said Rand, then hung up the phone.

His next call was to Charlotte. He'd previously mentioned

a desire to go out for a motorcycle ride in the morning, and wanted to see if she was interested in joining him. He got her answering machine, which annoyed him. Waiting less than ten minutes, he tried back. Hearing the recording once more, he hung up in frustration without leaving a message, then finally sat down with his glass of wine. He spilled a couple of drops on his suit pants, which pissed him off, but nonetheless got comfortable and decided not to budge until he'd finished his drink. Then the doorbell rang.

"Give me a break," he muttered. He couldn't believe the doorman hadn't rung the person up first.

"Who is it?"

The doorbell rang again.

"Oh, crap," he said as he got off the sofa and went to answer it. Occasionally someone delivering food got the wrong apartment. Depending on what they had, he might or might not send them in the right direction. He unlocked the bolt and then swung the door open, expecting a delivery person's face.

"What the fuck!" he said, his glass dropping and shattering.

It was Sylvia March.

# CHAPTER
## 35

Carla woke shortly after seven o'clock. It was cool and overcast—not bad for her morning jog. Reaching first for her mother's rosary beads, she started off the day with some peaceful prayer and reflection. Finally crossing herself, she rose out of bed, then spent a few minutes stretching and warming up before changing into her jogging attire. In spite of her regular runs through Central Park, it had been a while since she'd had a rigorous workout with weights, and she felt slightly out of shape. She could not wait to get back to her regular physical regimen.

She knew from her caller ID that Rand had tried reaching her twice last night. She'd been instructed, however, to pace herself and so had not yet returned his calls. So much was at stake now that the risk of saying or doing the wrong thing must be kept to a minimum by controlling her exposure to him. She was waiting to hear the latest from Liz before calling back, in particular whether the funds in her bogus account had been checked.

Leaving her apartment, she glanced at a detective parked in a car across the street. Anticipating her morning jog, his partner was waiting about a half-block away to follow her through Central Park. He kept a close eye on Carla as she ran her usual five-mile course, staying several paces back, and just before she reentered her building, he casually ducked inside a corner market to purchase a bottle of water.

She was at the front door when suddenly a car horn blared. Startled, Carla paused and looked curiously at the driver of the late-model black BMW sedan parked in the driveway. It was Rand. Though it was cloudy, he was wearing his Ray-Ban sunglasses, and smiling warmly, he gestured for her to come over to the car. Still breathing heavily from her run, her heart quickened even more.

"Hi," she said breathlessly as he rolled down the window. "What a surprise. What are you doing here?"

He held up a cup of gourmet coffee and a large cinnamon apple muffin.

"Breakfast at Café BMW," he replied with a grin. "Jump in."

She laughed. "I had breakfast at Café Harley once. It wasn't bad."

"This is even better."

"I can't believe you," she said, glancing down at her watch. "It's seven forty-five. What are you doing up this early on a Saturday?"

"Don't you remember I mentioned a ride in the country?"

"Yeah, but that was on your motorcycle. No fair," she said, chuckling. She was leaning against the outside of his car, and glancing past Rand she looked across the street. The two detectives were watching closely.

"Here," he said, holding up the coffee and muffin. "Climb in."

"I'm all sweaty," she playfully protested.

"That's what leather seats are for," he said.

"Well, this is awfully sweet of you," she said, stalling. *You're covered at all times. Don't worry.*

She opened the door, then climbed in the seat.

"I'm sorry," he said, handing her the coffee. "I should have gotten you some water."

"I hope you don't mind if I don't drink this right away," she said. "How long have you been waiting?"

"Not long. I asked the doorman if I could bring this up, and he said you were out jogging. So I knew eventually you'd be here."

"And that I am. Embarrassed as hell to be seen like this."

"You look beautiful. You always look beautiful."

She smiled. "Thanks."

At that moment another driver honked his horn, urging Rand to move forward. Rand rose his hand and slightly waved, then put the car in drive. But instead of parking at the end of the driveway, he kept on going, making a left turn onto the street and then another left turn into heavier traffic on Broadway.

"What are you doing?" Carla asked, laughing to cover her fear.

"Listen, I promised you a ride on my motorcycle. But since the weather's crappy, I thought we could just go for a ride in my car instead. Sound good? I can always open the sunroof."

"It sounds wonderful, Rand. But I have two problems. One, I'd really like to take a shower. And then, I told a girl-friend of mine I would go shopping with her later today, and I need to call her. I'd really appreciate going back to my apartment first."

"Call her from my cell phone."

"Well, I could do that. But I still need to take a shower."

"Not where we're going, you won't need a shower."

"What are you talking about?" she asked, a chill rushing through her. "Rand," she said, then laughed again. "I'm a sweat hog. Do you really want to be seen with me looking and smelling like this?"

He didn't say a word, only smiled at her with that same strange grin. Carla looked in her side-view mirror, relaxing slightly at seeing the detectives two cars behind them.

"This muffin is still warm," she said, then held it up to her nose. She was too nervous to eat. "It smells wonderful."

"I thought you'd like it. It's sweet and warm, like you."

"Wow! You're full of compliments this morning. What did I do to deserve this?"

He reached over and patted her knee. "Just because you're you, that's all."

He glanced in the rearview mirror, then back at Carla. "Aren't you going to eat it?"

"In a minute. I usually don't eat this soon after running." She glanced in her own mirror again. The car was still a short ways behind them, and when she looked ahead, she could see the light had changed to yellow. Rand slowed down as if meaning to stop. Then, just before it turned red, he punched the accelerator and raced through it, leaving the detectives stuck at the light behind them.

She waited a few moments, looked again, then took a deep breath. They were gone. She took a bite from the muffin, thinking.

"Mmmm. This is delicious," she said with forced nonchalance through a mouthful of food. "Thank you. Do you mind if I use your phone now?"

"Go right ahead. Here," he said, reaching in the glove compartment for his cell phone.

*It's Saturday morning. Do I call Liz Phillips at home? What if I'm scared for nothing, and he hits redial on his phone? I don't dare call headquarters.*

"What's the matter?" he asked.

"I'm trying to remember her number."

"Call directory assistance."

"No, I'll remember it. Just give me a minute. What time should I tell her I'll be back?"

"What time do you want to be back?"

"Well, originally I thought we'd be back by midafternoon."

"Tell her midafternoon, then."

"Where should I tell her we're going?"

"Does it matter?"

"No. I mean, it's just that *I'd* kind of like to know."

"That would ruin the surprise. But I think you'll like it. Just tell her you'll call her when you get back to the city. How's that?"

"All right."

His manner reeked of deception, and she decided it was worth the risk of calling Liz Phillips's cell phone number. The line rang repeatedly before the recording picked up.

"Leave your name and number," was all her message said. It seemed like an eternity waiting for the beep.

"Lynda," Carla said. "I'm sorry to have missed you. This is Charlotte. Listen, we should still be on for shopping this afternoon, but I've had a slight change in plans.

"Remember that handsome mystery man in my life? He met me at my building this morning in his BMW with coffee and a muffin the size of a sofa cushion, and is taking me on a surprise trip. I have no idea where we're headed, and I'm not sure exactly what time we'll be back in the city. He says midafternoon, so I'll call you when I get in. Hey, there's Bloomingdale's. You know, there's a sale on Emmanuel Ungaro today. We've got to check that out!" She caught Rand looking at her. Was she overreacting? If he was truly up to no good, why would he have even offered to let her use the phone? "I've got to go," she concluded. "I'll call you later."

She tried returning the phone to the glove box, when

Rand took it out of her hand, disabled it, then stuck the slim device in his pocket.

"Are you all set?"

"Yep."

"Well, then. Just relax and enjoy your breakfast. We'll be there before you know it."


Liz Phillips returned from an invigorating but abbreviated workout. Once she'd arrived at the gym, she realized she'd left her cell phone at home, and instead of returning to get it, she compromised by packing a typical two-hour routine into an hour and a half. When she finally picked up the phone, she discovered three chilling messages. One was from Carla; two urgent calls were from headquarters.

"I don't fucking believe this!" she shrieked. She didn't want to panic, as Rand had already mentioned taking Carla for a ride on his motorcycle today. But their plans hadn't been solidified, and it was certainly strange that he had showed up unannounced and so early in his car. And worse, the detectives assigned to follow them had gotten stuck in traffic. Even after cutting through red lights, they'd still lost him. She did not waste a second, calling Cliff Blackman and then bolting out the door for headquarters.

"She's scared, Blackman," she said upon seeing him. "I can hear it in her voice. Something's up!" she exclaimed in frustration, running a hand through her hair. "She said in her message that they were passing by Bloomingdale's. Which means he's probably headed east. Maybe to his beach house."

Liz was picking up the phone to place a call when she heard the beeping tone indicating there was a message waiting on her voice mail. Anxious that it might be Carla, she retrieved it.

The sound of haughty laughter from a recognizable throaty

voice practically made her hair stand on end. She closed her eyes and drew in a deep and frightened breath. "Oh, my God."

"What? What is it?" Cliff demanded.

"Blackman, we're in deep shit." She turned on the speaker and replayed the message.

"Your little Charlotte is dead in her web." The message was followed by wicked laughter and then an ominous click.

"Jesus Christ, that's Sylvia March," he said.

He had never seen such panic on Liz Phillips's face.

Another phone line rang.

"Yes," Liz shouted impatiently into the receiver. "Who saw them? Where?" She listened for a moment longer, then slammed down the phone.

"They were spotted exiting the Queens Midtown Tunnel two hours ago, heading east. Get your gun and get a car, Blackman. We're going to the Hamptons."

# CHAPTER
## 36

Carla sipped coffee tentatively, then asked Rand if he minded changing the music. She wasn't in the mood for hard rock.

"Whatever you want. I'm just happy to have some time alone together."

She found a soothing jazz station, and after leaning back, she gently stroked his arm. He seemed more like himself, making Carla worry that she'd sounded a false alarm. She had to believe that Liz Phillips would not overreact and do anything to jeopardize her safety. She also wondered again why he'd offer his phone if he didn't want anyone to know her whereabouts. Unless his strategy was to keep things seeming as normal as possible—for now.

One thing was clear. They were headed to the beach, and presumably his house in East Hampton. Carla glanced in the side-view mirror, and noticed they were the only car on this stretch of highway.

"You are so funny," she finally said, once more stroking his arm.

"Why?" he asked, a cocky grin crossing his face.

"You're full of surprises. I like that."

"You're not so predictable yourself, you know."

"Oh, really! In what way?"

"Well, to begin with, I've never met a woman who could help a man dodge a bullet. The last I heard, they weren't teaching that in prep school."

"It must be a Seattle thing. We're just a different lot than you—"

"You . . . Easterners?" he finished her sentence. "Or, is that Upper East Siders?"

*Why did he say that?* She laughed to diffuse a renewed nervousness. "What's the difference?"

"A big one. You could be from Brooklyn, or even Queens," he said, and looked directly at her, "and still be an Easterner. But there's only one Manhattan. And then, there's only one Upper East Side. Just like there's Seattle. But there's only one very exclusive community called the Highlands. You know the difference. Right?"

"Of course. But I think generally we're talking about the difference between West Coast and East Coast mentalities. Am *I* right?"

"Yes. And you're the expert."

Carla bristled at the tone of his voice and his strange logic. "I haven't offended you, have I?"

His eyebrows drew together, sarcasm framing his face, but for the moment he remained silent.

"Rand," she stated softly. "I apologize if I said something offensive."

"Don't worry."

*Don't worry about what?*

"How's your coffee? I hope it's not cold."

"No, it's fine."

"Aren't you going to drink the rest of it?"

"Actually, no. Maybe when we get to where you're headed, I can get some water."

He started to say something, but let out an ironic laugh instead. "Not a problem. Definitely not a problem."

*     *     *

An hour later they pulled up the driveway to his beach house.

"I figured this is what you had in mind," said Carla blithely. Though overcast skies threatened a downpour, his home looked welcoming. She smiled at the sight of it.

"Oh, really. And how's that?" he said. "I thought I was full of surprises, remember?"

"A la carte from Café BMW was surprising. But you love this place. I suppose that's why I guessed it."

It was impossible to read him. Superficially everything seemed fine. But absent from their discussion was anything concerning her potential investment in HTP Chemicals. They'd discussed it at length the last two times they were together, and finally she offered to contribute five million dollars toward the purchase price of the plant, then provided him with everything necessary to complete the requisite background check. Liz Phillips had provided repeated assurance that her alias was airtight. So why hadn't Rand mentioned it again? She decided not to bring it up first.

"Aren't you coming in?" Rand asked.

"Absolutely!"

"You know, I was thinking, since it's a little windy, it might not be such a bad day for a sail."

"Are you crazy?" she quickly retorted. "It's getting ready to rain."

"So?"

Carla felt desperate and almost blurted that she suffered from seasickness, but remembered that supposedly she grew up on the water and knew all about sailing.

She looked at her watch. "Rand, it's ten-thirty. It could be another hour before we get the boat out. I'm not sure we have time."

"Nonsense. We'd be out by eleven, sail till twelve-thirty, be back on the road by one, and have you home by three."

She sighed. "I'm not in the mood for sailing today."

"Hmmm. Well, come on inside. We'll just start a fire and hang out here for a while, then."

"That would be great. Thank you."

He took her hand and led her inside the house.

"Is someone here?" Carla asked as they walked inside, noticing that several lights were already on and that the house seemed warm.

"No wonder my electric bill here is so high! Must have been the cleaning lady. She is so forgetful." He went straight to the refrigerator and retrieved a chilled bottle of spring water. "Here. I'll be right back. I'm going outside for some firewood."

"Can I help?"

"No. You stay here and make yourself comfortable." A curious expression crossed his face. "Are you okay, Charlotte? You seem edgy. Come here."

He didn't wait for her response. Instead he stepped forward and took her in his arms. "You are so tense. I think you need a back rub."

"A back rub?" she said, easing away. "Go get that firewood first!"

"Yes, ma'am." He winked at her, then disappeared. She could hear him whistling as he made his way outside to the woodpile.

She sat down on the overstuffed sofa in the family room near the fireplace, but could not get comfortable. After gulping down several sips of water, she grabbed the kitchen phone and dialed Liz's cell phone. It had started to ring when Carla heard the door reopen.

"Shit," she said, quietly hanging up and heading back near the fireplace.

"You made yourself at home yet?" he asked as he reached the family room.

"Not without you," she said, smiling. He smiled back over his armload of logs, then resumed whistling some made-up tune.

"You sure are in good spirits," said Carla.

"Can't imagine why not," he said while unloading the wood. "I'm about to sit by a fire with the girl of my dreams. Do me a favor, please. Reach over and open those doors to the fireplace, would you?"

She never saw it coming. She bent over slightly, offering him just the position he needed to whack her on the back of the head with a log.

Standing over her prostrate body and observing the bloody wound, he laughed.

"What are you in the mood for *now,* Carla Jennings?"

"Slow down, Blackman. I think this is it."

Phillips rolled down the window and studied the property through a light drizzle. There was no mailbox, and as the house was set a good quarter mile from the road, it was difficult to see if any numbers were on the house itself. Phillips grabbed a pair of binoculars off the floor.

"Pull up," she demanded, "just a little." She peered at the house, put the glasses down and looked, then tried the binoculars again.

"Stay here," she said, then jumped out of the car. Darting behind one of the few trees lining the road, Phillips looked past the expanse of lawn through the binoculars. After spotting something she jumped back in the car.

"I see his car parked on the side of the house. Black BMW sedan."

"What do you want to do?"

"Call headquarters. Give me the phone." She got Detective Woods.

"Melissa, have you heard anything?"

"The U.S. marshals discovered someone matching Sylvia March's description purchased a ticket yesterday at the Milwaukee Airport. Destination New York City."

"Shit! Any other calls from Carla?"

"No."

"We are at his property, and I see his car. Be on standby to alert local officials we may need backup."

"Will do."

Phillips hung up.

"Sylvia March bought a plane ticket to New York yesterday. Blackman, park the car out of view. We're going in."

It was nearly impossible for them to move unnoticed. The front lawn to Rand's house was long and wide, and keeping the lowest possible profile meant taking a side approach. Once beside the house, they split up, with Phillips taking the front and Blackman covering the back. Crouching low and peering through windows as she went to the front door, Phillips detected no movement inside.

Reaching the front door, she tried the handle, but it was locked. She couldn't tell where Blackman was at the moment, but she needed the rear protected if they tried escaping, and knew she would have to enter alone. Phillips stepped back from the front door and took a deep breath. She couldn't even remember the last time she'd had to kick in a door. She hoped she still had what it took. With all the strength she could muster, she raised her right leg and forcefully jammed the door. It barely budged.

"Shit," she exclaimed, feeling tingling vibrations in her leg. She stepped back and tried once more, only this time with greater energy. Again she failed. Rand apparently had locked it with a reinforced dead bolt.

She was contemplating blowing the lock open with her gun when she suddenly heard the door begin to unlatch. Her gun drawn, she stepped to the side, breathing nervously as it opened. She felt both shock and relief at seeing Cliff Blackman standing there.

"The sliding glass doors out back were unlocked. The house is empty, but we've got real trouble," he said.

Phillips took a moment to collect her breath, then looked him straight in his dark eyes. "What is it?" she asked.

"A trail of blood."

# CHAPTER
# 37

After years of sailing together, Sylvia and Rand worked in wordless partnership on the water. They were both expert sailors, operating on instinct to accomplish whatever needed to be done. With a certain look, or nod of the head, they could communicate up-to-the-minute needs. Today they barely spoke, but for different reasons.

Their lives were now traveling on an unimaginable course. They were sailing to the Caribbean, with the intention of eventually making it to Costa Rica to obtain as much of their cash as possible. Soon they intended to drop Carla's body into the ocean.

*"She's a cop, Rand. Charlotte Desmond is a cop."* The revelation from his supposedly dead friend kept repeating itself in his head. *"Her name is Carla Jennings. She is the daughter of Commander Jack Jennings, who was recently killed. I've met her before. I know it's her.*

*"Think about it, Rand. What a coincidence that she shared a taxi with you that day, then just happened to show up at Cameron Bulloch's funeral, and go to the reception afterward. The cops found evidence that Cameron was buying his drugs from the Candy Connection and had that place under surveillance. I never told Carla specifically that I bought my own drugs there, but when she asked, I did men-*

tion a place up on Third. Once the NYPD had that information, they nailed me.

"Rand, they know all about you, and they didn't have to
get it all from me. They knew about HTP before they got to
me. Has Charlotte ever talked to you about HTP?"

He was speechless.

"Rand!" Has your dear friend Charlotte ever talked to
you about HTP?" she demanded angrily.

He'd shaken his head in disbelief. "I'm fucked, Sylvia.
I'm fucked."

"No, Rand. We're fucked. We need to get out of the city—
out of the country—now!"

"I should call Roman."

"Fuck Roman. He got us into this in the first place. Besides, don't you think your phones are tapped? Why give the
cops a heads up as to what we're doing? I say we leave
tonight."

She was right. But a towering rage burned inside him.
This meant his present life was obliterated. He chuckled at
the irony of Sylvia's presence; she'd always wanted to spend
her life with him, and now she'd have her wish.

"I'm not leaving, just yet."

"You're crazy, Rand."

"We're taking her with us."

"Now I know you're fucking crazy. She can't come with
us!"

"Cut the jealousy crap, Sylvia. She'll be dead by this time
tomorrow."

She wasn't sure what woke her up first—her flaming
headache or the fact that her body had just soared three feet
off the ground, followed by a head slam to the floor. Whatever it was, Carla awoke into darkness. It took several harrowing moments to discern the truth, that her hands and feet

were bound in rope and that she was inside some type of canvas bag. The sound of water and the perpetual rocking motion meant one thing—she was on a boat. Grateful, at least, that her cotton-dry mouth wasn't gagged, she took several deep gulps of the stuffy air.

"Oh, God," she whimpered, realizing Rand had tried to kill her. Obviously he was planning to dispose of her body. She could hear the angry flapping of something metal on metal, and sensed they were traveling at a brisk speed. Presuming, of course, they were on his yacht, she wondered if they were alone. Had Liz Phillips received her phone message?

There was no way of telling what time it was, or how long they'd been on the boat. Her hands were tied behind her back, and she felt an overwhelming urge to scream. Instead she just cried, then began imagining what might happen, wondering if Rand would even bother to see if she was still alive before tossing her overboard. And then she panicked. Squirming helplessly, she began kicking her bound legs in sheer anxiety until she wore herself out, only stopping when the boat seemed to hit another large wake and send her flying upward yet again. This time when she hit the floor, her shoulder broke the fall and she rolled into what seemed like a wall.

"Where in the hell am I?" she asked aloud, and then managed to sit up. Only then did she realize that in her frenzy the rope tying her hands had been slightly loosened. Taking several deep breaths to calm herself, she wriggled her hands back and forth, then repeatedly flexed her lower arms, eventually gaining enough space inside the rope to release her right thumb. She tried in vain to free the rest of her hand, until an aggravating cramp in her right arm made her stop. She lay back down on the floor, trying to apply pressure to it, when a wave of seasickness encompassed her.

*Oh, no!* she thought, horrified at being covered with puke. She propped herself up again, hoping that would ease her nausea, furiously resuming the struggle to free her hands.

"Shit!" Rand shouted after glancing at the knot meter. The Marine Forecasting Service had issued a small-craft advisory before they departed, something of minor concern while they were still in Mecox Bay. But upon entering the Atlantic Ocean, the wind velocity had picked up considerably, making control of the ship a greater challenge. The wind gauge measured 30 knots—nearly gale-force blasts. Sylvia had gone to scan radio weather reports, but even without a bulletin he sensed a northeaster blowing in. The rain was falling harder, and the temperature had dropped. He had sailed in bad weather before, and right now his biggest concern was trying not to get blown off their course. He kept a steady eye on the markers, and knew as soon as Sylvia emerged they were going to have to lower the jib. Thankfully, it was a power operated device that would take less than five minutes to furl.

His thoughts grew increasingly hostile as he realized none of this would have happened if not for Carla Jennings. As soon as the opportunity presented itself, he intended to drop her ass into the ocean.

"Fuck!" he screamed at the top of his lungs, releasing his rage into the wind.

Sylvia stuck her head out of the cabin. "What's the matter?" she said, concern in her face.

"Everything's just fine, dear," he replied bitingly.

"There's a nor'easter blowing in," she commented matter-of-factly, trying to hold herself steady on the door frame.

"Oh, really? What a surprise," he shouted.

She looked at him severely. "You'd better put the harness

on, it's going to get rough," she said, then disappeared into the protection of the cabin.

"Sylvia," he screamed. "Sylvia!" he shouted even louder, when at first she didn't respond.

"What?" she said, returning to the doorway.

"I need your help."

"With what?"

"The jib. It has to come down. You can either take over the wheel or furl the jib. Take your pick."

"The jib," she said, knowing full well he didn't want to leave his post. She climbed on board the deck, then carefully made her way to the bow of the boat by holding on to the rigging and railings. Once up front, she watched as the sail began its automatic descent, only it stopped one quarter of the way down. She hit the button again, but heard only the low whine of an engine missing its mark.

"Shit," she exclaimed. "What could it be?"

She'd furled countless jibs in her lifetime, and knew how to do it manually. With such fierce winds it was absurd to leave it up, as it could practically blow them to China. But under the present conditions, it was dangerous to manage the task. She had begun examining the rigging when a blast of cold water sprayed over the bow, causing her to momentarily lose her grip. She fell with an aching thud on top of a Plexiglas hatch, unaware that Carla Jennings had managed to free herself from the canvas sack in which they'd hauled her aboard the boat, and was looking directly up at her from below.

She was going to have to cut one of the lines. Unfortunately, she had left her knife down below. She thought to save herself some time by crawling down through the hatch, and began lifting it open when another gust knocked her down. She skidded a couple of feet in Rand's direction, and holding on for dear life, she decided to slide herself his way, avoiding the hatch altogether.

Carla, crouching on the floor, could hear Sylvia shout out to Rand.

"The jib is stuck. I'm going to have to cut it. Do you have your rescue knife on you?"

"Great!" he screamed back. "What next? I don't know where my knife is. You packed it."

"Not to worry," she said with forced confidence. "I can fix this."

Moments later Carla heard her rummaging around below. She looked at her own surroundings—a cabin crammed full of supplies—and realized that any moment Sylvia might enter this chamber in search of the knife. Carla had tried the door—it was locked from the outside. She looked at the hatch above. By climbing on top of everything, she could perhaps escape through it.

Carla heard a nearby door slam shut, and then heard Sylvia cursing at her inability to find the knife. Sensing this room was next, Carla slithered back inside the royal blue canvas sack. Seconds later, she heard keys rattle and the door open. Sylvia paused, apparently checking it out before entering the chamber.

"You fucking bitch," she said, then with unrestrained force kicked Carla in nearly the same spot she'd broken her ribs just a few months before. "None of this would have happened if it weren't for you. Can't wait to turn you into fucking shark bait."

To keep from screaming, Carla bit into her finger so hard that she actually drew blood. The pain seared through her, and the temptation to scream was so overwhelming that she almost wished she'd just pass out again. Instead, she focused on her breathing, forcing rhythmic breaths to rise and fall from her abdomen. In a few moments Sylvia seemed to find what she was looking for. She slammed the door shut again, then locked it.

Carla achingly scrambled out of the bag and gasped. The pain she was feeling was vanquished by one overwhelming thought—to get off the boat alive, no matter what. Sitting upright, fighting for balance, she began climbing on top of the supplies toward the hatch. Forcing the lid open, she was struck by a cold, wet blast. Still wincing in pain from the kick, she lifted herself up and onto the teak wood deck. Crouching low, Carla spotted a loose, wet rope and promptly tied one end of it securely around her waist and the other around a railing. She heard Sylvia emerge from the opposite end.

"I found it," she shouted.

"Hurry up," Rand exclaimed. "I'm fighting like hell to keep us on course."

"Aye-aye, captain," she responded lightly, then began inching toward the jib.

"Oh, shit," said Carla, who now realized she'd left the hatch open. It was the first thing Sylvia noticed when she reached the bow.

"What the hell!" Sylvia screamed, making her way to the opening and looking down below. Carla did not hesitate. She rose behind the woman, and with all the strength she could muster kicked her in the back of one leg. Sylvia buckled and fell to the deck. The knife slipped out of her hand and skidded Carla's way.

"Rand!" Sylvia bellowed at the top of her lungs, then lunged at Carla. At that moment the boat hit a large swell, and Sylvia slid full force into Carla, dragging them down to the deck.

"You fucking bitch, I'm going to kill you," Sylvia screamed, trying to pummel her.

An adrenaline rush pumped through Carla's body, and she

jammed the heel of her hand straight up Sylvia's nose. She heard cartilage crack. Sylvia went limp, and when the boat hit another swell, she rolled uncontrollably across the v-berth to the edge of the boat. With one final turn she dropped overboard into the vicious swells of the cold Atlantic Ocean. Within seconds she disappeared.

Carla rose and turned, looking for Rand, but he was no longer steering the boat. In fact, he was nowhere in sight. She was standing out in the open.

Ducking down, she caught the glint of steel and saw the knife with its serrated edges was stuck in some trim work. Plucking it out, she cut the rope holding her on board in one slash. She crawled to the hatch and stuck her head down below. There was no sign of him there. Lowering herself into the oddly shaped chamber, she closed the hatch behind her. She stood by the door and gathered her wits, trying to think clearly through her options, listening carefully for Rand. She didn't know what he was up to, and she held fast to the knife in her hand.

*The boat must be equipped with a radio. No matter what, I've got to call for help.*

The boat rocked hard, forcing her to grab the door handle for support. Amazingly, the knob turned and opened.

*Wait a minute! I know I heard Sylvia lock this!*

Carla slowly opened the door and peeked outside. The companionway was empty. There were four doors—all of them closed—on the way to the main cabin.

She closed the door and leaned up against it for a moment. Even if she knew anything practical about sailing, there was no way she'd be able to control this sixty-five-foot boat by herself. Summoning help was imperative. With the knife clenched tightly in her hand, she reopened the door and began creeping cautiously toward the captain's quarters.

*Good God, where is he? I wonder if he went overboard too?*

Carla sighed with relief after passing all the closed doors. Still seeing no sign of Rand, she headed toward the deck. She was halfway up the steps when suddenly she was forcibly attacked from behind. Rand had ambushed her and tried to tackle her. But he just missed, and instead grabbed her legs and started sliding her body down the stairs.

Though her chin banged hard and split open, Carla wrenched around and with brutal force jammed the knife she carried deep in his leg. His hands involuntarily flew up, and she scrambled madly for the deck. He screamed in pain as he pulled the knife from his leg. In seconds he barreled after her, but Carla was ready. Hoisting herself up on rails in the cabin's doorframe, she delivered a kick to his chest. He grabbed her leg and tried pulling her down. Holding strong, she raised her other foot and socked him in the jaw. Still, he stood firm, madness flaring in his eyes. Within seconds he had dragged her down the stairs and was on top of her, his legs pinning her arms, his hands firmly around her throat. At first all she could see was a blur, almost a strange, burning light inside her head. It hurt; it hurt so badly, and she was gasping for air. She tried feebly lifting her knee and hitting him in the back, but that only served to anger him more. His hands constricted so tightly around her throat that she couldn't even scream.

*"If you've got your eye focused on the attacker's weapon, then you're not concentrating on an opening—on a way to escape or hurt your opponent."* Master Tompkins's words suddenly rang through her head.

*An opening. Where in the hell is the opening?* And then she saw it. Carla raised her right leg into his back once more. This time he slightly shifted his weight off that side of her body, enabling her to free her right arm from beneath his left leg. With dead-on accuracy she slapped her palm on top of his left hand, and with all the might she could muster, put intense pressure between his thumb and index finger with her own thumb. He screamed. She'd nailed a vital pressure point that crippled him with pain. Immediately he loosened his grip on her neck, enabling her to fully grab hold of his aching hand and turn it so hard and fast that she knew any second it would break. Screaming in agony as his lower arm twisted nearly one hundred and eighty degrees, he quickly rolled off of her.

Kneeling just three feet away from her, clutching his hand, he looked up at her, then laughed.

"Get ready to see your beloved father," he said. She never gave him another chance. Rolling onto her stomach, and then practically levitating from the floor, she delivered a devastating kick right into his face. The thrust of it was so forceful that she not only broke his nose, but knocked all four of his front teeth back into his head. Blood gushed from his nose and mouth while the color drained right out of his face. His eyes rolled back and he fell face forward, passing out on the floor beside her.

Fearful that he might strike again, she slid away, watching him closely the whole time. At that moment, the *Reciprocity* hit another large swell, sending both of them flying upward. Carla landed directly on top of him. He didn't budge. He was out cold.

She lay frozen on top of him for a moment, then placed her mouth close to his ear.

"Listen carefully, you son of a bitch. You have the right to remain silent."

# CHAPTER
## 38

Carla looked anxiously around from her seat on the floor at Madison Square Garden to see if they'd arrived. Indeed, Jack Jr., Tommy, Robbie, her aunt, uncle, and some cousins, along with a few close friends were now settled in their seats.

Eight months following her harrowing adventure and Coast Guard rescue on the high seas, and the subsequent incarceration of Rand Emmerson, Roman Petrovsky, and various other collaborators, Carla Donnatella Jennings was officially graduating with a thousand other cadets from the training academy of the New York City Police Department. Her hair, restored to its natural dark color and wave, had been French braided for today's occasion, and in her formal dark blue attire, hat, and white gloves, she did not seem so different from all the other cadets.

But this was her day. She listened nervously to the various speeches and presentations of awards. And then her heart raced as she watched the commander of the entire force step up to the podium. The arena hushed as he began to speak.

"It is my privilege today," Joseph Stevens solemnly began, "to confer the award that honors our top graduating cadet; someone who the department believes has displayed excellence overall in every conceivable category—whether it be academic, physical fitness, marksmanship, or even general sportsmanship.

"Beyond the official considerations, this cadet demonstrated from the beginning an unwavering commitment to a dangerous undercover investigation that resulted in shutting down a multimillion-dollar international drug dealing network. In the face of tremendous odds, this rookie rallied to the cause with the extraordinary will, constitution, and perseverance that we believe symbolizes what it takes to serve and protect the citizens of New York."

He paused and took a deep breath.

"And I know that if he were with us today, her father would be as proud as I am right now to see this esteemed award bestowed on your classmate, and my new colleague, Carla Jennings."

Though the audience rose and the Garden echoed with applause, Carla sat still in a moment of quiet respect for the father she had lost. Finally rising from her front-row seat, she climbed the dais and performed the obligatory salute, then graciously received a warm congratulatory handshake as the commander handed her an award plaque.

Dressed in full uniform herself, Liz Phillips, who had been sitting with the commander and other department officials, rose and stood beside the commander while smiling warmly at Carla. Moving in front of her, Carla formally saluted. Phillips saluted her back, then, forsaking decorum, embraced the young woman. Tears filled both their eyes and, for a moment, Carla wondered if Phillips wasn't going to start sobbing. Instead, she stepped back and, reaching into her pocket, pulled out a black felt pouch.

"Oh, no," Carla said, her voice cracking.

"I know he would want you to have this," said Phillips, handing Carla her father's badge.

"Thanks," Carla whispered, clutching the shield in her white-gloved hand.

"You know, he was right," said Phillips, then winked. "With you in the ranks, I think it's time I started watching my back!"